Romancing the GIRL

CAMRYN EYDE

Romancing the Girl
By Camryn Eyde

camryneyde.com

Author Note

This story is unapologetically Australian.

Set on a rural sheep station, it's full of dust, dirt, flies, Aussie clichés and beer. A lot of phrases and slang may be confusing and bizarre to an international eye, so I've added a quick cheat-sheet below to help decode the Aussie language for overseas readers. Hopefully, the unique turns of phrase to this gloriously arid country don't take away from the heartfelt story being told within the pages.

Camryn.

Ute = pickup, and in this case, a four-wheel drive (four-wheeled drive) with a tray on the back.

Verandah = Veranda, patio, terrace. This has many names and is essentially an outdoor covered area that (in this story) wraps around the house. I prefer to spell it with a 'h' at the end.

Shopping centre = Shopping mall.

Final note, rabbits and foxes are considered feral animals in Australia and do a significant amount of damage to native wildlife and native vegetation. Farmers spend a lot of time and money trying to control them.

For
Every true blue Aussie giving rural life a red hot crack. It's tough out there.

With her arms open wide, she stood in the spring sun and let it warm her bronze skin. Halfway between the main buildings of the place she called home, she'd paused in her mission when the allure of heated rays became too much. The winter chill had finally left the property, the scattered grass no longer crunching with frost under her feet when she ran to the stables each morning to check her latest possession. A toothy grin sprouted on her young face when she heard the whinny of her horse. Today, she was finally allowed to train her, for today was a very special day. Today, Aimee Turner turned seven.

"Kite!" she called down the stable run as she continued on her path from the stone homestead to the wooden stables. Breathing in the cooler, hay-scented air, she hurried to the grey foal her father had brought to the property a week earlier. A horse was a big responsibility. It required care, feeding, training, riding, and nurturing. Like her seventeen-year-old brother and sister had done before her on their seventh birthday, it was time to take a step into maturity.

"What do you think you're doing?" her father said in a mock grumble as he joined her in the stable. Aimee ran to him and wrapped her arms around his waist. A second later, and her feet left the ground as the strength of her father lifted her from the dirt floor. "I heard a rumour that it's someone's special day today."

Aimee nodded and grinned.

"Yeah, mine," said a gangly boy joining them and ruffling the child's long brunette hair.

"Is not," Aimee said, swatting away her brother's teasing. "I'm seven," she said proudly at her father.

"Really?"

"Unh huh. And I get a horse."

"Is that so?"

"Yep. Kite," Aimee said, pointing to the grey foal looking at them with curious brown eyes.

"Kite? She doesn't bloody fly," her brother said as he moved past them to peer at the horse.

Their father playfully swatted at his head as he moved off. "You named your horse Arton Senna. Last I checked, it doesn't drive Ferrari's." Putting Aimee back on the ground, Gary Turner said, "Joey, put a halter on young Kite here. It's time Aimee started training her."

With a grin of pure glee, Aimee proudly took the guide rope from her brother when he passed it to her, and the three spent the early hours of the morning in the horse yards leading young Kite around in a circle.

Just as they were taking Kite back to the stables, a man ran puffing into the area by the homestead and started yelling.

"They're gone!" he screamed. "Katie and Mica, they're missing!"

"Joe, get Kite settled. Make sure Aimee brushes her down." Gary strode quickly to the distraught man in the middle of the quadrangle. While Joey moved off and called his kid sister over his shoulder, Aimee stayed still and watched her father talk to the stranger who had arrived at the property a few days previous.

He spoke funny. All clear and important. She remembered overhearing her parents calling them city slickers that were about to get a shock to the system. She got a shock once, from a low electric fence they used around the sheep paddocks near the homestead. Aimee wondered if her dad was going to push them into the fence. Idly frowning at that curious notion, she heard her father shout, "Gav!"

Aimee's attention moved to the shed behind her where Gav emerged from covered in the oil of the car he had been working on the past few days. "Yo."

"Get the boys together. We've got people missing."

Missing? Aimee ran to her dad, only to be overtaken by Joey who had been drawn from the stables by the commotion.

"Who's missing?" Joey asked as Aimee caught him.

"My wife and daughter," the stranger said. "I can't find them. They went for a walk and didn't come back."

At Joey's frown, his father said, "They're staying up at the old cottage. They must've got turned around." To the man, he said, "We'll find them. Just stay put." Jogging to the homestead, Gary was followed by two of his children, finding the third in the kitchen with his wife, Bridget. "Bridge, the Pollick girls are missing. They've been gone since yesterday afternoon."

That's all Gary need to say to his wife before she started gathering together things the searchers would need in their pursuit.

"I'll saddle up," said Joey, making for the kitchen door.

Gary stilled his son with a hand on his arm. "No, you won't. You stay here and mind Aimee."

"I want to come, too," Aimee said, putting her hand on her hips to mimic Joey.

"No, honey. Stay here and enjoy your birthday."

"I'm not a babysitter," Joey said to his father. "Sally or Mum can mind her."

"I'm seven."

"Mum's coming with me," Gary said. "You and Sal stay here. I need someone on the radio. You can do that for me, can't you mate?"

Joey glared at his father. "I can help."

"You can, by being here and looking out for your sister. It's her birthday, Joey."

"And for my birthday, I want to help look for the people."

Gary looked to Aimee and put his hand on her head. "No, little bug, stay here. We'll be back in time for cake."

Aimee spent the majority of her birthday alone. Joey hovered around the radio listening for news and snapping at his sister anytime she interrupted. Sally spent her time in the kitchen having been relegated with the task of preparing the meals for the family and crew that evening. With the exception of providing Aimee with lunch or a snack, she was too busy to play. Aimee best and only friend that day was the storm-grey foal in the stables. At least Kite was pleased with her company.

As the afternoon sun began to hang low in the sky, lighting up the insects skipping over the dry yellow grass in the paddocks around the homestead, the searchers returned unsuccessful. Greasy but buoyant, the stranger Aimee had spent the day glaring at from her bedroom window ran to the group returning from their search and she could hear him say that his plane was repaired. They could fly around in the last light of day and find them. Forgiving the man slightly for ruining her birthday, Aimee ran downstairs to the group discussing where to fly. She inserted herself between her parents and listened intently. A grid was soon established and Aimee shadowed them to the vehicle that would take them to the airstrip behind the homestead.

"Aimee, honey, head back to the house," her mum said, stilling her youngest daughter with hands on her shoulders.

"I want to come and help. I have good eyes."

"I know you do, honey, but Dad and I can handle it. Go back and see if your sister could get you a piece of your cake." Her mother looked over her shoulder to Sally watching from the porch.

"I don't want cake, I want to come!" Aimee said, trying to get into the car.

"I'm sorry, honey. Not this time."

"I want to help," Aimee said with a whine only children can create.

"That's enough," her dad snapped as he strode around the vehicle.

"Gary…"

He held a hand up to his wife. "Aimee, this is a job for grownups. You need to go back to Joey and Sally."

"I don't want to. I'm a big girl."

"Now, Aimee."

"But—"

"Now!"

Aimee felt the touch of her sister behind her. Usually comforting, this time, she was too upset with the man she idolised to accept any form of soothing. "But Daddy…" Aimee's chin began to wobble as her father strode away from her. Her mother gave her a kind look and tried to touch her shoulder. "I hate you!" Aimee screamed at her parents with a stomp of her foot. She stepped back and bumped into Sally before spinning away and running back to the house with tears streaming hot down her face. From her bedroom window she watched her parents and the stranger drive away in a cloud of dust. She lay her head in her arms and silently cursed them all.

***

"Where are you going?" Sally asked as her brother rushed past the kitchen with his backpack on.

"Joey, they said you have to stay here," Sally said, hurrying after him.

"Bugger that, Sal. I can help. Aimee doesn't need a bloody minder. Besides, you're here."

"Someone has to man the radio."

"So do it."

"I can't watch Aimee and be in the office."

"She's seven! She's bloody old enough to look after herself. Jesus, Sally." Joey turned around and jogged across the yards to the stables. He saddled the horse he received for his seventh birthday and charged to the north just as the sound of a light aircraft that brought the strangers to Yarrabee Station climbed into the sky.

Aimee watched him leave through the screen of her bedroom window. Joey was gone, Sally was downstairs, and somewhere out there were two strangers wandering around lost. Strangers that had been told to be careful. Strangers that had stolen her birthday away from her. Strangers that made her dad cross. Strangers that had ruined her special day.

Pushing off the sill, Aimee spun around and grabbed her My Little Pony backpack, and stuffed it full. In went the torch Gav gave her that morning, the compass her grandparents gave her last week before they left on their holiday, a blanket, jacket, and sparkly lip gloss Sally had loaned her unwillingly. Downstairs she crept to fill the remaining space with food and fluids. Wearing her favourite wide-brim hat and her favourite boots, she walked unseen from the homestead to the place where she'd be able to see the plane.

The path of its proposed route over the property was fresh in her mind, and if she hurried, she'd get to watch as they searched for the missing wife and daughter. Maybe she could even find them herself and she'd get even more presents. Grinning with that thought, Aimee began a long walk to the ruins of the old homestead, and wished more than once that Kite was big enough to ride. What could have taken fifteen minutes at the trot took her much shorter legs more than an hour.

She chuckled to herself when she finally made the old ruins and heard the sound of the plane the moment she arrived. Grinning, she hid low and watched it pass nearby before banking and going back the other way. Once it was too far away to follow with her eyes, she listened to the plane while casting her eyes around the landscape nearby. Intermittent patches of grass speckled the light brown dirt around the site of the old homestead. Rock, coarse and bleached, rose from the ground a hundred metres away to form an outcrop that circled the old ruins like a horseshoe. Spring warmth and a recent sprinkle of winter rains had encouraged dark green plants to grow and bud wildflowers that burst into colour along the ridge and all over the ground nearby. Smiling, Aimee emerged from her hiding place and gathered an armful of flowers to put on the old graves of her forefathers protected by a wire fence near the ruins.

Twice more she dove into her hiding place as the plane neared her position. The old, beige rock, harvested from the ground around her, stood tall and proud in places, and in others, crumbled as the mortar eroded beyond its ability to bind. Her favourite part was the tall chimney against the western wall. The strongest part of the old homestead, it provided the perfect cubby at the base. The wide chamber was the ideal size for a girl of seven to utilise as a secret hideout. Lined with the contents of her backpack, she nibbled at her food as the light of the day began to dwindle. Tempted to return home in the fading light, the sound of the plane still circling the property kept her in place. *What was the point of being home enjoying her birthday cake when there was no one home to sing her happy birthday?*

As the sun touched the horizon, the plane neared the ruins once more. Sneaking over to a low wall, she watched its approach as it returned to the homestead. The steady whine of the engines popped and stuttered and she saw a little puff of smoke come from the plane. *That couldn't be right?*

She stood up, shielding her eyes from the setting sun with her hand. The plane popped and dipped and soon, Aimee was stepping over the low wall watching as the aircraft wobbled through the air. *What was the stranger doing?*

Silence pierced the air like the ricochet of a gun. It was sudden, it was disturbing, and it scared Aimee with a chill right to her core.

"Turn it back on," she muttered as she began to take steps toward the flailing aircraft. "Turn it back on!" she screamed as it took a sudden turn towards the ground.

It was all over a second later. One moment the plane was gliding in silence, the next, it had pierced the low outcrop around the ruins with a sound that would terrify Aimee in her sleep for years to come. Shock at the booming crunch of metal against rock and dirt trapped

Aimee in place for several heartbeats. She blinked at the mangled pile trying to absorb what had just happened. Her parents were in that plane. Eyes flying wide, she screamed, "Mum! Dad!" and ran as fast as her legs would take her.

"Daddy?" she yelled when she heard the sound of a male voice as she reached the base of the outcrop. She began scrambling over granite burning orange in the dwindling light of the day, before her world turned upside down. The concussion wave of the explosion tossed her young body ten metres backward, instantly rendering her unconscious as she rolled across the gravelly dirt. By the time Aimee opened her eyes, the sky was filled with the distant glow of twilight. Disorientated, she blinked and rubbed her eyes, whimpering as the battering her body took registered in her nerve endings. Her head throbbed.

Trying to sit up, she noticed the smouldering mass on the hill. Her eyebrows furrowed together as she tried to make sense of what she was seeing. *Where was she?* Looking around as she slowly got to her feet, she saw the ruins. A familiar and comforting sight. Turning again to the smoke on the outcrop above her, she frowned once again. *What was that?* A gasp nearly knocked her over as her memory returned. *"Mum!"* she screamed. *"Daddy!"* she screamed with the same amount of desperation and fear that made the back of her throat ache. Clambering up the rocks to reach the plane, she was greeted at the top of the outcrop with nothing but the charred frame of the twisted aircraft. Fire still burned near the tail of the plane.

She wasn't fast enough to save them. "Mummy?" she said in a low voice choking with grief. "Daddy?" Her chin trembled and tears streamed across her skin. "No," she said, her voice cracking with emotion. Feeling herself overwhelmed with a darkness her youth couldn't comprehend, she did the only thing she knew how to do. Run and hide.

In the chamber that once housed fire, she shivered and sobbed while her hands covered her ears trying to block out the sound of the crumple of plane against rock. Back and forth she rocked trying to shake the memory of the plane taking its fatal gravity-assisted path to the earth.

Sometime that evening she heard the approach of several vehicles and noticed red and blue flashes of light. She blocked out the sound of the people discovering the fate of her parents. Aimee, caught in her own nightmares, was rendered paralysed as the word got out and the grieving began.

Daylight came and curled up in the foetal position, Aimee stared in a daze as the sun travelled over the sky and changed the shadows across the ruins. More cars came that day, noticeable to Aimee by the dust blowing across the ruins.

More days passed, and after hearing the sound of her name being called over and over again, Aimee was forced re-join the living.

Sally and Joey found her. Three days after their parents had been taken from their lives. The shell of what was once Aimee broke their hearts. Not only had they lost their parents, but they had let their little sister become a victim of a terrible tragedy thanks to neglecting a simple request by their parents. Joey's discovery of the wife and child safe and well on the day of the crash went unnoticed in the local newspapers as the community mourned.

It had taken years to learn the truth of what Aimee witnessed that night. The plane, taken down thanks to a loose fuel hose, had been clinically and swiftly diagnosed by forensic investigators. But Aimee's eye-witness account of that terrible night didn't emerge until the night before her seventeenth birthday.

***

Strangers from the city came to the property, and while tolerant of those experienced and weathered in the art of existence on the land, Aimee's ability to accept city folk was non-existent. People from the concrete jungle didn't get life on the land. They didn't understand how easily you could die. If venomous snakes or spiders didn't get you, then dehydration and exposure would. That day, when the strangers decided to wander off for a hike and got themselves lost, she snapped.

They were found an hour after they were reported missing nearly five kilometres from their intended destination. Aimee discovered them, after hearing Joey had come off his motorbike. By the time she returned them to the homestead, her voice was raspy with overuse as she tore strips off the strangers as she escorted them to the homestead.

Complaints about her abusive words shocked both Sally and Joey. Since the accident that took their parents, Aimee had been a quiet, reserved child, moving about her day with very little intrusion. After asking the backpackers to leave the station, Sally and Joey found their kid sister in the stables crying in Kite's stall. A blubbering apology fell from her lips before the truth came out about how she couldn't save her parents. How her parting words were filled with spite and hate, and about cursing them as she watched them leave her behind. She told them how strangers from the city terrified her with the possibility of stealing away more family members to their graves. The twenty-seven-year old twins sat down with her in the hay and comforted her as much as they could, but knew there was nothing they could do to mend their sister's heart break.

Regret would always itch within Aimee, but over some things she had control. With the blessing of her siblings, never again would naïve city fools be allowed unrestricted access to the property. From that day forward, Aimee swore to protect her family from outsiders. If you weren't from the land, then you weren't welcome.

CHAPTER ONE

"Bimbos, the lot of them."

"Aimee, shush."

Aimee rolled her eyes as her older sister elbowed her in the arm. "Look at them!" Aimee said, gesturing at the three city chicks as if they were flies that needed swatting. "Can you see any of them surviving out here?" Cupping her hands to her mouth, she shouted, "No malls out here ladies. No fancy beauty parlours. No coffee shops to gossip at. Hell, there's no freaking phone reception!"

Sally, shorter than Aimee by a couple of inches and wider by a good deal more, leaned into her sister and said with a growl, "Aimee, for Christ's sake, they'll hear you."

"Good. Maybe they'll turn their size-too-small lycra-clad arses around and leave."

Sally made a noise of disgust.

"What?" Aimee said, hating the whine she could hear in her own voice.

"You're a bloody pessimist."

"At least I'm not pimping myself out like Joey is. What an idiot."

"Shh…I want to hear this." Sally rubbed her hands together before blowing warm air into them. The morning was bitter, but lacked the blanket of frost across the ground as the approaching spring slowly warmed the air.

Aimee rolled her eyes again but kept quiet to watch the circus unfold in front of her. Her brother, Joey, was finally released by some chick putting powder all over his face. To Aimee, he looked like one of those metro ponces on TV. The makeup woman relinquished control of him to another lady in a severe business suit who sent Aimee a dirty look.

"And why is that pain in my arse back here?" Aimee said, scowling at the woman whose name she was still yet to learn.

Sally sighed. "Because she's the producer, remember?"

"All I remember is her swanning all over the property making pretty boy there look like a bigger ponce than he does now."

"Seriously, Aimee? That was months ago now. Get over yourself."

Aimee continued to scowl. Two months ago, a cameraman from the show and the producer had spent two days on the property filming stock images. Two days that Aimee had been blissfully busy elsewhere except for one incident that she tightened her scowl over. "She lost my best hat."

Sally groaned.

"What? It was barely broken in, and she had it for what? A day before losing it in the top paddock somewhere. She owes me."

"Will you *hush*," Sally said.

Aimee crossed her arms. The producer was now leading Joey to the three contestants who were all looking up at the homestead as though they'd struck gold. On the surface, they probably had every reason to think that.

The homestead was a magnificent stone two-story structure with four distinct wings. It looked grand and straight out of Hollywood. It boasted numerous bedrooms, a commercial-sized kitchen, more formal rooms than they knew what to do with, and a conservatory that lead into a large courtyard complete with heated pool. The place was a testament to the success of their ancestors, and was impressive even to Aimee. To the women salivating at it, it also meant money. Lots and lots of money. *If only they knew what running a station cost.*

Hovering around the group were two guys with cameras and another with a long stick with a fluffy thing on the end.

"What's with the skinned possum?" Aimee asked Sally.

"It's a microphone. Shh."

"Jeez!" Aimee had to quickly shield her eyes as another minion ran about with a reflective screen, managing to blind her with the sun. The producer gave her a tight-lipped glare. Aimee resisted the urge to poke out her tongue. One of the contestants looked over and Aimee gave her a little wave. Aimee's eyes roamed the remarkable assets of the woman, and as a result flashed her teeth and gave her a wink. The woman blushed.

"Hey," Sally whispered harshly in her ear. "No hitting on Joey's girls."

"Why not? You said they're here to find love. Why can't it be with me?"

Sally clucked her tongue. "The day you fall in love will be the day snow falls on Christmas day. Never going to happen."

"Excuse me, but could you refrain from gossiping for a moment?" the producer said.

"Excuse me, but could you hurry this up. This is a *working* farm, not a bloody prop for some pre-war soap opera. We need your pin-up boy over there to actually pull his weight and not just fawn about these…desperates," Aimee said back at her. The girls squeaked with offence. "There are men in the city, just so you know. They're the ones with the deep voices, moisturised skin and fancied up hair."

"Aims," Joey warned.

"This is so *stupid*," Aimee said. Turning her back on the entire production, she whistled for her four-legged companion and went to the stables to prepare her horse for the ride out to the west paddock.

"Hey, Aimsey, what's happenin'?" Gav, Gavin Munroe, called over to her as she walked past the sheds. The man, hairy on every piece of visible skin, was sporting his usual coverage of oil to his elbows, a dark blue work shirt unbuttoned to his beer belly, and boots without laces at the bottom of his thick legs. "Joey picked himself a bride yet?"

"Ugh. No. The idiot needs his head read for signing up for this show."

"The man wants some lovin', Aims. Let him be."

"He had plenty of *loving* with Tracey."

"Yeah…he shoulda trapped that when he had a chance."

"Hmm," Aimee mumbled and continued on to the stables where she had penned her horse earlier. Tracey, a woman who used to fall at Joey's feet, was the woman he should never have let go. Joey, the imbecile, decided he needed to sow some wild oats before getting tied down in family and the farm. He lasted three months in the city before crawling home to find Tracey had refused to sit around and wait for him. She was now working in the next town at the local vet and according to current rumour, dating the locum doctor.

It was his wild oats that started this mess, Aimee decided. Tracey broke his heart though he'd never admit it, and apparently the remedy to that was this brilliant scheme. Joey Turner, a contestant on the latest series of *Romancing the Farmer*. The thirty-four-year-old went into the city last month, met a bunch of girls and chose three to return to their farm for two weeks. Sally had explained that he eliminated a girl each week, meaning the contestant count would at least go down. The problem was that it was nearly lambing season, they had shearers booked for three days starting tomorrow, and the sorghum fields needed attention for planting next month. August, the last of the winter months, was the busiest one on the station. Why Joey decided it was a good idea to bring a circus to the property was beyond Aimee's understanding.

Aimee, busy shaking her head to herself, walked into the cool, crisp air inside the stables. The tallest building on the property, it provided a holding area with seven stalls at ground level, and on the mezzanine was an area converted into a loft space several years earlier. A loft space Aimee called home. Adjacent to a large paddock that let the horse stock they owned roam free when not being ridden, the stables had a series of stalls on either side of the centre run. Mainly used to pen horses they planned to ride in the near future, Aimee had coaxed her mare Kite from the paddocks at daybreak and put her in a stall. Across the run was River, a sedate horse her nephew Robbie wanted to ride that afternoon.

"I hope the desperates know the arse end of a sheep from its front," Aimee muttered as she picked up a saddle from its resting place on the stable wall. Her border collie, Mitsy, cocked her head at her and whined. "Exactly," Aimee muttered.

"Hey, my beautiful Kite," she cooed to the big grey mare snuffling at her pockets the moment she entered her pen. Kite nudged at Aimee's hands after glaring at the dog that marked its territory in her stall.

"Ah, crap. Sorry girl, the circus made me forget your sugar. I promise you double tonight, okay?"

Brushing down her horse, she felt at peace for the first time that day. Since daybreak, Joey had been pacing around the house like a nervous cat and Sally had managed to temper the usual boisterousness of her two children creating a strange, ominous atmosphere. A house Sally was being forced to share thanks to Joey and his suitors. The fact Aimee had to share a kitchen and amenities with three strangers didn't sit well either and forced her to reconsider putting a bathroom in her loft above the stables like Joey had suggested countless times.

"Guess I'll be using the emergency shower," she said to Mitsy, thinking of the shower in the machinery shed primarily used for chemical spills.

"Okay, set up in here. Use this quaint rustic look for the video diaries," said a loud voice that startled Kite, making the mare step on Aimee's toes and Mitsy jump to her feet.

"See if you can stack up some hay bales for a backdrop. Have some saddles and bridles draping over them."

"Oh, for the love of all things holy," Aimee mumbled, her face scrunched in pain as she hopped to the door of Kite's bay. "Do you mind?" she called out to the producer who was pointing at some hay bales stacked near the stable doors. Closing in on the petite woman, Aimee encroached on her personal space and crossed her arms with a glare.

The producer turned and rolled her eyes when she saw who had spoken to her. "Well, if it isn't the antagonist. If you don't mind, I'm on a schedule. I have a production to manage, and if you and your little horsey could stay out of my way, then I'm sure this will all be quick and painless." She turned her back to Aimee and tried to saunter out of the stables.

Aimee wasn't going to be so easily dismissed. Snatching the woman's thin arm in her hand, she whipped the woman around. Not expecting her to be so light, Aimee's strength from years of working the farm and managing horses came to the fore and the producer ended up crashing against her.

Both women gasped and stepped back, the producer's amber eyes flashing like a cat. *No*, thought Aimee, *a dragon*.

After an awkward pause at the accidental body bump, Aimee remembered her annoyance and pointed her finger at the woman. "This is a business, not a playground. If you want to set your lights and fluffy sticks up somewhere, you need to ask for permission first." Aimee put her hand down. "And you owe me a new hat."

The producer narrowed her eyes. "For your information, farm girl, I have a document that says I have creative rights for this show and for where I choose to set up my scenes on this property. Your brother, who I must say, was raised with a darn sight more manners than you, agreed to the requisites for this show and signed accordingly. I don't need to ask for permission because I already have it. As for your hat, buy a new one."

"Typical city attitude. Just go buy a new one," Aimee said with a great deal of petulance.

"It was a dusty piece of felt hardly worth three bucks."

"It was just getting worn in."

"It had a bloody great hole in the front of it."

"That's called a vent."

"It's called a moth hole."

Aimee squinted and was about to defend her hat once more when she spotted Joey rushing across the yard over the producer's shoulder, Aimee smirked. "We'll see about this circus now, won't we?"

The city woman crossed her arms and turned to the approaching party of production crew, farmer, and contestants. "I suppose we will. Enjoy being proved wrong. And that hat reeked of mouse urine."

"Whatever," Aimee mumbled to her. Joey reached hearing distance and Aimee called out. "What's this about this lot getting the run of the place? This isn't a doll house, Joe, it's a bloody working station. Tell them to get stuffed."

Joey glanced at the producer before zoning in on his sister. "Aimee, they're only going to set up in a few places, and I already said they could have at it."

"But she came bursting in here and startled the horses. Is their welfare suddenly less important than getting laid?"

Joey blushed bright red and the contestants snickered among themselves. Hooking his younger sister by the arm, he dragged her into the stables. "Look, Aims, we've talked about this. They're here for two weeks, it's good marketing for the farm, and who knows, maybe I get to meet the right girl for me."

"The right girl for you left because you wanted to dip your wick elsewhere."

Joey clenched his jaw. "Drop it, Aimee."

Hearing the warning in her brother's tone, Aimee took a deep breath and noticed the producer glaring at her. "I don't want them here," she said, trying not to pout.

"Stop being a brat. This isn't about you, it's about me. It's two weeks, for Christ's sake, so deal with it already." Joey swung around and walked back over to the producer offering apologies for his kid sister.

"I'm not a bloody kid!" Aimee yelled over to him, which garnered the producer's attention again.

She raised her brow with a smirk. "Oh, farm girl, your horse is escaping."

Aimee scoffed and turned back down the run to Kite's stall. "My horse is so not—crap!" Kite's grey backside rounded the doors at the other end. Doors that led to a different paddock. Doors Mike would have exited through a few minutes before she returned to the stables with a thoroughbred horse. Knowing exactly where Kite was going, Aimee broke into a full sprint through the stables with Mitsy hot on her heels. If the stallion caught a whiff of her, she'd be hard pressed keeping them apart. Emerging from the stables, her fears were answered. Trotting along the narrow fenced corridor, Kite was headed straight for the yard her niece's pony was in to visit her favourite friend, Raincloud. Unfortunately, the stallion, Handsome Boy, was yarded adjacent to the ponies, and sure enough, he started trotting over to the Kite, dragging the farmhand along behind him. Having asked Mike to halter him to take him to the younger mares he was supposed to breed with fifteen minutes ago, the disaster was set up and ready to unfold.

"Damn it!" she shouted. "Close the gate!" she called out in vain as the stallion rushed the opening and mounted her horse.

Mike was too late.

Mitsy barked in agreement.

"Get him off!" Aimee yelled. It was a futile order. The stallion was strong, and Kite had been through the breeding process before, so like a little hussy, she stood there and let herself be mounted.

Aimee growled to the clear skies in frustration. *Damn that stupid woman and that stupid show.*

CHAPTER TWO

"Tell me again how you managed to mate your old mare with a million-dollar stud!" Joey yelled at her that afternoon.

Sally stood beside him with her arms crossed. Danny, Sally's husband, was rubbing at his stubble with a grimace on his face. "He didn't want a bar of the bay mares. He took one sniff and walked away," Danny said, making Aimee cringe a little.

They had hired the stallion to breed from the younger mares they recently invested in. The hilly and rough nature of the property lent itself to horseback travel over four-wheel driving, and they had invested a significant amount of money to breed good stock.

"It was that producer's fault," Aimee said, defending herself. "She came in, yelled down the run, startled Kite, and she escaped."

"Who left the stall open, Aimee? Who was the one that felt the need to confront the production manager? Huh? You did. Don't you dare try and palm it off when you know fully well who's at fault here."

"They were—"

"Enough!" Joey yelled, effectively stilling the entire room. For a big man, he rarely raised his voice, but when he did, people listened. Broad and muscled from a lifetime of station work, he was the exact kind of man the city women were hoping to find. Dark, curly hair with dark eyes to match, a kind face with two-day stubble, and a heart of gold. She'd heard him called handsome before, and Aimee might be forced to agree, but right now, he was pissing her off. Apparently, Joey was just as irate.

"You've been acting like a spoiled brat all day. Get over yourself already, and grow up. These people are here for two weeks, and I expect you to be respectful and welcoming. In fact, it's now your job to escort the film crew around. Get them familiar with the property and what we do. If you can't do that, then maybe it's time you went back to uni. Maybe getting out in the real world will make you grow up a little."

Absolutely furious with tears burning in her eyes, Aimee glared at her brother as his threats cut her like a hot knife. She loved this place, and threatening to send her away was like stealing her home.

Unable to speak as her throat tightened, she turned on her heel and stormed out, but not before seeing the remorse in Joey's eyes, or the shock on Sally and Danny's face at the ultimatum.

The screen door slapped against the stone of the house as Aimee stormed out, only to be faced with the producer who ruined her day.

"Must you be so brutish?" the woman snapped, her hand clutched to her heart at being startled.

"Piss off," Aimee muttered as she pushed past.

"Charming," the producer called out to her.

Clomping up to her loft above the stables, Aimee flopped down with a grunt on the two-seater couch in the one-room space. Mitsy leaped up and settled on her stomach forcing the air from her lungs. "You know, you're not a bloody puppy anymore you big lump," she mumbled.

Content to leave the dog where she lay, she began unconsciously tickling at the soft chocolate-coloured hair behind her collie's ears. Her eyes found the picture of her parents hanging above the bureau. Taken a few months before their accident, they looked weathered and happy.

"Your son, Joseph, is threatening to send me away," she told them. "Bastard." Her lip trembling, she swiped at the tears in her eyes. "It's not my fault he let Tracey go. She was perfect for him, but *no*, he had to go screw around in the city."

Taking a deep breath, she stared at the photo, wishing for the millionth time that her parents were still here. Now twenty-three, Aimee was as much a part of her parent's property as the soil that grew their sorghum. She knew her life was going to be lived out on the three-thousand-hectare farm, and that constant kept her grounded. Leaving was never an option.

Not one to wallow in self-pity for any longer than twenty minutes, she hopped up from the couch and grabbed a beer from the small fridge beside the kitchenette, brushing off her despondency in the process. Leaning against the counter, she drained half the bottle as she stared absentmindedly around her living space.

The loft was small, but cosy and was a testament to her life on the land. A multitude of trophies and ribbons won at various riding events adorned her bookshelf. A unit overflowing with novels, biographies and other various non-fiction titles stood beside the simple television cabinet. Walking across to the bookshelf, she fingered the various spines, selecting a recent book of stories about inspiring country women. She pulled it off the shelf and walked to her bedroom. Separated from the rest of the loft by a low beige wall that ran just wider than the width of her queen bed, she tossed the book onto the spread and walked to the windows at the foot of the bed. Pushing them open, she sipped her beer as she stared out across the paddocks currently bathed in vibrant late-afternoon sun.

Finishing her drink, she grabbed her toiletry bag and a handful of fresh clothes, intending to go back down to the house to shower and grab a bite to eat. Despite the morning's shenanigans, including her eighteen-year-old mare possibly getting impregnated by the stud, she had eventually pulled the stallion away Kite and ridden her up to the north paddock with a station hand, Matt, to set up the yards for the shearing due to start in a few days. After that, it was a long day of herding sheep from the western paddocks to the central ones. Mitsy had performed beautifully alongside the more experienced sheep dogs her brother usually mastered, and Aimee had returned to the homestead in a buoyant mood. On her return, Aimee heard the bad news about the stallion not wanting to mount the other mares. She blew out a long puff of air and rubbed her hand down her face.

"Come, Mitsy. Let's go eat."

The dog scampered over to the door and bounded down the stairs into the stables below with great enthusiasm. The young collie took off towards the house and into a throng of people willing to lavish her with attention.

"Ah, crap," Aimee muttered, remembering there was a big welcome barbeque organised for that evening. Her mood, restored by her one-sided chat with her parents and a cold beer, slumped into annoyance again. Contemplating using the farmhand quarters instead of the house bathroom, her mind was changed as she saw the producer walk into the shared amenities across the yard. *House bathroom it is.*

"Hey, come give us a hand, will you?" Sally called out as Aimee walked past the kitchen.

"Sure. Let me clean up first," Aimee called back.

"Ah…" Sally's head poked around the kitchen door. "There's a queue."

"What?"

"The guests are using the bathroom."

"Ugh. Fine." Aimee plodded back to the kitchen and parked her fresh clothes on a spare space of bench. She sighed and asked, "What do you need me to do?"

"Sign that," Sally said, pointing at the paperwork on the kitchen bench.

"No. I don't want to be on the stupid show. Watching the circus is enough for me."

"They can't use any footage you're in if you don't sign it. You might get in the way of something important and pivotal to Joey's romance."

Aimee stared at Sally for a few heartbeats before bursting into laughter. Sally joined her. "Did you sign it?" Aimee asked after calming down.

"Hell no. No one needs to see this on TV." Sally gestured to her apron-clad body. She shared the same dark colouring as her twin, Joey, but none of his height. Shorter than Aimee, Sally was none-the-less a strong woman despite the curves she wore as a testament to motherhood.

"You're beautiful," Aimee said.

"I'm not—"

"I agree," Danny said, coming into the kitchen to pick up the tray of sausages Sally had out.

Sally pursed her lips and ignored her husband. He hesitated for a moment before leaving the way he came.

"You two having a tiff?" Aimee asked, picking at the cheese Sally was dicing.

"Something like that. Hey! Hands off. Instead of sitting there picking at the food, why don't you make yourself useful? Lettuce, tomatoes, cucumber, chopped and in that please." Sally pointed to a salad bowl. "Want a beer?" Sally asked as she shuffled about the kitchen.

"Sure."

Handing over the bottle, Sally rubbed Aimee's forearm. "You know Joe didn't mean it earlier."

Aimee pursed her lips and lifted a shoulder up and down.

Sally pecked Aimee on the cheek and lifted up the tray of meat from the kitchen table. "We both love you."

"Love you back," Aimee said automatically.

By the time the salad was chopped, the first carton of beer was drunk, and half the meat was burned or undercooked, Aimee finally got to escape to the shower. Squealing at the lack of hot water, she quickly scrubbed the day's grime off, along with a splatter of vomit from an overexcited niece she had twirled around the kitchen. Changing into black, skin-tight jeans, and a designer plaid cotton shirt fitted to her work-honed body, she regarded herself in the mirror. Purchased a month ago, she smiled at her reflection after pulling on her boots. It was nice to be out of her work jeans and baggy chambray shirts.

"Hey, Bug," Joey greeted her as she entered the back yard. Coloured party lights lit up the quadrangle of green grass and picnic tables, and soft rock music could just be heard above the noise of conversation.

"Hey," Aimee replied.

"You okay?" he asked, wrapping an arm around her shoulders and tugged her against him. "Sorry about before."

"Don't worry about it." Accepting the beer Joey handed her, she cracked the can and took a swig as she surveyed the party. "The kids in bed?"

"Yeah, Sally and Danny just went to tuck them in."

"Hey?" Joey said, turning to her.

"Yeah?" Aimee said, frowning at her brother.

"Do you think that Sal and Danny are okay?"

"Okay? What does that mean?"

Joey took a long swig of his beer. "You know what? Never mind."

Aimee rolled her eyes and scanned the crowd. "So…when do I get to meet the bimbos?"

Joey grunted. "First off, they're not bimbos. They're contestants vying for my undying love."

Aimee groaned. "That was pathetic."

Chuckling, Joey nodded. "They're quite nice if you give them a chance. That one," he pointed to a woman with one of the permanent workers, Chris. "That's Brittney."

"Brittney? Are you serious?" Aimee watched her for a moment. Fake red hair, long showy legs, and a narrow straight body gave Aimee nothing to linger over.

"'Fraid so. That's Tiffany." Aimee groaned as she looked over at the tall blonde with Gav. Another typical Joey pick. Tall, leggy, and thin as a pole. "And the one standing with Justine is Amber."

Who the heck was Justine? Aimee wondered as she picked out the final city woman. She was shorter, curvier and had short brunette hair. *Much more interesting and completely against type for her brother.* Fully armed to tease Joey about the bimbo-sounding names of his choices, Aimee was side-tracked as she stared at the woman she assumed her brother pointed out as Justine. She'd never seen her before, so potentially, she was part of the seasonal shearer's crew that had started to arrive, or part of the camera crew that she had failed to notice. Why, she didn't know, because Justine was smoking hot. Long, dark, curly hair caressed her shoulders and brushed the swell of soft curves at the neckline of her low-cut top. Her hips and legs, defined by a pair of tight blue jeans drew her attention for a long moment. Aimee then ogled her waist and chest covered in a silky looking tank top. The glasses perched on her nose added a cute, quirky quality.

"Earth to Aimee?"

Joey waved a hand in front of Aimee's eyes and she batted it away. "That one with Amber, that's Justine you said?"

Joey nodded. "Yeah."

"When did she get here?"

"Uh…today. You know that."

"She's gorgeous."

"What?"

Mitsy, who had been doing the rounds to look for treats anyone had dropped, stopped by the woman in Aimee's sights and wagged her tail. The woman smiled down at her and scratched her behind the ear. Aimee turned to her confused looking brother. "Is she here with someone?"

"Uh…what?"

"Christ, Joe, it's not a trick question. Is she part of the shearing crew?"

"No, she's with the TV show."

Aimee nodded. She hadn't paid the people with the producer much attention, so it didn't surprise her that she missed spotting her earlier. "I'm going in."

"Wait, what?" Joey said attempting to catch her arm. "Be nice!" he called out when that failed.

Frowning, Aimee stopped and turned back to him. "Of course, I'm going to be nice. I'm going to make her an Aimee Special."

Joey's eyes raised in surprise.

Heading inside to the private bar, Aimee quickly threw together a cocktail mix that never failed to be enjoyed. She'd used it more than once to woo a lady to her loft. She hoped Justine was otherwise unattached so they could enjoy an evening getting to know one another, and maybe teach the woman the art of lady-loving. Smiling as the drink was completed, she re-emerged from the house and spotted Justine standing alone by the hibiscus.

"Game on," she whispered to herself and walked over. "You look gorgeous tonight," she said as she sidled up to the woman who she was still yet to study up close. Mitsy's tail began to thump against the paved ground.

The woman widened her eyes with surprise. *Light brown*, Aimee noted. *Like caramel. No, like amber.* Aimee blinked. Those eyes looked familiar.

"Are you here with someone, or am I allowed to monopolise you for the evening? I promise you I'm interesting."

Shutting her gaping mouth, the woman frowned and tilted her head slightly.

She was definitely familiar. "Do I know you?" Aimee asked, cocking her head to the side in mimic.

She received a confused look in response.

Trying to salvage her attempt to pick the woman up, Aimee smiled and passed the drink to the woman. "I bought you a cocktail. I call it Aimee's—Christ!" The moment she touched the woman, static friction zapped her and so did her recognition of the woman.

"Interesting name," said the woman who took the drink from her. It was the lady she had secretly named the dragon. "It is poisonous?"

"Are you a chameleon or something? What's with the glasses? Where's the stupid bun and that ridiculous suit?"

"Ever the charmer, aren't you?" Justine said, shaking her head. "Firstly, I'm not currently working, so my work clothing is not currently appropriate. Secondly, have you ever heard of contacts, or is that technology too new for you?"

Aimee narrowed her eyes, thoroughly aggravated that she had lusted for this woman a few moments ago. "Funny."

Justine raised her eyebrows and inspected the cocktail. "You didn't answer my question, is this poisonous?"

"No, it isn't. It's the best drink you'll ever taste; however, since it's you, I want it back."

Justine held the drink away from her reach. "Best drink I'll ever taste, huh? That's a mighty statement from a farm girl."

"It's true, but you're going to have to miss out. Hand it over."

"No." Justine shook her head, making those soft strands of hair swish about and capturing Aimee's attention briefly.

Damn her and her stupid sexy hair.

"You must have made this for me for a reason," Justine said. "Pray tell, what was it?"

"What was what?" Aimee asked, confused with the question.

"Why did you make this drink, apparently the best I'll ever taste, for me?"

Clearing her throat, Aimee lifted her chin. "I didn't make it for you."

"I beg to differ. In fact, correct me if I'm wrong, but were you hitting on me?"

Sirens wailed in Aimee's head begging her to escape before she made a bigger fool of herself. "Hardly," she said, refusing to meet her eyes.

Justine was grinning smugly when Aimee dared to look back. "My, my, do you have a little crush on me, farm girl?"

"As if."

The words were lame and she knew it, and at Justine's chuckle, Aimee quietly said, "Piss off," before abandoning the barbeque entirely. Overwhelmed with embarrassment, and exposing herself for a fool, she stormed home with Mitsy on her heels. "God, I'm an idiot!" she said to herself. Groaning, she face-palmed herself a few times. "Idiot, idiot, idiot."

She promised herself to help her brother out and stay as far away from the TV clowns as she could. There was no way she'd be able to face Justine without turning bright red with mortification. Then she groaned, remembering how she was put in charge of showing them around.

"God damn!"

CHAPTER THREE

The pre-dawn light brought with it a quiet and cool serenity as Aimee rolled out of bed the next morning. Mitsy was curled on her mat in the corner of the room and came to life with a thump of her tail against the wood floor.

"Morning, girl," Aimee said on a yawn as she turned on the kettle, bouncing from foot to foot on the cold hardwood floorboards. "Let's head out first thing and avoid those city slickers, okay? Joey will have to make do," she said to the dog, who wiggled her way across the room for a pat. "That's a good girl," Aimee said on a chuckle as Mitsy wound around her legs happily.

Throwing on her usual jeans and a long sleeve shirt – today's choice was a blue plaid design – and her thick socks, Aimee made her coffee and descended to the stables after pulling her jacket from the peg by the door. *No stupid reality show was going to halt proceedings this morning*, she mused as she pulled on her battered work boots at the bottom of the stairs.

"Ugh," she said when she emerged from the stables. There, climbing aboard a Landcruiser Troop Carrier they brought with them, was the two-man film crew, the make-up woman who also ran about with the reflective board, and yawning contestants, complete with her brother staring over at her expectantly.

"Come along! We'll miss the sunrise," Justine called out to a particularly slow member of her crew. She paused on her rounds to each car when she spotted Aimee.

"Where are they going?" Aimee asked, striding across the yard and confronting her brother.

"Oh…Aimee…hi," he said, scrubbing at the back of his neck. "You kinda left early last night, but umm, we're taking the girls up to the top paddocks today." He grimaced at the end.

Deservedly so, thought Aimee. "They're mustering with us? Are you crazy? That'll take forever." The sound of quad bikes coming from the sheds had her putting her hands on her hips. "Bikes? You're using the bikes?"

"Yeah. They can't ride horseback."

"It'll spook the flock! Make them sit on a log looking pretty or something instead."

"They're here to learn about how we manage the farm. One of them may be the future Mrs Joey Turner."

"Then you should teach them we muster at Yarrabee Station on horseback, not on those things," said Aimee, pointing at the bike Gav rode over to the convoy of cars.

"Come on, Aimee, it's only for today…er…or maybe for the next week, but you know the dogs do most of the work. These things will just putter along behind the flock."

"Keep your excuses, Joe, I'm not interested," Aimee snapped walking back to the stables. Her brother had completely let his groin take over his head if he thought spooking the pregnant ewes was a good idea. Their sheep were healthy and settled for a reason, and if his prank lost them lambs, Aimee was never going to let him live it down.

Saddling Kite after brushing her down, a small cough caught Aimee's attention. Looking over her shoulder to see Justine behind her, she rolled her eyes. "What do you want?"

"I overheard what you said to Joey earlier. Do you really herd the sheep on horses?"

"Yeah, what's it to you?"

"Why?"

Aimee scrubbed at her face. It was too early to be confused. "Why what?"

"Horses and not vehicles."

Aimee huffed and put a bridle on her horse. "Because the flock is calmer and they're easier to handle. A good portion of the flock is also four months pregnant."

"How long does it take to reach the paddocks?"

"The ones where the sheep are? On horseback, thirty minutes at a trot."

"And in the cars?"

Aimee turned to look at Justine. She propped her hands on her hips and said, "You have to go around the creek and Lachlan Hill past the ag fields, so maybe twenty minutes or so. Depends on the roads. We haven't graded them for a while. Gav and the boys are starting that today so the shearers and the trucks can get up to the sheds."

Justine nodded and nibbled on her lower lip.

Aimee frowned down at her. "Don't you have someone to boss around? Those desperates won't know which is their best side if you're not there to tell them."

"They're not desperate. They're women looking for a chance at love."

"Yeah, by coming out here in droves to compete for a man's attention. Real classy. Definitely true love."

Justine shrugged. "Love can surprise you."

Caught between asking the woman to elaborate, or running her over with her horse, Aimee was left speechless at the woman's next question.

"Can I ride with you?"

Aimee barked out a burst of laughter. "Yeah, no. Not happening. If you fall off and break your neck, they'll think I topped you off."

"I think you'd be surprised at what I can accomplish."

Aimee stared at her for a moment, contemplating the latest situation. Seeing this city woman bounce and complain on the back of a horse over some relatively rugged country would be worth the murder charges. Aimee shrugged. "It's your funeral, and just so you know, I'm not going to run around after you. Saddle that horse over there properly, and you're welcome to trail along."

Justine followed Aimee's gesture to the brown horse in the stall across from them. "Okay."

Aimee let her jaw fall open. "What?"

"Let me tell my crew. Be right back."

With an agility Aimee didn't expect from someone in dress boots, designer slacks and pinched vest atop a white shirt, the woman ran lightly from the stables.

"Ah, crap." Resigned to the fact she might be stuck with the uptight woman, Aimee walked over to River's stall. Reaching for the saddle considering she had no choice but to get this woman on the horse, she felt her arms batted away.

"Allow me," Justine said, smoothly walking into the stall and talking softly with the brown gelding. It was the most easy-going horse the stables housed and was often the go-to mount for Sally's kids. Aimee's mouth fell open and stayed there as Justine ran her hands over the horse, gave him a brush and expertly fixed his saddle around his girth.

"What…how…what?" Aimee managed to mutter as Justine floated to the horse's back. "How the hell?"

Justine smirked down at her. "Coming?"

With a click of her tongue, the woman guided the gelding from the stables.

"Bloody hell," Aimee muttered, rushing over to Kite and leading her outside. "You can ride?" Aimee said a few minutes later after studying the woman's form. She was phenomenal. So balanced, so comfortable and so damn irritatingly good.

"Yes."

"Humph," Aimee murmured. Catching Justine's smug smile, she turned her attention forward. Passing the machinery shed, and a small yard, Aimee took them along the rutted two-wheel track leading to the homestead water tanks. "This is where it gets rougher, princess," she told Justine as they passed the tower holding the tank and descended down the loose shale slope on the other side.

"What is your issue?" Justine asked as the ground levelled out and they trotted their horses through open scrub.

Aimee scoffed to herself. "You need to be more specific. I have many."

Justine chuckled with a sarcastic note. "Yeah, that I noticed, but *specifically*, why are you so antagonistic towards me? It can't simply be because I lost your hat."

"I loved that hat," Aimee said, pouting for a little longer. After a sniff, she said, "I don't like city slickers."

"Yet you were trying to pick me up last night if I'm correct."

"You're not."

"I don't believe you."

"It was a case of mistaken identity. You looked like a friend or whatever."

"If you wanted to be my friend, then giving me a second-rate cocktail wasn't the way to go about it."

Aimee pulled her horse up. "Second rate? I'll have you know that cocktail is bloody awesome and I have a long line of women that will attest to that."

Justine reined her horse in as well and swivelled in her saddle to face her. "It was vile. Tell me, have you ever actually tasted it?"

Aimee pouted and shifted in her seat. "Not so much. I don't like spirits."

"That's pretty much all that was in it. I have a feeling you lured those poor women to your bed because they were drunk out of their skulls with straight…God, what was in it?"

"Vodka, bourbon and tequila with a splash of Irish cream."

Justine shuddered.

"And for your information, I don't *lure* women to my bed with that drink. It's an icebreaker—"

"More like a solid whack to the liver."

Aimee narrowed her eyes at the interruption. "It's my charm they fall for, not the drink."

"You can count yourself lucky for that. There's no way it was bringing me to your bed."

"Bringing you…what?" Aimee said with a stutter, picturing this woman beneath her and accidentally short-circuiting her brain. Justine smiled smugly, bringing her back to reality. "Shut up."

"I didn't say anything," Justine said, holding her hands up in innocence.

"You didn't have to, and for your information, I was not hitting on you."

"Thank goodness for that, because if that was charm, then it must be nothing but your looks to lure in this swath of women you're professing to have had."

"My love life isn't any of your business." Flicking Kite's reins, Aimee started the horse with a jolt and trotted off towards the paddocks. Halfway up the next rise, and hearing River's hooves against the ground behind her, she realised Justine had backhandedly called her attractive. *Damn her again, and damn the stupid tingle in her belly.*

***

Sally met the droving team at the northern yards at midday to provide a bevy of food for the film crew and the giggling girls hanging on her brother's every word. Sally had only been to the beach once in her life, and the lasting memory of that holiday was the flocks of seagulls trying to eat their lunch at the foreshore near Bondi Beach. You'd throw one chip in their direction, and the seagulls would swarm in pecking at each other to get to the morsel first. Joey's female companions reminded her of the noisy, squawking gulls determined to claim their prize.

Brittany and Tiffany were fierce in their competition to be the centre of Joey's attention. No sooner would one woman call out to him and stick out her chest and giggle than another would do the same. Amber, looking like she was growing tired of the constant battle, started to hang back and watch how the sheep moved.

"How far along are they?" Sally heard her ask Matt.

Matt, a nineteen-year-old junior farmhand, looked around to see if Joey was beside him, and turned back to Amber with a blush when he realised the question was directed at him. "Four months. One more to go. We're going to shear them up and fatten them up."

Wanting to watch Matt blush some more, Sally waved a greeting to Aimee as she rode her horse over. She was guiding another behind her, making Sally frown. *Where'd the second horse come from?*

"How'd the sheep go with the bikes?" Sally asked her.

Aimee grunted, unwilling to say that the mustering had been no different. The pregnant ewes looked as settled as they ever did.

Sally chuckled, reading her sister's answer. "What's River doing up here?"

"*She* rode him," Aimee said, pointing to Justine as she doubled on the back of a quad bike with her sound guy.

"Really? The suit did?"

Aimee bounced her head and chewed on her sandwich. Justine's skills on horseback were excellent, but there was no way she was going to convey that to Sally. "She hated my cocktail."

Sally frowned. "You made her an Aimee Special?"

Shrugging, she said, "Joey told me to be nice, so I was nice. Shame she's such a bitch. She said the cocktail was vile." Turning to face Sally, she said, "You've had it before. It wasn't that bad, was it?"

Sally made a popping noise with her lips. "Well…I'm not a big mixed drink fan, so…it, uh, wasn't my favourite drink ever."

"Ugh." Aimee let her head hang forward on her shoulders. "That's it. My sex life is over."

Sally patted Aimee on the back. "Trust me, you didn't earn yourself any favours with that drink, so obviously it was something else that your conquests liked. I'm thinking it's because you're you."

Refusing to acknowledge the conquest barb, Aimee said, "Me?"

Smiling kindly, Sally nodded. "Exactly. You're a beautiful young woman and you can be quite charming when you put your mind to it." Sally tucked a wayward strand of light brown sun-bleached hair behind Aimee's ear. "You look a lot like mum. Blue eyes, gorgeous hair and a complexion I hate you for." Sally patted her cheek. "Soft and blemish free. You suck."

Chuckling alongside her sister, Aimee let out a big sigh. "I accidentally hit on her last night."

"Who?"

"Justine."

"Really!" Sally's eyebrows shot up. "Where the hell was I when this was happening?"

"You were tucking in the kids. I'm surprised Joey didn't mention it. He was standing right beside me when I planned my great cocktail move." Covering her face with her hands, Aimee groaned. "I had no idea it was her. All I saw were curves, wavy hair, and lips worth kissing."

"Uh…Aimee."

"And those glasses she wears…damn. But no," she continued, still hiding her embarrassment behind calloused hands. "It turned out to be the one woman I'd sooner strangle. The Dragon."

"Aimee, darling, perhaps you should—"

"The universe is a cruel place. Someone like her should look so damn sex—oh Jesus!" Aimee, having pulled her hands away from her face looked up to see Justine standing in front of her with a smile on her face. "What the *hell*, Sal!" she whispered harshly to her sister.

Sally shook her head and held her hands up. "Hey, I tried to warn you. Not my fault. I'm going to go down to the hut to set up lunch." Sally gave Aimee a wink and walked over to her car past the crew hovering around the TV starlets.

"Lips worth kissing? Sexy? My, you do have yourself a crush, don't you farm girl?"

Let the mortification continue, Aimee moaned silently. "My name is Aimee," she snapped, sliding from her perch on the tray of Sally's ute.

"And how was I supposed to know that exactly?" Justine said, following her to Kite.

"You're a fancy producer, figure it out."

"I believe it's rude to call someone by their name before they've formally introduced themselves. Ever heard of a thing called manners?" Justine looked her up and down. "No, I suppose being raised by sheep and horses, you probably missed that lesson."

"I know exactly what manners are, lady. I exercise my right to use them as I see fit, and I'm not wasting good manners on people coming out here and acting like dictators."

Justine cocked an eyebrow. "You really do have yourself worked up, don't you? Perhaps I should remind you again that your brother is the person that instigated this little production, not I. Joey signed up to be on this show and whether he conveyed to you what that would entail during the dating phase, then, again, I'm not at fault for your ignorance." Stepping closer, Justine shoved a finger in Aimee's breastbone. "Save your antagonism for those who deserve it." Spinning around, she walked away, calling over her shoulder, "My name is Justine Cason, not dragon, by the way."

"My name is Justine...na, na, na, na," Aimee mumbled to herself petulantly, hating that Justine was right. Joey was the one she should be sniping at for this interruption in their normally peaceful rural life. She was hardly going to stir him up again after threatening to send her off to the urban life. Yes, she was twenty-three and perfectly capable of making her own decisions, but no, she wasn't about to disobey the law of the land. Joey, the officially named manager of the property, was to be respected.

It didn't mean, however, that she had to like him very much, and in protest against everything pissing her off, she got on her horse and dropped by the old hut where Sally was planning to set up for lunch. At least there the kids would welcome her without telling her to play nice with the city intruders.

Clicking her tongue, she urged her horse to a trot over the low, yellow pasture and over the undulations in the land. This area of Yarrabee Station was a stretch of grassy plains ringed by vegetated creek beds and rocky hills scattered in bushes. The grass was thick and tall thanks to above average winter rains, and the absence of recent stock in this paddock. Looking behind her before descending down the incline of a small hill, Aimee saw the sheep scattered across the paddock greedily eating the virgin grass. This would be their last opportunity to feed here until they rotated the stock back through in summer. Once sheared, the bulk of their stock was being driven to the top paddocks rich in new growth for the pregnant ewes, and already stocked with extra feed to accommodate for their growing bellies.

***

"Aunty Mee, Aunty Mee!" Caroline called as she escaped from her nanny's arms. The same woman, Miss Gerhardt, acted as teacher for Sally's family also.

"Hiya, Rolly," Aimee said, scooping Caroline up in her arms. "Have you been good for Miss Gerhardt?" Caroline nodded firmly, a serious frown on her face.

"Robbie's still studying?" Aimee asked Miss Gerhardt, realising for the hundredth time that she still didn't know the woman's first name. Asking always seemed rude, but her curiosity always remained.

"Yes." Miss Gerhardt looked at her ever-present fob watch then to the boy hunched over a book under the shade shelter of the hut. "He has fifteen minutes. Please don't disturb him."

Aimee shook her head. No one messed with Miss Gerhardt's schedule. As strict and routine-driven as she was, she was deadly efficient and remarkably patient with children. "Well, Rolly, why don't we go see how Rainbow Sprinkles is."

"No, silly! Rainbow Sparkles!"

Aimee grimaced playfully. "Oops."

Her four-year-old niece led her to a chicken and its makeshift pen. The chicken, a silky white bird, went everywhere with Rolly since coming to the child as a birthday present. Aimee listened to Caroline ramble on about the colour and size of the egg it laid a few days ago, the most favourite bugs it liked to eat, and the colour of its poo after it ate too much corn.

Chuckling at the child's observations, Aimee looked up in time to see Sally pull up along with the mess of women and film crew.

"Shit."

"Aunty Mee!" Caroline admonished.

"Sorry."

"Hello!" Caroline called out as she exited the chicken pen and ran off to where her mummy was offloading the containers of food from her ute.

Frowning as she closed the pen, and wondering who Rolly was talking to, Aimee came face to face with Justine. "Ugh. You."

"Swearing in front of children now?"

Curling her lip at being caught with her slip up, she brushed past Justine after securing the door. "What are you doing here?"

"I rode ahead and was told to follow the road to this hut, and then Heidi informed me you were over here with your niece and a spoiled chicken."

"Who the hell is Heidi?" Aimee asked, furrowing her brow as Justine fell in step beside her on the way to where the horses were tethered.

"Umm…Heidi? The woman I presume looks after your sister's kids."

Aimee stopped, forcing Justine to do the same. "Wait. You mean Miss Gerhardt?"

"Yes. Heidi Gerhardt." Justine cocked her head and looked at her strangely.

"Her first name is Heidi?"

"Umm…yes?"

"Huh." Aimee let that soak in for a moment before continuing to the horses.

"You didn't know?" Justine stared at Aimee gathering in Kite's reins. "Seriously? How is it you don't know that?"

That's none of your business." Leaving Justine no room to interrogate further, Aimee mounted her horse and clicked her tongue to get Kite moving.

***

Sally watched her sister ride off and huffed. *She was skinny enough without skipping lunch.* Cutting a glance to Justine, she wondered what had transpired between the two for Aimee to have left. Picking up a tray of sandwiches, she walked over to the woman staring at the paddocks.

"Lunch?"

"Oh!" Justine swung around with her hand on her chest.

"Sorry."

"No. It's okay. I was a million miles away." She looked at the tray. "Oh. Thanks." Taking a sandwich, she took a bite.

"Is she bothering you?" Sally asked.

"Who? Aimee?" Justine shook her head. "No. She's unpleasant, but nothing I can't handle."

Sally nodded. "She's usually really easy to get along with, but for whatever reason, this has got under her skin." Sally gestured to the film crew swarming around the girls and Joey as they ate lunch. She doubted anyone needed to televise someone eating an egg salad sandwich.

"We'll be gone before she knows it and she can get back to snarling at whatever the hell she usually snarls at."

Sally laughed. "Actually, you'd be surprised. Aimee rarely behaves like this. Sure, she can get protective, but whatever you two have going on is something else."

Justine shook her head and ate more of her sandwich.

"Maybe it's because you insulted her cocktail."

Justine cringed. "It was disgusting."

"I know." Sally began to chuckle.

"Does she really use that to lure women?"

"She likes to think so, but really, it's because she's a beautiful, charismatic young lady. That's what they fall for."

Justine chewed on more of her lunch as the pair of them watched the women by Joey's side fend off a swarm of flies intent on eating their sandwiches. "She doesn't think she's beautiful, does she?"

Sally tilted her head at Justine. *What an odd question.* "No, she doesn't. I don't know what she sees when she looks in a mirror, but it's not what everyone else sees. She over-compensates. Always has."

"Because of what happened when she was a child?"

Sally took a deep breath and glanced back over at her brother. She had no doubt the story of their childhood had become part of the show. "I think so, yes. It was hard for everyone. Especially Aimee." Looking back at Justine, Sally placed a hand on her forearm. "Give her some time. She'll come around."

Justine scoffed. "I find that unlikely. She hasn't held any punches in telling me where to go so far. I doubt that'll change."

"Well, looking on the bright side, you only have to put up with her for two weeks. If one of this lot turns out to be 'the one' she gets to put up with her forever."

A shared smile turned into a chuckle and then laughter, gaining the attention of the women swatting flies.

"Mum?" Sally's eldest said as he walked over with eyes on the container of sandwiches.

"Here." She gave him the entire container. "Share some with Caroline and remind her not to share it with Rainbow Sparkle. Chickens shouldn't eat chickens."

Robbie screwed his nose up. "Gross."

Justine and Sally sniggered at him as he moved off to where his sister was trying to catch flies with Miss Gerhardt.

"Do they know her name?" Justine asked.

"Who's name?" Sally said.

"Heidi. Do your kids know her name is Heidi?"

Sally frowned and looked over to the kids and the woman in question. "I think so. Why do you ask?"

"Aimee didn't know."

"What?"

"It's why she left. She didn't know."

"You're kidding?"

Shaking her head, Justine left Sally to it as she returned to the shade.

Sally turned to the direction Aimee had taken and shook her head. *How the hell had Miss Gerhardt lived on the property for so long without Aimee finding out her first name?*

CHAPTER FOUR

"Oh for God's sake! Can we move this along?" Aimee yelled at the film crew huddled by the gate leading to the yards beside the shearing shed. She looked at her watch and huffed for the twelfth time. It had taken a decade to get across the fields, and now Justine had the city girls playing sheep farmer by the gate. Watching the women squeal and leap about in fright as dozens of sheep ran past them and into the shearing yards had been entertaining at first, but doing three takes of the same thing by making the sheep run around in circles was ridiculous. "Come on, Joe! We've got flamin' work to do!"

Aimee heard Justine yell 'cut' before the women herself stormed over to her. "Will you please keep the commentary to yourself? I don't want to be up all night trying to edit your impatience out of the soundtrack."

"Then hurry up already. Surely you've got enough footage of them falling on their arses to fill up an entire show by now. I need to get back to the homestead and make a start on the million other jobs I have to do. All you're doing is wasting time."

"Feel free to leave whenever you like."

"And leave you alone to find your own way back? No thanks. I may want to get rid of you, but I'm not being blamed for your death when you wander off and get lost."

Justine pursed her lips as Joey walked over to them.

"Aimee?"

"What?" she snapped at him.

Joey clenched his jaw for a moment. "Why don't you go sort the feed."

Furrowing her eyes, she shook her head. "Matty's doing that."

"Then help him."

"But I have to—"

"I'm not asking."

Taking a long, dusty breath through her nose, and scowling at her brother, she said, "Fine." Turning her attention to Justine, she put as much heat behind a glare as she could, and felt a curious tickle of pleasure as Justine matched it. Aimee may not like the woman, but she had plenty of gumption.

***

They finally yarded the flock and called a three-hour hiatus on filming as Joey and a few farmhands were forced to do last minute maintenance on the water pump. Work that the cameramen wanted to avoid lest their equipment get doused in sprays of water. Aimee, thankfully, avoided the task also, having been charged with escorting Justine back to the homestead to prepare the film schedule later that day.

Her brother had a date of some sort with one of the girls and Aimee was under explicit instructions to show Justine the creek south-east of the house to scout a good location. Aimee chuckled to herself and hoped they didn't mind being swarmed by insects. Aimee almost wished she could be there to watch Justine hop about trying to swat flies away as dusk approached.

Giving the woman in question a side-long glance, Aimee once again admired her form on a horse and with curiosity burning at her, she finally asked, "Where did you learn to ride?"

Justine looked at her blankly having been staring out at the fields of grass they rode through. "Hmm?"

"I said, where did you learn to ride."

"Oh…uh, pony club."

The woman looked back to the landscape and Aimee rolled her eyes. *Of course, it was pony club. Silly her. How very city of the woman.* Leaving Justine to her daydreaming, and probably admiring the amount of space there was outside of the city, Aimee remained silent for the remainder of the ride home.

"You're a grown woman," Justine pointed out after taking off River's saddle.

Aimee, who was reaching for Kite's brush paused and looked over at her. "What are you on about now?"

"Heidi. How did you not know her first name?"

Shaking her head at the absurd choice of topic, Aimee brushed Kite down and said over her shoulder, "It's called respect. She was very specific about how she wanted to be addressed when she first got here. I just did what I was told."

"How long has she been here?"

"Ten years or so. Why? Want to do an immigration story on rural teachers now? Isn't a desperate farmer interesting enough?"

"She's a teacher?"

Aimee dropped her hand from Kite's flank and turned to stare at Justine. "Why do you care?"

"I'm just trying to figure it out. You say the woman has been here for ten years, yet you don't even know her name. Doesn't that strike you as odd?"

Aimee bristled. "Not really. A lot of people come out here and prefer to remain private. It's their prerogative." Miss Gerhardt was practically part of the paintwork she had been at the station that long. She came to the station when Aimee hit high school and guided her through her schooling with a patience Aimee had taken for granted. After watching her work with Robbie and Caroline, she began to appreciate the tolerance the woman possessed. A tolerance she herself didn't have. Especially with townies.

"So she teaches your sister's kids?"

"Yes."

"Did she used to teach you, too?"

"Yes."

"What's that like, not going to a proper school?"

Aimee threw her brush onto the shelf. "I didn't know any different, so I wouldn't know."

"So you're a loner?"

Shutting Kite's stall door roughly, Aimee stared at Justine. "What's with all the questions?"

"I'm curious what life out here is like. Especially considering you lost your parents so young. I can't imagine—"

"Wait. You know about my parents?"

Justine frowned in confusion again. "Of course. It was part of Joey's backstory. The tragic passing of his parents when he was seventeen. The way he stepped up to run the station with his grandfather and raised his seven-year-old sister. It's an incredible story. I think he shed a few tears at the interview. It was very moving."

"I bet it was," Aimee muttered, her back teeth clenching. This wasn't a conversation she ever liked having, even with her siblings, so listening to the producer talk about it so casually ignited her anger.

"I saw the edited piece the other day for the first time. I mean, I saw the uncut version, but the edited piece with the soundtrack was truly heart wrenching."

"I'm glad you found so much entertainment in our tragic past. Real classy." Aimee pushed past Justine fully intending to storm off but was waylaid by a hand on her arm.

"I don't find it entertaining at all. It's incredibly sad. To lose both parents so young…" Justine shook her head. Dropping Aimee's arm, she said, "I think that was the reason he got so many interested women. Women love a broken soul. They think they'll be the ones who can save him."

"Save him? From what? He *is* happy." Stepping toe-to-toe with Justine, Aimee said with a growl, "We don't need saving."

"Oh, I'm sure *you* don't," Justine said, emphasising her words with a shove to Aimee's shoulder. "After all, you're the tough station chick standing there thinking you've got it all figured out, but really all you are is a scared little brat with a superiority complex."

"You know nothing about me."

"Trust me, that's a positive."

Aimee narrowed her eyes to glare at the smaller woman scowling up at her. Justine's cheeks were flushed, her eyes shone, and after a quick glance south, Aimee could see her chest heaving against the tight shirt she wore. A flush of lust ripped through Aimee at the thought of taking the woman against the stall door behind her. Just one small movement and she'd kiss that snarl right off those painted lips. Justine cleared her throat and Aimee came to the sudden realisation that she was staring at lips that were now parted and being wet with a flicking tongue. *Shit!* Aimee jumped back like she'd been stung and curled her lip. *What the hell had she been thinking?* This woman was a viper, not someone to lust after. Aimee stormed away trying not to notice the way Justine's features had changed when the air shifted between them. How those amber eyes melted, and how her chin tilted subtly north bringing their faces closer.

"You idiot," Aimee muttered to herself as she fell against her closed door, trying to ignore the buzz of excitement rocketing around her body, as well as the heat of embarrassment burning her cheeks. Slumping to the floor, she held her head in her hands and shook it. *Fool.*

***

Sally lifted the last box from the back of the ute and caught the drift of heated words on the wind. Pausing, she cocked her head and tried to source the direction. A second later, Justine was striding out of the stables. Groaning, Sally rolled her eyes to the clear blue sky above. Aimee was clearly being her charming self again. Taking the box to the kitchen, she dumped it on the floor and made her way over to the stables.

"Mitsy?" she said, looking at the woebegone-looking animal standing guard in front of Aimee's door. If dogs could stick out their bottom lip and look pathetic, that's exactly what Mitsy would be doing.

"Aimee?" Sally said, knocking on the door.

"What?"

Rolling her eyes again, Sally let herself in. Mitsy nearly knocked Sally over to reach her owner. "Shit!" she said, startled to find her sister sitting on the floor right beside the door. "What in *heaven's* name are you doing?"

Aimee fended off Mitsy's need to lick her face and said, "Meditating. What does it look like?"

Ignoring the sarcasm, Sally said, "What happened with you and Justine this time? I could hear you two across the yard."

Getting up off the floor, Aimee said, "She's a nosy bitch who finds our past tragic or some such crap. I don't want her here. I don't want those bloody bimbos here. And I want Joey to get over himself. Someone's going to get *hurt*, Sal."

Sally took a deep breath and put her hands on her sister's shoulders. "No one is going to get hurt. We're too careful for that. You're too careful. I know you don't like it, but this is temporary. It's not like we don't ever have strangers out here, Aims. People come and go all the time."

"Yeah, but they're people that work on stations. They know the risks. These idiots are just like…like them. They'll wander off and get themselves killed, just like…" Aimee shook her head and lowered her eyes. "I don't like this."

"I know, sweetheart," Sally said, pulling her sister in for a hug and grateful that she got one in return. Aimee was hard to predict when the subject of their past came up. She swung between wanting comfort and wishing for solitude. "Look," Sally said, leaning back. "Joey will keep an eye on the women and crew. You'll look after Justine when she's looking around the property, and I'll be doing what I can to watch them, too. Gav, Mike, Matt, and Danny are always around and always on radio. Between us all, if something goes wrong, we're all there to fix it. Okay?"

Aimee stepped back and wrapped her arms around herself. *Classic isolation technique*, Sally recalled the psychiatrist mention once.

"No one will get hurt?" Aimee said.

"That's right." Watching Aimee take a deep breath, Sally reached out and rubbed her arm. "Why don't you have a cuppa before you take Justine out to the creek?"

Aimee nodded. "Hey, Sal?" Aimee called out softly as Sally turned to leave.

"Yeah?"

"Did you know Miss Gerhardt's first name was Heidi?"

Sally frowned at her. "Of course, I did. I was the one who hired her."

"Oh…right."

"You didn't know."

Aimee shook her head. "I never wanted to ask. She's bloody intimidating."

Sally chuckled. "That was the point. How else were you supposed to pass high school with honours? She's the only person that could keep you in line back then. You've always been intense, especially since…" Sally tapered off, wary of her sister's triggers. "Well, you know. You were a highly-strung child."

Aimee gave her sister a thin smile and looked at the floorboards. "Yeah…I guess."

Sighing, Sally came over and wrapped her little sister in another hug. "You okay?"

Aimee nodded into Sally's shoulder.

"They'd be proud of you. You know?"

"Don't," Aimee said, pushing her sister away.

Sally cupped her sister's cheek. "I love you, Bug."

"Yeah, yeah," Aimee said, swatting playfully at her sister's hand. "Love you back. Now go away. I have a producer to find."

***

After lingering for as long as she could in the loft, Aimee made her way back down to the stables. Finding it free of anything with less than four legs, she sighed in relief. It was one thing preparing yourself to face the woman she almost attacked with her lips, it was another thing entirely to face her for real. Shutting her eyes, Aimee took a deep breath.

"There you are."

Aimee's eyelids shot open and she physically jumped. Justine strode into the stables looking as serious and dragon-like as ever.

"I haven't got all day to wait for you to do…" Justine waved her arm at the stairway to the loft. "Whatever it is you do up there. I have a bloody production to run, and time is of the essence. I need to get the film crew to the next location to set up, and if you're too busy sulking about like a hormonal teenager, then point me in the right direction and I'll find my own way."

Aimee noticed Justine refused to meet her eyes. Briefly confused, Aimee stepped closer to the incensed woman to find Justine jolt and step back quickly. *Interesting.*

"Well?" Justine snapped.

Aimee puckered her lips in thought at Justine's behaviour.

At her silence, Justine cleared her throat and crossed her arms. "Well?"

"Say please."

"What?"

Aimee took a step closer and Justine nervously held her ground. *Very interesting.* "Use your manners, or is that something city folk don't have time for anymore?"

"My…?" Justine took a long inhale through her nose and fisted her hands. "Will you *please* get off your arse and take me to the bloody creek."

"With pleasure," Aimee said, shooting the woman a grin before pushing past her into the mid-afternoon light. "Come on then, we haven't got all day."

***

Dust lingered on her tongue as the parched earth churned around them in the wake of the four-wheel drive's turbulence when they stopped. Mitsy leaped off the tray into the cloud and set to work with her nose, heading toward the creek. The creek was more of a partially wet line of sand squiggling its way across the landscape. Trees clung to the banks with their roots pushing deep below the surface to reach the permanent underground water. On the surface, grassy clumps were brittle and brown because their shallow root systems were inadequate to flourish without rain. Beside the creek was a rustic, disused cattle yard. Large logs from the pioneer days of the station stood firm and strong as they formed a fenced area where cattle and sheep were once herded for transport. In the bright light of day, the place looked barren and dead, but Aimee knew that when the sun approached the distant hills, the place glowed like a picture. *A perfect date location.* She glanced at the nearby pool of semi-stagnant water. *With the exception of blood-sucking insects in summer.*

"Why have we stopped?" Justine asked.

"This is where Joey will take contender number one."

"*Here?*"

"Yep," Aimee said and climbed out of the car. Immediately swatting at flies that always seemed to occupy this part of the property, Aimee smiled to herself. *It may not be mosquito season, but there was no shortage of flies with a penchant to bite.*

"You're kidding, right?" Justine asked, following. Shielding her eyes from the glare, she looked at the stagnant pond clinging to the surface beside the yards.

"Nope."

Justine put her hands on her hips, which had the effect of stretching her shirt across her chest. Aimee tried not to look, but since the altercation in the stables, her hormones were piqued. She couldn't deny she found the woman attractive. Convinced the interest went both ways considering Justine's bizarre behaviour earlier, it was worth her time to find out. Justine's attention was on the pathetic excuse for a creek as Aimee approached her with a sly grin on her face.

"You don't approve?" Aimee asked, making Justine step back in surprise at her proximity.

"Definitely not."

"Not a fan of romance?" Aimee took a small amount of delight at the pause this gave Justine. The quick glance at her lips didn't go unnoticed either.

Justine ignored the question. "What else have you got?"

"What's wrong with romance?"

Justine huffed. "It's unrealistic. Grand gestures that may or may not win the heart of the person you're interested in seems like a big risk to me. Why can't people just admit their attraction and act on what they feel without wasting time?"

Aimee smiled and moved closer, pleased to hear Justine take a sharp inhale.

"There's got to be somewhere else we can go?"

Aimee raised an eyebrow.

"*That* is unacceptable," Justine said, gesturing at the old yards.

"You're just going to have to trust me."

"*Trust* you?" Justine snorted. "Sorry. No. I'm confident you'd do what it takes to sabotage this for your brother, so I'm not going to approve this derelict pile of wood for a suitable filming location."

Aimee pursed her lips. "I'm not sabotaging anything."

"That says otherwise," Justine said, pointing at the old yards.

"*That* is going to look amazing later, and honestly, that's more than the woman deserves. The station isn't a film set. It takes time, but the beauty will reveal itself. Be patient."

Justine scoffed. "Patient? What? Like you, you mean?"

Aimee took a long breath through clenched teeth. In lust, she may be, but this woman was irritating. "This is it, princess. Deal with it." Aimee strode to the driver door and climbed into the car, put it in gear and threatened to move off.

After a glare that looked like it should have pierced her skull, Justine climbed in, slamming the door for good measure. "You're impossible."

"You're a bitch."

Justine made a weird exasperated sound and crossed her arms while muttering under her breath.

***

As the homestead neared, Justine said, "You know what? Give me the keys. I'll drive myself around."

Aimee let out a bark of laughter. "You will *not*."

"I'm perfectly capable of—"

"Getting yourself killed. The answer is no. You're not to go anywhere on this property without an escort, do you understand me?"

"I'll have you know I'm not a bloody child. Unlike yourself, I'm a responsible adult capable of navigating through life without chucking a hissy fit every five minutes."

"A hissy fit?" Aimee shook her head and braked harder than she really needed to as they returned to the homestead yards. Both women were tugged against their seat belts. As Aimee's body jerked backwards, she turned the car off and yanked the keys from the ignition. "You know nothing about me, lady, and the answer is still no. I don't care how old you are, you don't know the place and getting hurt or lost is easier than you think, not to mention the fact the snakes are starting to warm up and move." Aimee shoved the car door open and after securing it firmly in place, she stormed off to the stable. Gav came out of the shed at the same moment, took one look at Aimee's dark face and turned back the way he came. Aimee gave him a scowl for good measure.

"Hey!" Justine called, jogging after her. "I'm not done speaking with you."

Aimee stopped in the shade deep inside the stables and crossed her arms to watch Justine stride in to join her. Her hair was askew from the drive in the car. No air conditioning meant winding down the windows, and with the ruffled hair and the flushed angry look on her face, the woman was an imposing figure.

"Must I continually remind you I'm here to film a show your brother is part of. It means accessing the best locations the property has to offer to meet my filming schedules."

Aimee looked down at the woman that had invaded her personal space. She may be imposing, but she was also short. Leaning down slightly, she said, "Hate to break it to you, lady, but the sheep don't care what label you're wearing or what your filming schedule is. Why don't you go back to where you came from and leave us the hell alone?"

"I'm here to do a job and unfortunately, I have to rely on you to get it done. You're a rude, arrogant bitch blaming the world for your lot in life."

Aimee stepped closer still, enjoying the exhilarating rush the proximity gave her. "Excuse me? This coming from the uptight city chick coming out here in her ridiculous suits and demanding free reign over our lives. You're a typical city idiot thinking you can come out bush and make it bend to your will. New flash, all it gets you is pain and misery. And for your information, I love my life."

"I can see that, what with all the whining and pouting."

Curling her lip, Aimee leaned in almost touching Justine's nose with her own. "I hate you."

Justine took a few deep breaths and said with a croak in her voice, "And my dislike for you is equally as fervent."

Aimee shook her head and scoffed. "God, you can't even talk like a normal person." Her eyes fell to Justine's lips as a sliver of tongue moved out to wet them and Aimee's breath caught. Time slowed as her heart pounded in her ears and her heaving breath mingled with Justine's.

Justine's eyes flicked across Aimee's face, settling on her lips. "And your grunting is practically ineligible," she whispered.

Staring each other in the eye, neither made a move to step back. Quite prepared to strangle the woman if it came down to it, Aimee's heart thudded wildly as she stared at those soft-looking, parted lips below her. Leaning in, and daring the woman to move, she whispered against Justine's lips, "I really don't like you."

"Will you shut up." Justine grabbed at Aimee's lapels and crashed their lips together.

It was electrifying, desperate and wet. It was unexpected passion and lust. Mutually moaning as their tongues met, Aimee shoved Justine against the stall door and needy hands clutched at her clothing. The impromptu make-out session only increased in its desperation and fingers sought out skin-on-skin contact. After yanking Justine's shirt from her pants, Aimee cupped a bra-clad breast before Justine broke the kiss to breathe out, "Wait."

Aimee stepped back as though electrocuted. *What the hell was she doing?* "I'm sorry. I shouldn't have—"

"There you are," Sally said, walking into the stables and making both women leap out of their skin. Sally stopped and frowned. "You all right?"

"Fine," Aimee said, doing her best to stand with trembling legs.

"Did I interrupt something?" Sally asked Justine.

Justine patted down her clothing and cleared her throat. "No. You were looking for me?"

"Actually, no. I was looking for Aimee."

"Oh. Okay. Umm…" Justine cleared her throat again, gave her a curt nod and quickly vacated the stables leaving Sally frowning after her.

"What was that all about?" Sally asked.

"Buggered if I know," Aimee said, willing her pulse to slow down before it buckled her at the knees. "What do you want?"

"I need a hand with the trailer. The hitch is stuck again."

"Right." Aimee brushed past her sister and headed to the vegetable garden out the back of the homestead. Taking her frustrations out on a hitch that refused to let go of the four-wheel-drive, she managed to pop it loose. Even though victory was hers, Aimee continued to scowl at the tow hitch. *Why did she kiss Justine?* "Of all the stupid, God damn foolish ideas…" she muttered to herself. One minute, she was livid with the woman, the next, she wanted to participate in the sexual energy that she emanated. Face palming herself, Aimee shook her head. *Why did I kiss her?* Never before had a woman made her question herself. As her head continued to shake, a thought crossed her mind. Aimee's head snapped up and her jaw dropped. Looking in the direction of the stables, a slow smile began to form on her face. *Justine* had been the one to pull them together. *Justine* had been the one to initiate the kiss. "Well, God damn."

CHAPTER FIVE

Joey was smiling when they reached the old yards. The sun was low and the place lit up like a scene from a Banjo Patterson novel. *Man from Snowy River, eat your heart out*, he thought. He glanced at his companions to find the camera crew breaking apart the beauty around them into lighting levels, contrast angles, colour saturation and sound checks. Joey shook his head and looked at his date. Brittney was scowling at the dust on her shoes and swatting vigorously at insects swarming around her face. *Should have brought the bug spray.*

About to walk over to where the crew had laid out a blanket, some hay bales, and a chilling bottle of wine, he noticed Justine. She was standing still admiring the scene with a faraway look on her face. Changing his trajectory, he walked beside her and said, "Beautiful, isn't it?"

Jolting to life, Justine turned to him and said, "Y-Yes. It is." The smile Justine flashed him looked stiff.

"Everything okay?"

"Certainly. Now…if you'd take your positions on the rug with Brittney, we can get the show on the road."

"Righto." Giving Justine a curious glance as he walked away, Joey's contemplation was side-tracked as Brittney launched herself at him.

"Hi, handsome." Brittney threw her arms around her neck and kissed his cheek. Her hands slid down his back to the seat of his jeans before she pulled back.

Blushing at the attention, Joey managed an awkward smile at the blonde woman before escorting her to the mat laid out on the ground that would have once been ankle-deep in cow dung. His eyes took in the ruins of the old cattle yards; one of the few landmarks left of an endeavour his grandfather attempted in the early nineteen hundreds.

"Ugly, isn't it?" Brittney said.

"The yards?"

Brittney nodded. "You should burn it down or something."

"I…"

Joey was saved from trying to find an appropriate response to Brittney's inappropriate suggestion by Justine clapping her hands to get everyone's attention.

"Okay. Sound check."

The man with the microphone stick nodded after checking Brittney and Joey's personal mics as well as his own.

"Lighting." Justine glanced at another crew member and received another nod. "Okay, then. Joey, Brittney, I want to you sit there for a moment and take in the scene while we roll some footage, and then you can start conversing. Have you got the conversation suggestions with you?"

Joey gave her the thumbs up.

"Do I really have to ask about babies and stuff? They're so…icky."

Everyone stared at Brittney for a couple of heartbeats.

"Icky?" Justine asked.

Brittney's grimacing face gave her the answer.

"Fine. No. Talk about rural life instead."

"Rural life? What's that?"

"Living in the bush."

"Oh…like this place? How it's in the middle of freaking nowhere. I mean, seriously, why would you want to live out here?"

Joey and Justine gaped at her.

"Ah…okay," Justine said. "Let's just stick with the notes and go from there." Giving Joey a look somewhere between bewildered and apologetic, Justine called action and let the car crash go on permanent record.

***

While Joey was off dating contestant number one, Aimee went to the main house in search of a snack to see the other two lazing by the pool through the kitchen window. It was a beautiful and balmy afternoon and the pool was heated, so Aimee didn't blame them. She almost wished she could dive in and freshen up also, but she had predator traps to set before the sunlight completely disappeared. Foxes had begun to move in as lambing season approached. Snatching a snack from the pantry, she wandered out to the pool to play nice with the girls for a couple of minutes.

"Hi. Enjoying yourselves?"

"Oh, definitely. This is the life, isn't it?" said the one without an ice pack on her backside.

The other wiggled a little. Aimee still couldn't figure out how she had managed to be nipped by a sheep. "Sometimes," Aimee said, taking a bite of her snack. "We don't get a lot of free time to enjoy it, though. Life on a station is pretty much dawn to dusk. Sometimes night," she added, thinking of doing some spotlighting soon to hunt for feral animals.

One of the women, Aimee thought was Amber, frowned. "Seriously?"

Aimee nodded. "The animals don't take holidays."

"Even weekends?" the other one, Aimee assumed was Tiffany, asked.

"Even weekends."

"Ugh. That must suck," Tiffany said.

"Not really. You don't really notice to be honest, and when you do have time off, you seriously appreciate it."

Tiffany looked at her dubiously.

"Anyway…I better get back to work. Enjoy your afternoon."

"Oh, we will," Tiffany said with a broad smile.

"Enjoy your work," Amber called out to her.

Aimee shook her head as she walked to the machinery shed. *If any of these women became a permanent part of the station, she'd eat her own hat…if she could find it.*

"Aims, problem," Gav said as she entered the shed.

"With?"

Gav beckoned her with his finger and led her to the big fuel tanks at the back of the shed. One for diesel, one for unleaded petrol, and several oil drums stacked beside them. "Tap them."

Frowning, Aimee did just that. Both tanks sounded hollow. An inspection of the drums showed most were empty. "What the hell? What happened to the order?"

Gav shrugged. "Ask the boss. I put it in last month."

Aimee pursed her lips. Last month Joey went to the city to pick his girlfriends. "What else hasn't he done?"

Taking a deep breath, Gav rattled off a list that ignited Aimee's fury. The station only ran efficiently when everyone did what was asked and expected of them. If one person started to slack off, then it put everyone else at risk. Fuming, and with nothing she could do about it at that very moment, she decided to see to the tasks she had to finish before tackling her brother's jobs.

Throwing on her backpack filled with a water bottle, a clipboard, handheld radio, and various tools, she pulled on her helmet and kick-started her motorbike. The bike roared to life and she looked to her canine companion.

"Stay Mitsy."

The dog whined.

"Be good." Tearing across the yards, she headed south. Preferring horseback over machines, she couldn't deny the thrill of the speed her 250CC Yamaha gave her. Especially when she was angry. Cutting across the countryside through several paddocks, she navigated a path for her front tyre as the land zipped by. Grassy for the most part, hidden in the tall, green grass of the pastures being rested from the grazing stock, there were hidden sandstone outcrops and stumps of old dead trees that had succumbed to fire many decades earlier. Hilly and uneven, she forged her way through paddock after paddock before reaching the southwest corner of their boundary to start the steady routine of riding the boundary fence line looking for holes while making her way to the traps. Near to the homestead, the fences had been upgraded from wooden posts and wire, to metal posts, strainers and spacers. Straight and true and only a few years old, the difference in the older paddocks was noticeable. Posts, cracked and weathered with age stood with a lean to this side or that, making the sagging barbed wire meander along a path that should have been baron in a five metre strip on both sides. The neighbouring property looked freshly cleared, but on the Yarrabee side, Aimee found nothing but firebreaks on the verge of being overgrown jungles along the entire southern flank of their property. She added it to the list of jobs Joey had failed to accomplish over the winter season, and grumbled at herself for not noticing it sooner. Grading the fire breaks took days…days that they wouldn't have available for a month or two. "Damn you, Joey," she muttered as she turned back toward the homestead as the sun dipped over the horizon.

***

She walked into chaos.

After a huge welcome by Mitsy, she found Brittney in the kitchen being attended to. The woman was covered in a mix of red welts and lavender-coloured dots of calamine lotion.

"Bugs bad?" Aimee asked trying not to smile.

Joey gave her a warning glare, seeing the humour in her expression. "Not now, Aimee."

"Where's the next big date, Romeo? The veggie garden?"

Joey scowled. The vegetable garden lovingly attended to by Sally was covered in fresh horse manure thanks to Aimee unhitching the trailer, and the thought of it had her chuckling.

"Make yourself useful and give Sally a hand. She's got the rotisserie on."

Aimee forgot everything at those words. Joey's mismanagement could wait. "What? Why wasn't I told?" Nothing was better than a rotisserie meat in her mind, so grabbing a beer, she made haste to the barbeque on the side verandah, laughing when she saw Mitsy was already there soaking up the heavenly smells.

"Sally, my beautiful sister," she cooed as she followed the heavenly scent.

"Oh, hello. Joey told you what's for tea I'm assuming."

"Oh, yes." Draping an arm around her shorter-statured sister, Aimee gave her a kiss on the temple and sniffed at the cooker.

"Did you see Brittney then?"

"She looks like a map of the stars."

Sally chuckled. Moments later, her two kids came screaming past on their bikes. Robbie led on the BMX, and little Caroline came flying past on her trike looking very determined. "Hey! Try not to run anyone over!" Sally screamed at them.

"Yes, Mum," came the chorus in response.

"So, how are the love interests going?" Aimee asked. "Did you know one got bitten by a sheep this morning?" Aimee shook her head. "Idiot."

Sally laughed. "Well, one has a bruise on their backside, one is covered in bites, and I can only presume the other is faring well enough." A scream greeted them, and moments later, Robbie came around the corner on his next lap. "Robert James Higson! What just happened?"

The boy came to a sudden, but sheepish stop. "Umm…Rolly kinda road-killed a bimbo."

Sally's eyes flew wide and Aimee tried not to laugh too loud. Sally swung on her. "Do you hear that? Bimbo! That's your bloody fault. As for you!" She rounded on Robbie. "Call anyone a derogatory name again, and I will make sure you can't sit down for a week your backside will be so red. *Both* of you," she said, giving Aimee a glare for good measure. "Robbie, go and make sure Caroline hasn't killed the poor woman. I told you kids to slow down."

"It wasn't our fault. She fell down in front of us."

"Fell down?" Aimee asked.

"Yeah. She came out of the sunroom and tripped over them big spikes she walks on and Rolly ran her over. Bam. It wasn't our fault," he repeated in a whine.

"She tripped on her heels?"

Robbie shrugged. He was twelve, so to be fair, he probably didn't care what the hell the woman was walking on.

"Look after this, will you?" Sally said to Aimee before stalking off to assess the damage.

"Did she really just fall down?" Aimee asked him.

"Like a shot rabbit. Rolly hit her straight in the face."

Aimee laughed and patted her nephew on the head. "Run away before Mum catches you."

"I'm on it."

Smiling at her nephew, she watched him bolt for the water tank. His favourite playground.

"What's the damage?" Aimee asked when her sister returned ten minutes later.

"Tiffany is now sobbing in Joey's arms with a bag of peas on her fat lip."

Aimee's shoulders shook with silent laughter, and after glaring at her for a moment, Sally joined her. Soon they were doubled over with tears streaming out of their eyes.

"What a circus," Sally said through her laughter.

Wiping her eyes as Sally basted the meat again, Aimee caught sight of Justine walking from the shearer's quarters. She had unfinished business with that woman though she had yet to decide whether she needed to offer an apology or demand an explanation, after all, she hadn't been the one to instigate that kiss.

Justine paused when she noticed Aimee's attention was on her and the two women had a brief staring contest. Justine wrenched her gaze away and continued towards the TV trailer and soon disappeared inside it. Feeling both dread and a spike of excitement as Aimee contemplated the woman inside the trailer full of TV's and equipment, she downed the remainder of her beer.

"I better go freshen up. Need beer. Stay, Mitsy." She caught Sally's curious look before hurrying away.

***

"What happened out there?" Danny asked as walked in from the carnage in the patio. "One woman was covered in bites, one has an ice pack on her arse, and the other has a bag of frozen peas on her face."

"What do you care?" Sally snapped as she threw things into the sink.

"Bloody hell, can't a guy ask a simple question?"

Sally took a deep breath and glared at the dishes, daring them to wash themselves. They didn't. Yet another disappointment in her life. With a huff, she spoke to the man who had disappointed her the most. "Joey took one of them to the old yards and she was bitten by swarms of bugs. One was bitten by a sheep and the other was run over by your daughter."

"In the face?"

Sally turned to find her husband looking confused. "The woman fell down in front of her. Caroline drove straight into her."

Danny looked shocked for a second before bursting into deep laughter. Sally smiled at him. How she had missed that sound. As he fetched a beer from the fridge, Sally looked him over. Still firm and muscly despite his growing age, the man looked exhausted. Dark bags hung under his eyes and his greying whiskers were longer than he usually kept them. Sally was pretty sure she looked just as haggard.

Popping his beer bottle open, Danny leaned against the kitchen bench. "How are you?" he said quietly.

Sally shrugged. "As good as I can be, I suppose."

He gave her a sad smile. "Look, about what happened, I—"

"Who ordered rotisserie lamb?" Joey yelled as he came into the kitchen carrying a giant tray of meat.

Thankful for the interruption and not willing to listen to yet another apology, Sally leapt at the distraction. "I did. Put it over here."

Joey put it down, grabbed himself a beer and stood beside Danny. "Where's Aimee? I thought she'd be hovering over this thing like a blowfly."

The three of them looked around to find nothing but silence and their own company.

"Weird," Joey said, sipping her drink. "All the more for us, though!"

Sally shook her head with a smile and instructed the men to carry various bowls out to the patio. Once alone, she looked out the kitchen window to the loft. *Surely her sister wouldn't be too far away.*

Walking back to the kitchen after depositing a plate of pasta salad on the long table on the patio, Justine came in with a faraway look on her face.

"Hey, you're just in time," Sally said.

"Hmm?"

"Tea's on the table."

"Oh. Sorry, I was in a world of my own."

Sally nodded, raising her eyebrows as she piled sauce bottles and other condiments on a tray. "Did that world have Aimee in it?"

"What?" Justine said rather defensively.

"Aimee. Were you plotting her demise?"

"Oh. No. No plotting for me."

"Where's the lamb!" Aimee yelled as she barged through the kitchen door.

Sally watched on as the two women gave each other a stiff, awkward greeting. She was certain Aimee just blushed.

Sally's frown deepened as her eyes flicked from one woman to the other. She didn't have time for whatever game they were playing now. "Well, don't just stand there, make yourselves useful," she snapped a moment later. Pushing the condiment tray at Justine, she shoved another one at Aimee and braced her hands against the kitchen bench when she found herself alone. *Hold it together, she chanted in her head.* Patting down her apron, she took a deep breath followed by long, purposeful steps into the fray.

***

"So you've got shearing on Thursday?" Sally heard Justine ask her brother when she placed the potato salad on the table between Justine and Aimee. She briefly scanned the area for weapons in case the two women decided to start another battle.

"Yep. Those sheep don't like being trapped up for too long, so we shear as soon as we can. Five o'clock start tomorrow to get the rest of them in the yards."

Justine nodded and brought a piece of lamb tentatively to her lips. "So, I was thinking in that case, we could have the film crew in the sheds and maybe get the girls doing some shearing before the real shearing starts?" Justine asked after swallowing her mouthful.

"Oh! Shearing!" squeaked one of the girls. "I would love to cuddle a sheepy."

Sally rolled her eyes as she walked around the table to find herself a plate. Brittney was truly a ditzy child.

"Not me," grumbled Amber.

"I'd like a go at shearing a sheep," said Tiffany.

"Out of the question," Aimee said, answering Justine as her brother indulged the contestants with a smile.

"I wasn't asking you," Justine said, sounding defensive for reasons Sally didn't understand. Judging by the dark look crossing her sister's face, it had something to do with Aimee.

"Well I'm *telling* you, it's out of the question. They're likely to cut the sheep up and I, for one, don't fancy spending all day stitching them back together. We need to dip them soon, and we can't do that if they're injured. I'm not running the risk of any of the pregnant ewes getting an infection. It's not going to happen. Tell her Joey."

Joey cleared his throat. "Maybe they can have a small go, *but*," he said loudly over Aimee's objections. "But Aimee is right. We can't afford to stress or injure the flock, so they can mostly do skirting and baling."

"Thank you."

Aimee poked her tongue out at Justine.

"Mature," Justine muttered with a scowl.

"Do we have to go up there at five in the morning? I'd have to be up at three if I want to make myself look presentable," Tiffany whined around the peas she insisted on keeping on her nose.

Joey shook his head. "I'll ask Aimee to take you up after her water run."

"What? No." Aimee shook her head with vigour.

"Aimee," Joey growled out, giving her a clear warning to play along.

"Water run?" Justine asked.

"She's checking the bores and troughs in the stocked yards along the western fence to make sure they're still full and working," Sally answered for her brother as he conveyed signals to Aimee to cut it out.

"Oh? Is that something we can film the girls doing?"

"Sure," Joey said loudly after Aimee scowled at him.

Sally froze. *What was Joey playing at?*

"No, Joe," Aimee said, cutting her brother a glare.

"Unless they know how to ride horseback, then that's probably not a good idea," Sally said, widening her eyes at her brother. He gave her a curious frown.

Justine nodded and looked thoughtfully at Aimee. "Can I come? I can scout potential scenes for the next few dates."

"I don't see why not," Joey said. Aimee began shaking her head at him, but he chose to ignore her. "There's some beautiful country out that way."

"Can I come too?" Robbie asked from Sally's side.

"Joey," Aimee and Sally said in unison as Joey answered: "Yeah, mate, you can."

He frowned at his sisters. To Justine, he said, "Aimee could show you the old ruins."

"No," Aimee snapped.

God Almighty, Sally fumed. *Was his head completely void of thought? Did he not know what tomorrow was?* "Joseph Trent Turner!" Sally shouted, cutting in over the top of everyone. Sally screwed up a napkin and pegged it at her brother as everyone else froze. The sudden silence was dizzying.

"What? What'd I do?"

"Think real hard brother-dearest."

Aimee shoved her plate away. "You know what? It doesn't matter."

"Yes, it does," Sally said putting a hand on her shoulder.

"Shit," Joey mumbled as realisation dawned on his face. Getting to his feet to lean across the table, he said, "Aimee, I'm—"

"No. Don't worry about it. Robbie and I can show the *producer* the sights. You want me to play nice, then fine, I'll play nice." Aimee fixed Justine with an angry look before pouting down at her beer bottle.

"What is your issue?" Justine snapped.

"I don't know what you're talking about," Aimee muttered.

"You're acting like someone is trying to take your toys away. Grow up and stop being such a princess."

Sally sucked in a breath of air and held it.

Some of the contestants sniggered.

The various farm hands and shearers averted their eyes and found a great deal of interest in their beer bottles, for most knew exactly what the significance of tomorrow was, which was more than Sally could say for her brother.

Aimee pushed back so hard her chair slapped the cobblestones making Sally cringe. *Here it comes*, she thought. *Nuclear Aimee*.

Sally almost fell over with surprise when Aimee whispered, "I've had enough. Goodnight."

Joey stared up at her looking guilty. "Aimee, I'm sorry, I forgot."

"Whatever," she mumbled, glancing at Justine as she made to leave.

"Aimee—" Justine started to say.

Aimee held up her hand. "I'm fine. See you in the morning."

What was going on with this pair? Sally thought. *One minute they were awkward and blushing, the next they were at each other's throats, and now, now was just weird.*

Rushing to see Aimee before she had a chance to escape, Sally caught her at the kitchen door and said, "Honey, you sure you're okay?"

"Oh, I'm just wonderful. He's letting them shear sheep and he practically ordered me to take sight-seers on to the ruins tomorrow. *Tomorrow*, Sal!"

Sally rubbed her hand up and down Aimee's arm. "You know he understands, okay?"

Aimee shrugged her touch away. "Yeah, I know."

"He just wants you to show her around. Don't read too much into it, okay?" She was positive Joey had forgotten about the significance of tomorrow's date thanks to his hormonal urges to mate.

Aimee took a deep breath and she sagged her shoulders. "Am I really being a princess?"

Sally rubbed her arm. "Yeah, you are, but tonight, you had a pretty good reason."

Aimee took a deep breath. "Yeah."

Sally smiled and kissed her cheek. "Go rest up. Maybe you'll be back to your normal grouchy self in the morning."

"Ha, ha," Aimee said, shaking her head at her sister.

Watching Aimee leave without barely touching her meal, Sally swung around and scowled at Joey, who shrunk into his seat guiltily. Beckoning him to her with a curl of her finger, she waited in the kitchen for him.

"Are you insane?" she snapped the moment he entered.

"Hey, I forgot, okay? It's been hectic around here."

"It's hectic around here on a daily basis. God, Joey. You know how important tomorrow is to Aimee."

"Yeah, yeah, I know." Joey scratched at his short-cropped hair. "It's been seventeen years, Sal. Don't you think it's time she moved on?"

Sally sighed sadly. "It's her thing, Joe. It helps her. I can't imagine what it must be like."

Joey was silent for a moment. "Do you think she still has the nightmares?"

Sally shrugged, recalling how they took it in turns to nurse their young sister in the depths of the night after the death of their parents. "She hasn't said anything." Sally shook her head. "Look, Joe, I know you've got this romance thing going on, but try not to forget the important things."

"I know. I'm sorry."

"I'm not the one you should be apologising to."

"Should I tell Justine and Robbie to stay behind tomorrow?"

Sally gnawed at her lip. "No."

"No? *Really?*"

Sally nodded, frowning at the curious exchanges she had witnessed behind Justine and her sister. "Yeah. Leave it. Maybe you're right. Maybe she needs to start finding a way to move on and I think having Robbie and Justine there will help her."

"I get the Robbie thing, but Justine? Aren't they more likely to go at each other with a pointy stick?"

Sally chuckled. "Probably." Searching the fridge for a beer, she handed one to Joey. "How was the date today? I didn't get a chance to ask with all the damaged noses and swelling bites."

Joey glanced at the door leading to the patio and he leaned in close to his twin. "Horrible. I'm not sure Brittney is all there, you know? She told me to burn down the old yards because they're ugly."

Sally chuckled and shook her head. "So who's next?"

"Tiffany."

"You taking her to the creek again?"

"Ha. Ha. No. Maybe the sunset over the old shearing shed on the hill. Might get Aimee to take Justine up there tomorrow arvo."

That was a nice choice. "Well, good luck to you then."

"Cheers."

"And don't forget to apologise to Aimee," Sally shouted after him as he returned to dinner.

CHAPTER SIX

After managing to coax Kite from the horse paddock and stabling her, Aimee headed to her loft and made headway into organising the next few weeks to take up Joey's slack. A soft knock on her door made Aimee rise from the couch and had Mitsy wiggling herself inside out with glee at the arrival of a visitor. She opened her door to find Justine on the other side with a jug in her hand.

"Hi. Is it okay if I come in?"

Aimee paused for a long time as she considered the wisdom of letting her pass. Mitsy was making a nuisance of herself and kept knocking her backside against Aimee's knee as she greeted Justine with an overwhelming happiness only a dog could feel. Justine smiled at Mitsy and gave her the attention she craved. Watching the way Justine petted Mitsy relaxed Aimee, and she decided to take the risk and moved aside so Justine could enter.

"Look, I'm sorry about earlier," Justine said after putting the jug down and facing Aimee. "I'm not really sure what happened, but judging by the reactions from your brother and sister, it was something profound."

Aimee took a deep breath and let it out with a rush. "It's not your fault my brother is an arsehole. An irresponsible one at that," she added, looking over at the list of jobs that needed immediate attention.

Justine's eyebrows arched.

Aimee huffed out a breath. "What is this?" she asked, looking at the jug.

"A Justine Special. Try it."

Giving Justine a side-long glance, Aimee sipped at the concoction. It was sweet and powerful. Coughing, she choked out, "Potent."

"Not half as potent as your rocket fuel. Trust me."

Aimee put the drink on the coffee table. "I like to do things big."

"I noticed. So…what happened at dinner?"

The master of avoidance, Aimee sipped at her drink again and shrugged. "People ate?"

"Ha. Ha. Funny. You looked…dare I say it…upset. What happened?"

"Nothing. Just a forgetful brother. It'll be fine."

"What's he forgetting?"

Everything. "What are you? The inquisition?"

"No, I'm…umm…" Justine frowned and averted her eyes for a moment. "I'm just curious."

"Well don't be. I'm fine," Aimee said, dismissing the matter with a wave of her hand.

"Mmm. So you keep saying."

"It's the truth."

"I don't believe it."

Aimee huffed and stalked away. "Believe whatever you like. It's time for you to leave."

"Hey," Justine said, following Aimee and spinning her around with a tug of her arm. "What's going on?"

Aimee hesitated. Instinct made Aimee want to run and generally avoid any form of interrogation, but the concerned look on Justine's face looked genuine and devoid of pity. Everyone else gave her that placating look. The one that screamed 'poor traumatised child.' Justine's ignorance was, for once, something that ran in her favour.

"Aimee?" Justine asked, squeezing Aimee gently on the arm.

"I…it's nothing," Aimee said after a few moments of silence. "Your show just happened to turn up here right in the middle of shearing, and we're a few weeks away from lambing, so we're trying to improve the condition of the flock. The crops out west are due to be planted, and the fields aren't prepared yet. So, in short, it's busy. We've just got a lot going on."

"I get that you're busy, but we're not trying to get in the way of you doing your work. That's the whole point of us being here. To throw the potential suitors into the thick of it to see if they're cut out for this lifestyle."

Aimee scoffed. "They're so not."

Justine chuckled. "Unfortunately, I'd have to agree with you, but it still doesn't explain the attitude earlier."

Aimee let out a long drawn out breath. "I don't like wannabes."

"Wannabes?"

Aimee shrugged. "I guess. The point is, those girls don't know the land and I don't want Joey to do something foolish."

"Foolish? Like marrying them?"

Aimee laughed. "No, that's not going to happen. Trust me."

"Then what are you getting at?"

Aimee glanced at the picture of her parents on the wall. "People get hurt easily out here. It's not a resort, it's a working farm. It's hard work, it can be dangerous, and I don't like to take risks."

Justine's eyes scoured her face before she answered. "I figured that out, but Aimee, some risks are worth it."

Tilting her head to the side, Aimee tried to decipher what risk Justine meant. After coming up with no answers, Aimee said, "Not if people get hurt. No risk is worth that."

Justine took a deep breath. "Well then, we'll play it safe."

"Good idea."

Looking to the floorboards at her feet, Justine took a deep breath before raising her head. "About earlier today…" She nibbled at her lower lip. "I'm sorry about…well…taking advantage of you like that. I've never done anything like that before and…umm…" She huffed out a breath of air and shook her head. Looking back up at Aimee, she said, "I really don't know what to say."

"That's a first."

Justine narrowed her eyes. "I can't say I have a lot of experience with this kind of situation, so forgive me if I'm struggling. You're more than welcome to say something."

"Like what?"

"I don't know. Like I said, I've no experience with this."

Aimee cocked her head. "Wait. You think *I* do? Is that what you're saying?" Aimee put her hands on her hips. "Typical. You see a woman in jeans and work boots, and automatically assume she's a lesbian, is that right?"

"No, but being hit on with that revolting cocktail, and being kissed the way you kissed me definitely screams experience. I'm not blind, I can tell you're interested in me."

"*Interested?*" Aimee scoffed. "You need to get over yourself. Not everyone out here is as desperate as my brother."

Justine shook her head and huffed with frustration. "You can't help yourself, can you? You just have to be a bitch."

"The alternative is to let people like you think you have the upper hand."

"Upper hand? This isn't a *competition*." Justine looked at her through black-rimmed glasses and ran a hand through her wavy, damp hair.

Aimee tried not to notice the way she revealed a bronzed neck and shoulder, but her peripheral vision did it for her. Justine was wearing a red singlet top over a red bra judging by the second strap on her shoulder. The sun had darkened the neckline a little, leaving the shoulder a smooth olive complexion.

"Aimee…" Justine said with a sigh. "I don't know what to do here."

Aimee, slightly distracted by Justine's beauty and the breathlessness of her words, answered with a shrug of her shoulders.

Justine tightened her eyes when she realised that was the only answer she was going to get. "Helpful. Good chat."

Justine shoulder-charged her on her way to the door, and after righting herself, Aimee spun around and said, "I'm sorry."

The effect was immediate. Justine froze. "You're what?" Justine asked as she turned her head to look back at Aimee.

"If you're looking at me for answers, I'm sorry, but I don't have any. Contrary to what you believe, this is new to me too." At Justine's confused look, Aimee clarified, "Yes, I'm a lesbian, but whatever that was between us earlier isn't normal for me." Aimee looked down and shuffled her feet. "I…umm…" Aimee shrugged her shoulders again and looked at the wooden door beside her. *It needs paint*, she thought as she tried to ignore Justine's approach.

"You what?"

Furrowing her brow, Aimee looked at Justine. "I don't know." Justine held her gaze for so long that Aimee was forced to look away as her face heated.

"What would have happened if your sister hadn't interrupted us?" Justine asked.

Aimee shrugged again. She shivered as Justine closed the space between them.

"Show me," Justine said.

Feeling a rush down her body and an instant tingling in her belly, Aimee found herself incapacitated for a brief moment. An incapacitation that proved the difference between them being found decent, or bare and sweaty against the wall.

"Aims?" came the distinct voice of her brother a millisecond before she was about to make her move.

Aimee jumped away from Justine with a curse word. Justine took a couple of quick steps backward and nearly body-bumped Joey as he ran up the stairs.

"Oh." He stopped and frowned. "Justine?"

"I was just sorting out times for tomorrow." She looked at Aimee and raised her eyebrows. "So…six?"

Aimee suppressed her confusion and said, "Six."

"Okay. Goodnight."

"Night."

Aimee blinked the daze out of her eyes and glared at her brother. "What do you want?"

Joey's jaw hardened. "I was told to apologise."

"For what? Being an inconsiderate bastard?"

Joey shook his head and stepped closer to his little sister. "You know what, forget it. If you want to act like a martyr for the rest of your life, then have at it."

"Like you give a damn, Joe. You're too busy being caught up with your need to hump every woman you can find. New flash, Tracey isn't coming back, and screwing around isn't going to help that."

"This has nothing to do with Tracey, so back off. This is, as usual, about you. It always is. Here's your news flash, Aimee. It's been *seventeen* years. *Seventeen.* It's time to stop doing this to yourself every year because nothing…*nothing*, is going to bring them back."

Aimee shoved her brother away. "Piss off. You weren't there, and you have no idea what it was like to feel so helpless. You've gotten over it, good for you, but I can never get that image out of my head. You're not the one that wakes in a cold sweat hearing the echoes of screams that will never go away. You don't taste the bitterness of smoke that burned them alive. Nothing drowns out the sound of the explosion that tore our lives apart. Nothing!" Standing back far enough to slam the door in her brother's face, she could hear the desperation in his apologies through the door.

"Aims, I'm sorry! I didn't mean it!" He tapped softly on the door. "Please open up."

All he got in response was the click of the deadbolt Aimee had never had the need to use before.

"I'm sorry," Joey whispered. Slowly, he descended the stairs to find Justine at the bottom looking bewildered.

"Is she okay?" Justine asked.

Running a hand through his hair, Joey said, "Yeah."

"She didn't sound okay."

Letting out a huff of air, Joey looked up the stairs. "No. She didn't."

"Should someone go up there?"

Joey shook his head. "She deals better when left alone in this mood."

"A mood you put her in."

Joey scowled. "She started it."

Raising an eyebrow, Justine said, "Mature."

Joey sighed. Justine was right. *He sounded like an immature child.* Taking a deep breath, he looked up the stairwell and felt guilt clutch at his chest. "What's done is done. It's best to leave her for now."

"You're sure?"

Joey nodded. "I'm sure. Goodnight, Justine."

"Goodnight," she said, lingering by the stairs for a little longer, but eventually following Joey from the stables.

CHAPTER SEVEN

Jogging down the stairs at half five the next morning feeling like she got very little sleep, Aimee walked in to find she'd been beaten to the day. Justine was standing in front of Kite petting her nose and tickling her under the chin. Kite, the floozy, had her eyes half closed and her head tilted up to soak in the attention. Mitsy wriggled her way over to demand a pat that she quickly received.

"Traitors," Aimee muttered to the animals as she made her way to Justine's side.

Justine smiled. "They're friendly, unlike their owner." Justine winked.

"I'm friendly."

Raising an eyebrow, Justine stopped patting Mitsy and said, "You look dreadful."

"Thanks. You look…" Justine had her hair loose and her glasses on. Her jeans were tight and her long-sleeved loose shirt revealed a skin-tight singlet below its unbuttoned front. Aimee swallowed.

"I look?" Justine said, stepping closer.

Aimee remained silent as she tried to find the words she needed.

"Is everything okay?" Justine asked after inspecting Aimee's face again.

"Sure."

Aimee made her way down the run and out into the frosty morning to reach the horse paddock to retrieve the two horses that eluded her the night previous.

"Did you sleep?"

Aimee stopped and frowned back at Justine. "What do you care if I did or didn't?"

"I…overhead you talking to your brother last night."

Every tired muscle in Aimee's body stiffened as she opened the latch to the gate.

"You have nightmares?"

Aimee shoved the latch back where it came from. "You mean you were snooping? Looking for more tragic stories to put on the tele." Taking an aggressive step towards Justine she said, "My life is none of your business, and if so much as a sniff of my private life goes to air, then the least you can expect is a lawsuit." Aimee spun back around and began to pace. "You have no right to sneak around listening in on other people's conversations. They're private and none of your god-damned business."

"Aimee, stop." Justine reached out and took hold of Aimee's forearm.

Snatching it back, Aimee said, "Stop? Stop what?"

"*This*. I assure you I'm not going to put your private life on television, and I didn't deliberately listen in on your conversation. I was on my way down the stairs when you started yelling at Joey. I can't help hearing what I did."

Aimee crossed her arms and clenched her jaw. "What did you hear exactly?"

"To be honest, I'm not sure. I have no context to it, but I did figure that whatever it is, it's deeply upsetting, and can therefore only assume it has something to do with your parents."

Aimee averted her gaze, giving Justine the opportunity to move closer and once again touch her arm.

"I'm sorry."

"For what?" Aimee said quietly.

"I'm sorry you lost your parents so young. I'm sorry for upsetting you unintentionally, and I'm sorry for being here."

Aimee's gaze flicked back to Justine in question.

"I know you don't want me here—want any of us here. It wasn't our choice."

Aimee took a deep breath and looked at the hand touching her. Justine removed it when it became the focus of attention and Aimee wished she didn't miss the touch. "I…" Aimee huffed. "I shouldn't have gone off at you like that."

"Is that an apology?" Justine asked when the silence lingered.

Aimee gave a slight shrug.

Justine stepped closer. "I'm not your enemy."

Aimee scoffed to herself. "You're not my friend, either," she said, looking up.

"No. I'm not. Which makes me…?"

Swallowing to reintroduce moisture to her suddenly dry mouth, Aimee found herself transfixed by Justine's questioning eyes. *What was she if she wasn't friend or foe?* Justine inched closer and Aimee wet her lips as she tried to formulate a response. "You're…" Aimee said too breathlessly for her liking. *She sounded like a love-struck fool.* Trying to sound more assertive, she cleared her throat and tried again. "You're—"

Robbie ran out of the stables and made a bee-line for his aunt, forcing the women to step apart. Wrapping his aunt in a tight hug, Robbie let Aimee go a moment later to fetch his horse from the paddock.

"Umm…" Aimee cleared her throat when she looked up at Justine again. "You're taking that one," Aimee said to Justine, pointing to a black and white mare trotting toward the commotion. Robbie put a halter around her neck and led both horses he had rounded up to the gate.

"Okay."

"Umm…you know where the saddles and stuff are?"

"Yes."

"Right." Aimee nervously played with the collar of her jacket. "So…umm…you're good?"

The corner of Justine's mouth tipped up. "I'm good."

"Umm…okay then."

Justine began to step past Aimee, but paused long enough to whisper, "You're blushing."

***

"Ready, buddy?" Aimee asked as Robbie mounted River just as the sun started to peek over the horizon and send welcoming warm rays through the stables.

"Yep," he answered, the sun shining through the steam coming from his breath. Winter had yet to relinquish its grip.

"Right. Meet you out front, okay? I'm going to check the city slicker hasn't broken her neck on Skycatcher."

"My name is Justine," Justine called out, making Robbie and Aimee snigger.

"Off you go," she said, patting River on the rump. "How's it going?" she asked Justine as she rounded Justine's horse.

"Good," Justine replied with a grunt as she tightened the girth strap.

"Skycatcher's a little young and flighty, so watch her."

"Thanks." Justine smiled and mounted the tall horse. "Ready."

"He's a good rider," Justine commented to Aimee a few hours later as Robbie cantered across the broken ground of the foothills. They had just navigated their way to a series of water troughs and bores to check their workability, and were now headed towards the old homestead.

Aimee nodded.

"You've gone quiet."

"I'm always quiet."

The gentle clicked of hooved feet against dirt and rock kept them company as they saw Robbie's stead disappear over a hill with Mitsy in tow.

"So…where are these ruins?"

Aimee clenched her jaw and shifted in her saddle. "Just…" she cleared her throat. "Just over that hill where Robbie went."

"What are they ruins of?" Justine asked after they reached the flat ground.

"The old homestead," Aimee said as they came into view. Nestled inside a ring of low scraggly gum trees, the stone walls of the old homestead were in various states of disrepair, and the chimney still stood tall. Behind the dilapidated building was a smaller hut of stone and an old wire fence protecting several gravestones. Aimee climbed off Kite and let her graze in the grass still hanging onto a green tinge from the late winter rains and walked over to the homestead. Sitting on a low wall having long lost its fight against gravity, she stared out over the graveyards and the view to the west.

"Is he okay?" Justine asked, joining her and pointing to Aimee's nephew. He was wandering the hillside nearby with Mitsy doing circles around him with her nose to the ground.

"Yeah, probably looking for wildflowers."

"Your ancestors?" Justine asked, pointing to the graveyard.

"I suppose so."

"I apologised, remember?" Justine said, sitting down on the stone.

Aimee turned a confused look on her. "What?"

"You've barely said boo since our spat this morning, and you haven't insulted me for at least two hours now."

"Sorry, I'll try and pick up my game."

Justine glanced over at Robbie before she reached out and took Aimee's hand. "Are you okay?"

Aimee looked at their joined hands. *When had they reached a level of comfort for Justine to initiate this kind of contact?* Unwilling to question it, she left her hand still. "Yeah. Thanks. I'm okay."

"So no hard feelings about this morning?"

"None. It's just...I'm not used to company here, that's all."

"This place is special to you?"

Aimee nodded. The place was etched on her psyche in more ways than one. "Dad loved it here. Said the way this place still stands is a testament to how strong and resilient our blood and connection is with this property. Yarrabee Station was founded by my great-great-great grandfather. I couldn't imagine being anywhere else."

Justine squeezed her hand. "I'm sorry for inviting myself along today."

"It's fine." Aimee looked across at Justine and smiled. "I'm sorry about last night," Aimee said in reaction.

"Sorry?"

"For being so...bratty?"

Justine chuckled. "Somehow, I doubt you can help it." Justine looked over at the graveyard. "Though, I think I'm beginning to understand why. You're protective."

"Protective?"

Justine bounced her head in the affirmative. "The girls have come here with no experience, and we're trying to throw them in the deep end of station life without any sort of training. It puts people and your livelihood at risk."

Aimee's mouth dropped open. She didn't expect Justine to get it.

Justine smiled at her stunned expression. "I see it every weekend."

"Every weekend?"

"I train horses and riders, and travel around to equestrian events in my spare time. I see parents try to force their children to perform in arenas beyond their capabilities and it not only puts their kids at risk but the horses as well."

Aimee nodded in agreement, now having the insight of why this woman was so accomplished in the saddle.

"Anyway," Justine said with a shrug. "I'm thinking that's how you feel about what we're trying to accomplish with the women your brother selected."

"Exactly."

"However…"

Aimee rolled her eyes, earning an elbow to the ribs.

"However, I need to do my job, which means exposing these women to the reality of a farmer's life."

"Entertainment isn't a good enough reason to risk the livestock or the lives of the desperate women."

"They're not desperate."

"They couldn't get any more desperate if they tried."

"You have to be the most prejudice, one-eyed person I've ever met. What happened to the good ol' Aussie saying of a fair go?"

"That only applies to people who earn it, not women coming out here, looking at the property through eyes with dollar signs stamped on them. They laze about the pool thinking how wonderful the life is when they have no bloody idea."

"Which is my point exactly. They need to be exposed to the work done out here."

"Fine, then have them go strain fences and change the oil on the vehicles, just keep them away from the livestock."

"It's a sheep farm—"

"Station, actually."

"—and…do you mind?"

"Not particularly."

"Figures." Justine put her hands on her hips and took a breath. "The point is, sheep are the major resource on your station, and that's how this segment will be marketed. Sure, cover the girls in oil, but I figure since you're shearing today, then nobody will be doing anything else. Am I right?"

"No, actually. Miss Gerhardt will be doing lessons with the kids and I'm doing a water run and—"

"Save it. We're shooting in the sheds today. End of story."

"Fine. Take your pictures, but if anyone gets hurt, then I hope you have your affairs in order."

Justine shook her head. "Big talk for a little farm girl."

"Little?" Aimee pressed herself into Justine's personal space and looked down at her from her three-inch advantage in height.

"Figuratively speaking. You act like a toddler half the time. Seriously, what's with the constant attitude?"

"I don't like people trying to fit in when they clearly don't. It gets people hurt."

"Hurt?"

"They take stupid risks and innocents get in the way." Aimee let her eyes shift to the graveyard over Justine's shoulder.

Justine frowned and followed her line of sight to see Robbie with an armful of wildflowers on his way down from the hill. As Aimee tried to move past her, Justine held her back. "I promise you, I'm not going to let anyone take unnecessary risks."

Aimee sighed.

"Besides, I'm sure you won't let me. Am I right?"

Aimee looked at the woman with the raised eyebrows and couldn't help but concede with a smile. "Maybe."

"Like you could help yourself."

Aimee crossed her arms and scowled playfully down at Justine. "I still don't like you."

Justine burst into laughter. "Sure. Keep telling yourself that," she said, leaning up on tip toes and kissing Aimee on the cheek before moving over to Robbie who was now in the graveyard.

Aimee narrowed her eyes at the amused woman's back and shivered at the joy that coursed through her at the sound of Justine's laugh. The woman had an uncanny ability to stir emotions in her she thought were dormant or non-existent. Sighing, she went to pay her respects to the graves, uncertain whether Justine was going to be the ruin of her.

***

Robbie disappeared the moment they reached the stables when Aimee offered to brush down his horse for him. Justine tended to her own steed without complaint and had moved over to assist Aimee when she was done. Brushing River's flank, Aimee accidentally bumped against Justine, feeling a blush from head to toe as her arm recognised the feel of the other woman's breast.

Leaving River's stall and feeding each horse a sugar cube as a treat, they were side-by-side next to Kite when they both turned to each other after a minute of silent contemplation. Aimee had still yet to determine where Justine fit because no one lusted like this after a friend or an enemy. Having no experience on how to navigate the torrent of emotions she couldn't name, Aimee decided to look at it from a risk assessment point of view. Risk humiliating herself and acting on her lust, or risk mental impairment she was bound to suffer for not acting on her need to kiss this woman again.

The sound of a grinder starting up in the nearby machinery shed took Aimee's attention away from Justine's lips. *When did she start staring at them, and how long was she doing it?* Aimee cleared her throat. "Umm…so…shall we go get the desperados on the road?" She gave Justine a smile and a wink.

Justine rolled her eyes. "They're not desperados."

"Yeah, yeah." Aimee smiled and walked across the quadrangle to the house. The *quiet* house. It was eight in the morning and none of Joey's girls were awake. *Terrific.*

***

A couple of hours later and the morning was beginning to wane, just like Aimee's patience. Driving the contestants to the shearing sheds after returning from the ruins should have been easy, but trying to corral three women used to sleeping in and having a lazy coffee just to wake up was infuriating. Justine had to step in more than once and politely request the women hurry up.

The drive to the sheds was brief thanks to Gav's work on the road, and relinquishing control of the women to Joey's care should have been a smooth transition. Instead, Aimee was forced to show them in turn how to catch a sheep, while inside the sheds, Joey was apparently giving another girl shearing lessons.

"No! Listen. Just walk up to the damn thing, hug it, and drag it backwards."

Tiffany looked on horrified as Brittney took hesitant steps towards the flock cowering in the corner. This was attempt number seven and the sheep were spooked.

"Okay, now quickly grab it," Aimee said when she was close enough to touch one. Brittany dove forward as if she was rugby-tackling the poor animal, and grabbed hold of its back half. The scared animal baaed and kicked its legs, dislodging Brittney with a solid thump to her breasts and ran off, leaving her with nowhere to go but face-first into a pile of fresh droppings. Aimee grimaced. "Umm…no. Not like that."

Brittney picked herself up slowly, wiped some droppings off her face and started to scream.

"What the bloody hell is going on out here?" Joey said, rushing from the shed, followed by a cameraman. He found Aimee biting her tongue, Tiffany crying, and the cameraman on duty outside the sheds doubled over with laughter. "Aimee?"

"Forget this, Joe. They don't get it."

"I'm not doing that!" Tiffany yelled at Joey.

Joey assessed Brittany's condition and said, "You don't have to."

Tiffany looked appeased and calmed herself down.

"Why don't you head inside and help Amber layout wool?"

Tiffany nodded and walked inside as Brittney raced out of the sheep yard dropping dirt and droppings as she went. She made a path between Aimee and Joey and screamed, "You're all insane!"

Joey and Aimee watched her storm away and then back to each other.

"One down, two to go, Romeo," Aimee said.

Joey groaned. "Not now, Aimee."

"Everything okay out here?" Justine asked as she joined them. "Where's Brittney?"

"She's wiping crap off her face…literally." Aimee chuckled to herself.

"Aimee," Joey said, giving her a shake of his head.

"What? She is. And you know what, they all will at some point. Want to know why? Because they don't fit in out here. Can't you see that?"

"Aimee, give it a rest, or I swear to God…"

"Swear as much as you like, Joe, but you know as well as I that this is a bloody circus that's done nothing but distract you for months." Aimee held up her hand and started listing off issues. "None of the firebreaks have been graded since last season. I checked with Gav yesterday, and the fuel hasn't been ordered. Apparently he's also waiting on you to approve an invoice for some fencing wire, a new clutch for the old Cruiser, and so I just found out, the bloody disc planter hasn't been booked for the sorghum. I don't know about you, but I don't fancy hand-seeding a couple of hectares."

Joey clenched his jaw and crossed his arms. "You are more than capable of arranging all of that yourself."

"Yes, I am, however, I didn't know it needed to be done. We all have our jobs, Joey, and that is one of yours. The responsible thing to have done is to ask me or Danny to take care of it, but clearly, this bloody production takes precedence over everything else."

"I'll take care of it."

"Don't bother, it's already done."

"Fine."

"Fine!" Aimee glared at him for a moment longer before turning to Justine. "You want to see the old shearing shed?"

Justine snapped back to life after being riveted by Joey and Aimee's argument. "Give me five minutes?"

When Justine raced off, Joey said, "So…umm…how'd it go this morning?"

"Like you care," Aimee spat before storming off to her car. She yanked the car door open and slammed it shut. Gripping the steering wheel with white knuckles, she tried to stop the burn in her throat and the fluid building in her eyes. "Damn you, Joey," she muttered.

"Ready," Justine said, climbing in. "You okay?"

"I'm fine."

"I can tell." Justine gestured to Aimee's face.

Aimee swatted at the rogue tears on her cheeks. "He's being irresponsible."

"I gathered."

Still annoyed and with a need to vent, Aimee said, "He's so caught up in this bullshit that he's forgetting the important stuff. The generators need diesel, but there's only enough there for another week or two. The sorghum is supposed to be planted next month, but the bloody disc planter isn't available until December. *December!* It'll be too hot by then and the crop won't yield as well. We had planned to build a new paddock after the lambs were born, but none of the equipment has been ordered, and we're behind on payments to the bank." Aimee leaned forward and rested her forehead on the steering wheel.

Justine reached over and ran a hand back and forth on Aimee's shoulder.

Frowning to herself as her heart rate slowed, Aimee noticed the lack of questions or placating words coming from Justine. The simple act of her touch allowed Aimee to take a deep breath or two and calm down without having to explain her feelings. The counsellors were all about talking it out. Sally and Joey had been the same and had probably been prompted to do so on professional advice. Ever since she was a child, when she was upset or quiet, they'd interrogate her or offer the solution. *What's wrong? How do you feel? Can you explain why you're upset? Maybe you need more sleep. Maybe you need fresh air. Maybe we should call the doctor.* All Aimee ever wanted was to be left alone to sort through it herself, and over time, Sally and Joey had finally understood that. What had taken her siblings years to understand, Justine had managed to figure out in a day or two. The comfort Justine's touch provided was overshadowed by the confusion it created. *How can one person be so calming?*

Straightening up and keeping her head low, Aimee took a deep breath. "Sorry," she said quietly a few moments later.

Justine, who was yet to move her hand, gave Aimee's shoulder a squeeze in response. "So…where are these old shearing sheds?"

Chapter Eight

Making a clicking sound in her cheek, Aimee urged Kite up the gentle hill. The gradient wasn't steep, but she had challenged Justine to a race after the woman suggested they ride. A suggestion she gladly agreed to. Mitsy beat them both. From the old shearing shed site, there was a good view of most of the homestead yards. Hopping off Kite and letting the mare follow her nose to a patch of grass Aimee considered the scene below her. Beside the stables were the horse yards, and from where she stood, she could see Mike fighting with the stallion. She grimaced. That wasn't a good sign. Joey was going to be furious if none of the other mares were mounted. Not that he had room to argue. Next to the stables was the water tank and the machinery shed, and on the other side was the homestead. Her eyes followed the line of green that ran past the yards and into the distance toward Roper Creek.

"It's so lush," Justine said as she joined Aimee, bringing with her the light, fragrant scent Aimee was starting to dream about.

Clearing her throat, Aimee said, "Enjoy it while it lasts. That's usually a lot drier by now. We had good rains this winter. Lots of feed out in the paddocks."

Justine nodded and turned on the spot to survey the old shearing shed. "Is this thing safe?"

"It's been standing for nearly a hundred years, so in my opinion, no." Aimee grinned. "Didn't stop me from playing here as a kid though. Come inside, I'll show you."

The floors creaked as they walked into the dusty wreck of the shed's shell. Sunlight pierced past the holes in the tin roof through the dusty interior to the floor. Old sorting tables lay in various states of disrepair and old hand clippers hung on a couple of walls. The wooden slats making up the walls of the building were letting in the light breeze from outside thanks to missing or shrinking boards.

"It's…dusty."

"It's a wreck."

"Then why—"

Aimee took Justine's hand and tugged her to the ramp where sheep were once herded to reach the shearers. "That's why," she said when they walked out to the area hidden by the building earlier.

In soil fertilised by layers of sheep dung, several low native trees grew against the building and in a circle around the old holding yard. In the middle was a shaded patch of grass kept short by the lone resident...a goat. "That's Billy."

Justine raised an eyebrow. "Inventive name."

Smiling at the amused woman, Aimee said, "He's a miniature goat that we use as a lawnmower. He's on picnic spot duty this week."

"And from that, I assume this is the picnic spot?"

"Yep. It's shady, it's grassy, and you get to see that." Aimee once again initiated contact and drew Justine to the middle of the grassy patch. Walking behind Justine and putting a hand on each shoulder, she lowered her head to Justine's and pointed through the trees. "When the sun sets, that lights up." The view on the other side was of rolling hills with the distant ranges keeping guard on the horizon.

"Like the cattle yard," Justine said, turning her head slightly.

"No. Better," Aimee whispered back. Their cheeks were side-by-side and with a slight movement, Justine's lips could have been hers to claim. For a moment, she considered doing just that, but she was still feeling self-conscious about her mini-meltdown in the car. That, and Mitsy chose that moment to charge across the grassy area barking at her arch enemies, the miner birds that had begun dive-bombing her the moment she showed her brown and white nose.

Backing away, Justine turned and smiled up at Aimee and Aimee couldn't help but feel the pleased buzz in her stomach for impressing the woman, and nor could she stop the blush crawling up her neck as she recognised her feelings as more than just lust. She was intrigued, entranced, and undeniably infatuated. Aimee quickly looked away. *I'm Aimee, big bad station chick, I don't do crushes*, she reminded herself. "Got all you need?" she asked as she walked around the building to find Kite.

"Almost," Aimee heard Justine whisper to herself.

Aimee stumbled. "Umm...so...you want to ride a little?" She turned around to see Justine shaking her head. "Okay. Back to the house then. I bet you have umm...work stuff to do?"

Justine shook her head again.

"Oh."

"Aimee…" Justine walked closer and took a breath. "Are we— is this…" She adjusted her glasses and smoothed down her hair. "Is there something here. Between us?"

"Umm…" Aimee looked to the side. "Between us? Like…what?"

"Like since that kiss, I can't stop thinking about doing it again."

"Oh. That kind of something." Aimee nibbled on her lower lip. "I thought you didn't believe in—uh…romance, or whatever." Aimee was sure the burn of the blush rushing through her face was going to ignite at any moment.

Justine took a deep breath. "I don't." Raising her eyes to Aimee's, she smiled. "I'm not asking to be romanced."

Oh, what the hell, Aimee thought to herself and lowered her mouth in a swift, possessive motion.

Justine's arms were instantly around Aimee and pulling her closer. It felt like they picked up where they left off the other day.

The kiss was all lips, tongue and fire. Spinning Justine against the wall of the shearing shed and hoping it didn't collapse, Aimee bent her knees so they were eye-to-eye and pressed her body against her.

Justine responded by clutching at Aimee's bottom with one hand while tangling her fingers in the hair at the nape of Aimee's neck with the other.

Aimee's hands were on Justine's hips, at her sides, over her breasts, against her neck, in her hair, and eventually following the same course downwards until she gripped the back of Justine's legs and lifted her from the ground. Using her body to brace Justine's weight against the wall, Aimee continued kissing the inviting warmth of Justine's mouth and began to grind slowly against her.

Justine wrapped her legs around Aimee's waist and rolled her hips to match Aimee's tempo.

Their carnal dance continued for several minutes, and forced to breathe, Aimee's mouth was soon on Justine's neck while the woman began to shudder and utter encouraging moans into her ear.

A second later, the spell was broken when hot, snuffly air and whiskery lips hit them both in the side of the head.

"Jesus, Kite," Aimee snapped as she was forced to drop Justine to her feet and move away from the mare. One look at Justine made Aimee tip the corners of her mouth up. The woman's glasses were askew and she was biting her lips in an effort not to laugh. It didn't last, and the sound of Justine's laughter did strange things to Aimee's insides. Distracting herself from identifying those emotions, Aimee pulled Justine back against her and kissed her slowly, deeply, and far more languidly than she had intended.

"Wow," Justine said when Aimee pulled away.

Aimee tried to catch her breath and find an explanation for how good that just felt.

"Aimee?"

"Yeah?"

"Take me home."

***

They took the horses on the short ride back and settled them into their stalls. Closing Kite's stall, Aimee nibbled at her lower lip as she watched Justine. Twice now they'd started something they couldn't finish. It was an experience Aimee hadn't had before, and around Justine, every sense was heightened. Her scent, light and sweet, was becoming quickly addictive, and Aimee's eyes couldn't help but wander over the woman's body when she wasn't looking. Studying the curves of Justine's backside in the jeans she had chosen to wear that day, Aimee tried to imagine the sight without the denim covering it. Glancing up as Justine's body twisted in her direction, Aimee found herself caught in the act.

She blushed as she tried to formulate the words to invite Justine into her bed. *How does one say, please let me see you naked?*

As Justine walked over to her, it appeared words weren't necessary. Pulling Justine tight against her, she mapped the woman's mouth with her tongue. Justine tasted like berries and felt spine-tingling in the way she moved against her. Needing and wanting more, Aimee began to tug at the woman's polo shirt, trying to remove it from her jeans.

Justine pulled back and put a trembling finger on Aimee's lips. "Not here."

Blood and lust pounded through her body at the suggestion behind those words. "My bedroom is close," Aimee said.

Justine nodded and yanked her up the stairs. They barely made it inside the loft before they reattached at the lips.

"Bed?" Justine asked into her mouth.

Answering Justine by dragging her across the room and around the low partition, Aimee pulled off Justine's top and pushed her to the bed. Scattering clothing around the bedroom, they came together like a storm. Violent, exhilarating, and intense.

Covering Justine's naked body with her own, Aimee plunged her tongue into the woman's mouth and possessed the air in her lungs. Breaking away with a gasp, Aimee descended on Justine's neck, lavishing the soft pale skin with nips, licks, and sucks of her pulse point. Fingers clawed at her back and gripped her arms as Justine canted her hips upwards. So frenzied was Aimee, she granted the woman's silent pleas and dropped her thigh against her searching pelvis. The moan that followed made Aimee tremble and seek her own pressure to the point throbbing between her legs.

Wet and slippery, they continued to grind against one another until it wasn't enough. Pushing her fingers through damp curls, Aimee unapologetically thrust into Justine and made the woman emit the most delightful scream. Aimee's forehead dropped to Justine's collarbone, and she worked her fingers in the woman whose sounds of pleasure were doing all manner of naughty things to her body. Twisting and curling, she felt Justine tense for a long moment, and then she was suddenly thrashing her hips against Aimee's hand. Crying out nonsense words, Justine's inner muscles clenched around Aimee's fingers in orgasm. The culmination of sensations broke the walls of Aimee's building pleasure, and she tumbled down right alongside Justine. She'd never experienced anything quite so intense before and never had she orgasmed with such little attention from her bed mate.

I'm in so much trouble, Aimee thought to herself as she carefully slipped her fingers away from Justine. They lay together, chests heaving, staring at the ceiling. Soon, the craziness of the entire situation hit Aimee, and she couldn't help the wave of chuckles that overcame her.

"What?" Justine whispered beside her.

Looking at the woman, Aimee smiled and indicating the pair of them. "This. It's insane. We apparently don't even like each other."

"That's because you're impossible." Aimee's heart flipped when Justine smiled back in the most honest, expressive, gorgeous smile she'd ever witnessed. A sliver of pink tongue poked out between bright white teeth. *The dragon was a chameleon. A chameleon with a sexy-as-hell smile.* Aimee kissed the look right off her face.

Consuming each other again and again until their energy ebbed to exhaustion, they tangled together and drifted into unconsciousness.

***

Blinking her eyes open and finding Justine tucked up against her, Aimee smiled. Then Mitsy jumped up on the bed and licked their faces. *Who let her in?*

"Aimee!" Sally screamed across the loft, jolting her out of her peace.

"Shit," she muttered. Reluctantly untangling herself from Justine, Aimee yanked on her jeans and undershirt. "What!" she yelled at her sister when she rounded the partition.

"Where is she?"

"Who?"

"The production woman."

"The dragon is missing?"

"She's supposed to be up at the old sheds with Joey, but no one's seen her since you took the girls up to Joey this morning. Please don't tell me you dumped her body somewhere."

"Then I suggest not looking down the old well."

"Jesus, Aimee, you didn't."

Aimee threw hands up. "What do you take me for?"

"I wouldn't put it past you. You two are bloody volatile. Seriously, what's with the instant declaration of war on this woman?"

Aimee shrugged. "She's a pain in the arse."

"Yeah, only to you, but I think that might have something to do with being downright horrible to her. Now, where is she?"

"Well, I'm sorry to disappoint, but I have no idea where she is. Perhaps she wandered off and fell down the old well all by herself. What do I care?"

"Ugh." Sally turned and stalked off to the back door. "Some help you are."

Sally moaned. "If I find her down that well, there'll be hell to pay."

"So don't look there then."

Sally muttered her way out of the loft leaving Aimee alone with Mitsy and Justine.

Walking behind the partition, she sat on the bed and smiled shyly at Justine, who was sitting up wrapped in a bed sheet and patting Mitsy.

"Dragon?"

She shrugged. "Blame the suit and the eyes. You dressed so severely and your eyes are amber and reminded me of a predator, like a panther or something. Only I like cats, so I went with a dragon."

Justine shook her head. "You really are peculiar. Do you know that?"

"I try."

They smiled at each other, soon finding the need to touch. Leaning in simultaneously, they shared a lazy kiss that bordered on becoming heated. Justine pulled back with a sigh.

"I better go."

"Do you have to?" Aimee asked, unable to stop touching the woman, placing soft kisses across her bare shoulder.

"Unless you want to be charged for murder, then yes, I do."

Aimee chuckled against her skin. "Okay."

Justine was smiling at her when she cupped Aimee's cheeks to draw her gaze back to those amber eyes. "This…" Justine looked at the messed up bed. "…was really unexpected."

Aimee nodded in her hands, having a feeling she knew what was coming. The age old goodbye after a one-time fling. The urges sated after a quick romp. It was her norm, her modus Operandi. "Mmm. Let me guess. It was a one-time thing? A mistake?"

Justine grazed her cheek with her thumb. "No. Definitely not a mistake, just…really unanticipated."

Aimee's eyes widened. "Okay, I didn't expect that."

"Neither did I," Justine replied letting out a long breath.

"So…?"

"So…" Justine leaned in for a chaste kiss. "I have to go and prove your innocence."

Aimee moved back to give the woman space to swing her legs out of bed. Having not been afforded the time to sit back and study Justine's features during their afternoon sexual marathon, Aimee felt her breath dissolve watching her dress. Lean, bronze, and curvy, the woman was a true beauty. She was staring at the swell of breasts shaping the shirt and vest Justine put on when fingers clicked in her face.

"I'm up here."

Aimee smiled and stood, pulling Justine against her for a brief but passionate kiss.

Justine pulling herself away with a rush of breath. "Wow. Okay. I need to go before…"

Aimee gave her a cocky grin earning herself a narrow-eyed glare.

"Yep, leaving now." Justine picked up her shoes and headed for the door.

"Uh…maybe…you know, you could, like, later…" Aimee swallowed. A casual lover who had never bedded the same woman twice, this was new and scary territory. "Maybe we could…umm…catch up later. Or you could come back here and umm…we…" Aimee huffed.

Justine blinked at her. "I'm assuming you were asking me back for…what? A drink or something?"

"Yeah. Something."

"I will, but under one condition."

"Yeah?"

"No more cocktails."

Aimee grinned. "Deal."

"I'll see you then?"

Aimee accepted Justine's parting kiss and watched her go with a lovesick expression on her face. Left staring down an empty stairwell, Aimee sighed to herself and smiled. Shaking her head, she shook off the amazement that she'd only officially met the woman who lost her hat a couple of days ago, and the snarky little firecracker whose neck she wanted to ring more than once, had turned out to be the most passionate and satisfying lover Aimee had ever known. They did say there was a thin line between love and hate.

CHAPTER NINE

The next day was a hive of activity. The shearers began to arrive in dribs and drabs, and slowly took over the shearer's quarters over the course of the day. Sally relocated the film crew to the house, with the soundman and the cameraman being forced to share a disused formal dining room, and Justine making a bedroom in the office that housed a large couch. Aimee was off with Gav clearing the fence lines at the south and mustering more sheep into pens for the shear, and Joey was up at the shearing shed with the contestants and the film crew. With everyone scattered across the property, it was left to Sally to clean up after the breakfast rush.

An hour later, dishes were done, benches were wiped, and a cake was cooking in the oven. Sally took a moment to take a deep breath and enjoy the quiet.

It was short-lived.

Robbie crashed through the kitchen and attacked the fridge making Sally scream. "Robert James Higson! You were not raised in a barn or on a bloody speedway track! Slow down, or so help me God, you'll be scrubbing toilets for a month."

The boy, who had frozen the instant he saw his mother, cringed.

"Where's the fire?" Sally asked him.

"I was hungry," he said sheepishly, holding the fridge door open.

"Well, pick something before you let all the cold air out," Sally said, pulling off her oven mitts. "How was the filming this morning?" she asked, knowing Robbie was hovering around the camera men and his uncle. That, and he loved helping out the shearers. He was truly his father's son.

He shrugged. "Fine."

Sally resisted the urge to roll her eyes at the summary from a twelve-year-old.

"Mum?" he mumbled around a bite of apple.

"Yes, honey?" Sally asked, searching her cupboard for icing sugar. "Drat," she mumbled when she couldn't find it.

"Huh?" Robbie frowned at his mum.

"Sorry. Icing sugar. Go on, honey, what did you want to say?"

"When people hate each other, do they hold hands?"

"Uh…" Sally blinked. "Not usually, no."

Robbie nodded and frowned.

"Why do you ask?"

He shrugged.

Sally huffed a breath of exasperation. "I swear, getting information out of you and your father is like wringing out sandstone in hope of finding water."

"What?"

"Never mind." Sally put her hands on her hips and bit her bottom lip as she stared at the cooking cake through the oven door. "Robbie, fancy doing me a favour?"

"Depends."

"On?"

"Can I have a soft drink?"

Extortionists. That's what her children were. "Soft drink is for weekends only."

"Yeah, but—"

Sally raised a hand. "However, I really need icing sugar. So if you could duck over to Miss Gerhardt's cottage and see if she has some, then yes, you may have a can of drink. One. Singular."

He rolled his eyes. "Yes, Mum. I get it. Just one. Geez."

Ruffling her son's hair, she said, "I need the icing sugar first. It's in the flour box. Pink label. Fine white powder that tastes like sugar."

"Mum," he whined, escaping her touch. "I know what icing sugar is. What do you take me for?"

"An impertinent son?"

He made a face and snatched a biscuit from the tray Sally had baked earlier.

"Hey!"

"Back in a minute," he called out, rushing through the door.

"Woah!" Justine said, taken aback as she tried to enter the house.

"Sorry," Robbie said on his way past her. "Mum, I'm taking my motorbike."

"Helmet!" Sally shouted after him.

"Yeah, yeah," came the distant reply from Robbie.

Sally shook her head and smiled at Justine. "Kids."

Justine laughed. "Yep. Hey, umm, have you seen Aimee around?"

"No, sorry, she's out in the paddocks this morning."

"Oh."

"Why?"

"Oh…umm…I was thinking about getting some more stock footage of the area around where Joey took his dates. I was hoping Aimee could show me around."

Sally knitted her eyebrows together. *Why did Justine sound shy all of a sudden?* "I'm sure she won't mind. She shouldn't be too long."

"Oh. Good. Umm…I'll go and sort the cameras then." Justine pushed open the kitchen door. "Thanks."

"You're…welcome?" Sally said, trailing off as Justine strode away. "Weird."

***

Dirty and grimy after playing in the dust and with bales of hay all morning, Aimee returned to the homestead with the intention to wash with record speed. She told herself she wasn't desperate to see Justine after not having seen her since the previous afternoon thanks to being commandeered by Gav yesterday evening.

Aimee prided herself on not relying on anyone. She was a woman that knew her mind, had grand plans for the future, and had long mapped a road towards it. She had learned how to be independent early and had a fierce work ethic to match. Still, she was reeling over the new dimension Justine had added to her life in the past forty-eight hours and hadn't been able to get her out of her mind all day. More than once she had been so distracted by the woman with amber eyes, that she had twice over-shot the track she was supposed to be driving on, cleared several hundred metres of the wrong fence line before she realised it, and took three attempts at shutting the gate on her way back to the homestead. Thanks to her absentmindedness, she'd been the butt of Gav's jokes all day long. *Bastard.*

"Looking schmick," Gav said as she walked out of the homestead wearing her best jeans and a close-fitted tank top.

Aimee groaned.

"Trying to impress someone?" he said, hurrying to walk beside her as Aimee tried to make a break for it.

"No."

Gav laughed. "Which one? The one with the big knockers?" he asked, holding his hands in front of his chest. "Don't think Joe will be too happy about that."

Aimee frowned and looked at Gav. "Huh?"

"Hittin' on his women."

"Hitting on…" It dawned on Aimee that Gav thought she was making a play for one of the contestants. "Well, hey, you know me and generous…" She copied Gav's previous hand gesture of big bosoms.

Gav slapped her on the back and gave a hearty laugh. "Good luck, mate. Be thankful you can't be castrated."

"What?"

Gav gestured to the trailer the TV crew brought with them. "That production woman, whatshername, she'd cut off your balls for messing with those pretty girls."

"I'm not messing with anyone."

Gav winked at her. "Sure. Make sure Joey doesn't find out you're after his chicks," he said loudly as he walked away.

"Jesus," Aimee whispered under her breath as she turned the corner into the stables. "Oh, crap," she said, finding Justine in the shadows with her arms crossed and eyebrows raised. It had been a curious sixteen hours since she'd last seen the woman thanks to Gav's idea to go rabbit shooting the previous evening. Aimee's thoughts had barely strayed from the sight of Justine in her bed, eyes closed, head tilted back and making mewing noises that made her private areas clench. Usually a crack shot, every rabbit they found last night had gone back to its family safe and sound, and free to destroy more of their productive land in the process, much to Gav's amusement. Now, with Gav's inappropriate teasing and her sudden shyness, Aimee struggled to say, "Umm…hi."

Justine inclined her head in response.

Calling Gav a few choice names under her breath, Aimee said as brightly as she could, "What brings you here?"

"I was waiting for you, actually, but if you have other plans…"

"I don't," Aimee said, shaking her head and moving closer. "I have no plans."

"Good to know." Closing the gap between them, Justine surprised her by yanking her close and kissing her soundly. Either the woman was possessive and jealous, or Aimee wasn't the only one affected by their impromptu love-making session yesterday.

"Upstairs," Justine ordered.

"Yes, ma'am."

Frenzied, they disrobed as they crossed the room and the moment Justine pinned Aimee to the mattress, the intensity shifted. The desperation dissolved, replaced by something far more unanticipated. Blind need moved over for lingering looks, soft caresses and an overwhelming desire to be closer and more intimate.

The feelings exploding inside her were terrifying, but tempting. Giving in to them, Aimee flipped Justine to the bed and slowly made love to her. Each touch was deliberate and took the writhing woman to the edge multiple times before having mercy and letting her soar away on an orgasm. It was the most tender Aimee had ever been, and the fact that ability was inside her was thoroughly surprising. Her encounters to date had been quick and detached. They scratched an itch, and none had wanted more, nor had she needed it. This petite woman changed the game entirely.

Thoughts evaporated as Justine tenderly took her to heights that had her gasping for air and wondering whether she'd ever be able to recover. Aimee's eyes fluttered open long after her body stopped shuddering with bliss to find Justine looking down at her having taken the lead in the payback.

Justine shook her head slowly as she mapped her face with her fingers. "You're incredible."

Smiling on an exhale, Aimee tangled her fingers in thick dark locks. "You're not so bad yourself."

Justine smiled and kissed her. Resting her head on Aimee's forehead, she sighed heavily. "Where did you come from?"

"I've been here the whole time."

Justine pulled back a little to search Aimee's eyes. "I suppose you have."

Cupping Justine's cheek, watching as the woman turned her head to kiss her palm, she said in a moment of rare vulnerability, "I'm glad you found me."

Justine nodded. "Me too."

Aimee smiled and pecked her on the lips. "If this is why you were waiting for me, I'm not complaining."

Smiling back, Justine shook her head. "Actually, I need you to escort me around the property to get some stock footage this afternoon. Apparently, I'm not allowed to wander off on my own."

"So this was incentive?"

Shaking her head and caressing Aimee's cheek with a soft hand, Justine sighed. "No. This was everything I've ever dreamed of."

"Cheesy."

"Shut up," Justine whispered, bringing her mouth back down to Aimee's and initiating another round of love-making.

***

Sally sat down for a cup of tea after Miss Gerhardt called to say Caroline had completed their studies for the day, and could she take her to the dam for a swim. With the unexpected free time, she pulled her tablet off the charger and sat down to read the latest gossip from the online magazine she had downloaded last week.

With a heavy, pleasurable sigh, Sally lowered herself into the soft padding of the cane chair on the front verandah and felt the pressure release in her feet. Standing on a slate floor all day preparing Aimee's special surprise made her feet ache. *Thank goodness for the station cook they hired at this time of year who would be taking care of the meals for the shearers and farm hands.* The film crew was eating up at the shearer's quarters also, meaning she only had dinner to prepare for her family and Joey's girls, yet still, that was at least ten people to cater for. Sally slumped into her chair at the idea of preparing that much food. Her feet needed a break. Spotting Aimee and Justine drive back into the quadrangle, Sally nibbled at her lip. Perhaps she needed to get the contestants involved in the kitchen. It was, after all, an important part of the day. In fact…

"Justine!" she shouted, waving at the woman as she turned around. Holding up a hand in acknowledgement, she finished off her conversation with Aimee and walked over.

"Afternoon."

Sally smiled. "Fancy a cup of tea," she said, gesturing to the steaming pot on the coffee table.

"You sure?" Justine noticed the tablet and reading glasses perched on Sally's nose.

"Absolutely."

"Well then, I'd love one."

"So I see you found Aimee," Sally said after pouring Justine a cup of Earl Grey.

Justine cleared her throat and looked over to where Aimee was disappearing into the stables. "Ah, yeah. Yeah, I did. Thanks."

"And she didn't mind helping you out."

"Ah…no. Not at all." Justine took a sip of her tea.

Justine's face looked flushed.

"You okay?" Sally asked.

"Yeah. Good as ever. You?"

Sally blinked a little. "I'm fine."

"Good," Justine said with a nod and another sip of tea. "That's good."

A little bewildered by Justine's odd behaviour, Sally tried to change the subject. "How did the girls do this morning?" Justine looked like she relaxed a little.

"Wonderful. No one was bitten by anything and Amber sheared a sheep without nicking its skin."

Sally cocked her head with surprise. "Wow. I'm impressed."

"So was Aimee."

Sally raised an eyebrow. "Aimee?" *Surely the woman meant Joey?* "Aimee was there?"

Justine tucked a strand of curly brown hair from her face. She had stopped wearing it in a tight bun and had spent the past few days tying it back with an elastic hair tie. It softened her face significantly, and she looked nothing like the dragon Aimee claimed her to be. "Ah, no. I told her about it when she drove me around the property." Justine cleared her throat again. "To be fair, it took a bit to translate Aimee's praise, because honestly, I thought she was being her usual charming self when she said 'good to hear it didn't bleed to death for once.'"

Sally chuckled. "Sounds like Aimee. Typical backhanded compliment."

Justine laughed softly and said, "Yeah."

Sally went on immediate alert at the almost breathless and reminiscent way that word sounded. *Surely this woman wasn't fond of*

Aimee? They looked more likely to duel with pistols at dawn than make anything representing friendship, but Sally filed that look and that softly spoken word away for future reference. "Now, I asked you over here to ask you a question, if that's okay?"

"Fire away."

"Well, an important part of running the station is the behind-the-scenes work. It's not just shearing and dipping and fencing and cropping and ag sales and so on. There's a lot of mouths to feed, supplies to manage, and the book work is horrendous."

"You want the women to do your accounting?"

Sally tipped her head back and laughed. "Oh, dear, how I wish."

Justine shrugged through her chuckles. "Amber is an accountant."

Sally cut off mid-laugh. "Seriously?"

Justine nodded. "Seriously. She's currently unemployed, though, as she's back at uni studying nursing."

Sally's jaw dropped. *Well, there you go.* Sally made a mental note to tell Aimee about her and perhaps she could stop thinking of them as air heads. Shaking her head, Sally got back on track. "What I was going to suggest, is that they could help out in the kitchen. I usually cook for my lot and Joey and Aimee, but with the girls and yourself, there's more to do."

Justine nodded. "That's a good idea. You know, I don't mind helping out. In fact, I'd like to. Aimee keeps grumbling on about us being freeloaders, so I'm happy to pitch in if it means shutting her up."

Sally laughed again. "Good luck with that. My sister is an eternal pessimist. She'll find something else to whinge about, trust me."

"I don't doubt that."

Laughing softly to themselves, they looked up in unison to see Aimee, guiding Kite from the stables and back into the paddock.

While Justine continued to watch her sister, Sally stood. "Come on, if you're serious about helping, I could use a hand."

"Sure," Justine said, standing.

Sally walked off, assuming Justine was trailing her. When she opened the door, however, she turned to find Justine still over at the outdoor setting staring at Aimee's back. "Coming?" she called out, smirking when the woman jolted from her reverie with a blushing face. *There's definitely something going on there*, she thought to herself. Shifting her eyes to Aimee, she wondered if this interest went both ways.

***

"You know, I was rather concerned for your safety yesterday," Sally said to Justine in the kitchen a short while later. "We didn't know where you were after Aimee brought you back to the homestead."

"Oh…I was just…reading."

"We checked your room."

"I went for a walk. Lost track of time."

Sally put down the tray she was holding. *Bloody city folk had no idea how seriously life was balanced out here.* Relieved that the woman had been stupid rather than topped off by her sister, Sally said, "While I get the need for privacy, and hell, the need to have a break after dealing with Aimee, it's important out here that people know where you are. Trust me, the alternative is unpleasant."

"Alternative?"

"We've had people go missing out here before. Make sure someone knows where you are, okay?"

Justine nodded. "Will do." Justine bit her lip and looked at the potato in her hand.

"Especially this time of year," Sally mumbled to herself.

"This time of year?" Justine frowned at her.

I said that out loud? Sally was prevented from answering when Robbie burst into the kitchen at lightning pace again. "For God's sake, Robbie!"

"Sorry, Mum," he said, shrinking his head into his shoulders. "Here's the icing sugar. Can I have my drink now?"

"As soon as you tell me why it took you two hours to fetch this," Sally said, holding up the bag of fine sugar.

"I went to the dam with Rolly and Miss Gerhardt."

Clucking her tongue, she said, "Righto. Go get your drink. And thank you!" she called out as the boy bolted the moment she said 'go.'

Sally revealed the cake tin beneath a tea towel, Justine said, "A cake? What's the occasion?"

"Aimee turned twenty-four yesterday."

"*Yesterday?* Why didn't she have her cake then?"

Sally was quiet for a while and Justine watched her collect bowls from the cupboards. "Yesterday is a little emotional. It was the anniversary of our parents' death."

Justine blinked. "Oh. I'm sorry, I didn't know."

"I hardly expected you to, but as you could imagine, it's hard on Aimee, so we have her birthday today instead. That's what the bath thing is all about."

Silence filled the kitchen as Sally prepared the icing for the cake and lost herself in memories.

"Can I ask what happened? Joey said in his interview that they were in a plane crash?" Justine said.

Sally let out a long sigh. "Yeah. It belonged to a family that decided to do the country change thing before it was popular. They flew in one day after getting some work on the station, and a few days later, the mum and kid went missing out in the ranges. Went for a walk to look for flowers. We all looked for them, but with no sign. The guy, who had been servicing his plane, fixed it and suggested they fly around and cover more territory. You can imagine he was beside himself, so his attention to detail was lacking." Sally fiddled with the measuring spoons. "Aimee begged mum and dad to go with them, stating it was her birthday, so it was her right to go. Dad wasn't having it and they had a little tiff. He laid down the law and she was devastated. She took off to her special place and we didn't see her for a few days."

"A few days?"

"Yeah. Joey was supposed to be looking after her, but he went out on horseback to continue searching. He found the mum and kid up near the stock route. They were exhausted but fine, but when we couldn't contact our parents or the dad to tell them, we got worried. That's also when we realised Aimee had gone missing." Sally hesitated but continued her story. "The plane had a loose hose, so the report found, and came down out by the old ruins. That's where the wreckage was found late that night."

"The graves," Justine said, obviously recalling the ones Aimee and Robbie had placed flowers on.

"Aimee was nowhere to be found, and Joey and I were frantic. We just lost our parents and we had lost Aimee too." Sally wiped a tear from her eyes. "We found Aimee curled up inside the ruins a few days later."

Justine gasped. "Her special place."

Sally's eyes narrowed wondering how the city woman knew that. Thinking that Aimee must have mentioned it, she let it slide. "Exactly. She saw the accident."

"Oh, my God."

Sally kept her eyes on her mixing bowl. "She does the water run on her birthday every year because she likes to go to the ruins and visit mum's and dad's grave." Lowering her eyes to the bench, she said, "Aimee refused to come inside the house after we found her because mum and dad were no longer here. It took a long time before she was ready to come inside again."

"It sounds like she is lucky to have a brother and sister like you and Joey."

Sally gave her a sad smile before looking away. Rubbing her fingers across the bench to wipe away non-existent dust, Sally said, "It took a lot of patience and love for her to work through her grief. It wasn't an easy time, but we did everything we could to help her; however, the station never stops. No matter how much the loss hurt, we had to keep on top of this place. Joey had to take on more and more responsibility as our grandparents began to look towards retirement, I took on the role of Aimee's minder, but in time, I started my own family. She's strong though. So strong. I don't think I could have worked through it the way she did. Years of nightmares and counselling and—" Sally looked up to see Justine's hand over her mouth and stiffened when she saw Aimee over Justine's shoulder. "Shit," Sally muttered, bracing for her sister's reaction.

Justine quickly swung around, dislodging the tears in her eyes. "Aimee?"

Aimee stood stone still with her eyes on Justine.

Sally was terrified of her response knowing full well that she didn't like her personal life being discussed, and had a feeling she might need to throw her body in the line of fire. Tensing to defend herself and Justine, she let her head jerk back on her neck as Aimee's eyes, sometimes the only feature she expressed herself from, softened. *What the hell?*

Sally glanced at Justine. She looked teary and like she wanted to hug her sister. *Hello*, Sally thought.

Clearing her throat, Aimee said, "I have a little tradition for my birthday. You can join me if you like?"

"Oh?" Justine said, cocking her head.

"Aimee!" Sally gasped as understanding dawned on her. "Don't you dare!"

With a cheeky smirk, Aimee held out her hand. Justine took it tentatively clearly unsure of the protocol in front of Aimee's family. "It's fine, Sal. If it all goes pear-shaped, I'll just dump the evidence down the old well."

Thrown by her sister initiating personal contact, Sally was left standing alone in the kitchen. Coming to, she swore under her breath and ran off to look for Joey.

***

"So…do I want to know what this tradition is?" Justine asked.

"Nope." Aimee smiled and squeezed Justine's hand when she groaned. "Let's just say it's something Joey showed me on my tenth birthday. Are you afraid of heights?"

"Ah…they're not my favourite thing, but I manage. Why?"

Walking into the machinery shed, they turned a few heads when they saw the two sparring women hand in hand.

"Ah…you okay there, Aims?" Gav asked.

"I'm good." Letting go of Justine's hand, she took a box down from the shelf.

"Oh, Christ," Gav moaned.

"You know, this isn't sounding particularly appealing right now," Justine muttered to Aimee.

"Trust me, it's fine."

"I'll go get the mattress," Gav said, departing the shed.

"Mattress?"

"Landing pad," Aimee explained, heading outside and in the direction of the water tank.

"Umm…I suddenly remembered I have a shoot to prepare." Justine turned and began to walk away the moment Aimee strapped a harness on herself and looked up to the top of the water tower they walked towards.

"Hey!" Aimee grabbed her back. "It's fun. Trust me."

"Well, how about you go first and I'll judge from that?"

Aimee narrowed her eyes but conceded. "Fine, but you have to climb up with me with a harness on."

Ascending the ladder to the water tank's base, Justine gripped on tight as the ground looked small beneath them. Across the yards, Gav had put a mattress against the side of the machinery shed, and Aimee clipped something to a cable linking the shed and the water tank.

By the house, Sally held back her cheering children and Miss Gerhardt looked up at them with a bored expression. The film crew gathered with their cameras at the commotion.

"God. This is insane!" Justine complained as Aimee hooked herself to the cable.

"No. It's fun, and Joey only lets me do it once a year."

Justine just shook her head.

Grinning, Aimee said, "So I'll go, then you follow me down. Okay?"

Justine shook her head. "Nope."

"Or…" Aimee said, pressing Justine against the water tank and kissed her while linking their harnesses together. "Or," she said, pulling back. "We go together."

Justine looked down. A single loop held them together.

Aimee raised her eyebrows to prompt an answer from Justine.

"Fine. Together."

With Justine hands on Aimee's hips, she moved them around Aimee's waist and held tight.

As Justine buried her face against Aimee's neck, Aimee said, "Ready?"

"No," Justine whispered. A few moments later, Justine added, "Just get this over with."

Aimee wrapped her arms around Justine and fell backwards off the tower.

Justine screamed the entire way down the zip line.

Trying not to go deaf, and holding the woman tight, Aimee enjoyed the ride down right up to the moment they hit the mattress. Hitting it with her back, Justine's weight pushed the air from her lungs and she was sure something snapped. Justine tried to back away, but tethered to Aimee, all they managed was to topple over one another. Whatever damage Aimee had done burned as she landed on Justine.

"Oh, my God, I'm alive," Justine muttered to herself as Aimee tried to unhook the harness with a grimace on her face.

"What the hell is wrong with you!" said Joey as Aimee rolled off Justine. "You could have killed her!"

"Whatever you do, don't over exaggerate," Aimee said to him as she got to her feet, holding her hand out to Justine to help her up.

"What were you thinking!" Joey yelled at her before turning to Justine. "Are you okay?"

"I'm fine."

"See, she was perfectly safe," Aimee said, trying to stand tall and ignore the pain in her ribs.

"You are bloody insane!" Joey screamed. "You're lucky that cable held you both up," he said, pointing to a cable that had been joining the water tower and the machinery shed for two decades. "As of now, it gets taken down. I can't have you taking this stupid risk every year."

"Well, excuse me for trying to have some fun."

"It's suicidal."

Aimee rolled her eyes. Wrong move.

"What has gotten into you," Joey snapped, shoving a finger in her face.

Noticing the way Justine stepped closer to her, Aimee said, "Back off, Joe."

"I will do no such thing. You can't just push someone off the tower. Enough is enough."

"Or what?"

"Or you're off this property."

Aimee scowled at him. "Do whatever you like, Joe. We both know you're going to anyway."

"And what the hell is that supposed to mean?"

"Figure it out," Aimee said, storming off and trying not to cradle her ribs like she wanted to.

Joey mimicked his sister and stormed off in the other direction, leaving the witnesses blinking with shock.

"Ah, what just happened?" Justine asked Sally.

"Are you okay?"

"Of course." Justine smiled. "That was terrifying, but rather exhilarating."

Breathing out a sigh of relief, Sally looked in the direction of her siblings and bit her lip. "If you'll excuse me for a moment, I need to talk to Joey."

Justine moved aside to let her pass, and Sally could hear the excited tones of one of the cameramen behind her as he talked to Justine.

CHAPTER TEN

Joey paced the verandah, beer in hand, as he tried to calm the storm inside him. Aimee had gone too far this time. Going in tandem from the tower was a stupid move and she should know better. What was worse, moments before he discovered what Aimee had done, he'd had a heated argument with Gav about everything that was being neglected, and found himself lacking. *How had he let it get this bad?*

Growling, he turned to find Sally behind him.

"Christ!"

"Here, a fresh can." She handed him another drink.

"Thanks." Cracking the can, he sat heavily in the cane chair nearby. "What are we going to do with her Sal?"

"With who?"

"Aimee!"

Sally nodded. "As far as I can tell, no one got hurt."

"She nearly killed Justine!"

"Hardly. Aimee would never have done that little trick if she didn't think it was safe. She's safety obsessed, you know that."

Joey scrubbed his face with a hand. "That's not the point. She's being a brat and I'm fed up with it." He huffed out a breath and leaned his head back. "Why can't she just grow up already?"

"Joe, she *is* grown up. She's twenty-four. She's an honours student. She's independent. She's smart and she's an asset to the station. She's everything we raised her to be."

"I don't recall teaching her how to be a bitch."

"Joseph!"

"*What?* She's being difficult and rude. What did Justine ever do to deserve that the attitude she's been chucking about? Or the girls for that matter. Or me!" He groaned. "Maybe she should get off the property for a while. Get some perspective."

Sally took a long breath in. "I'm not sure—"

"I can't have her carry on the way she is. Her behaviour is unacceptable, and while I don't want to lose her, I think it's time she spreads her wings."

"By forcing her off the property? Oh, smart move, Joseph."

Curling his lip at Sally's sarcastic tone, he said, "She needs to re-evaluate herself."

"At the expense of her free will?"

"Bloody hell, Sal. You're making it sound like I want to disown her."

"That's exactly how she'll see it. Why don't you try talking to her instead of giving her ultimatums? You've both hardly spoken since the circus rolled into town."

"I've been busy." Joey bit down hard on the inside of his cheek. His excuse wasn't going to ride for much longer when his sisters discover how much he'd let everything slide. Aimee had only uncovered the tip of the iceberg. Thank goodness she hadn't looked at their finances too closely.

"We always are."

Joey stood. "Look, Sal, the fact is, Aimee has a lot to learn and a lot to offer at school. Maybe I should have suggested she go back to uni full time before this lot got here. I could have done without her constant attitude."

Sally followed her brother to her feet. "She's protective, Joe. That's all. If you just take a moment to think about it, you'll see she's trying to make sure nothing goes wrong."

"I'm the one that does that, not her. *I'm* the manager here, not her. If she has an issue with the way the film crew is operating, then she comes to see me. She doesn't, however, get to whine and pout like a spoiled child and drag people off of water towers."

"That's not—"

"Save it." Joey turned on his heels and walked away from his sister. Sally was forever coming to Aimee's defence like the clichéd good-cop-bad-cop routine. Yes, Joey was proud of Aimee, but she could be a downright cow when she put her mind to it. Shaking his head, he crossed the darkening yards looking for Justine, finding her in the back of her van in front of an array of televisions.

Headphones on, she was staring at footage of the flying fox calamity of earlier.

"Ah, hello?" he asked loudly, rapping on the van door.

Justine jumped and threw her headphones off. "Oh, hi, I didn't hear you."

"You were working." He gestured to the screens.

"Uh…yeah. I was about to go through this morning's footage."

Joey nodded. "Right. Umm…I just wanted to make sure you're okay, you know, after earlier. I'm really sorry about what Aimee did."

"She didn't do anything. She had my permission."

Joey frowned. "Oh."

Justine gave him a thin smile and raised her eyebrows. "So?"

"So…" He scratched his head.

Justine cleared her throat. "Any ideas on something you'd like to do with Amber?" she asked, picking up a notepad. "I need some video of private interactions with her, plus a date, and then on Friday we need to discuss which woman you're going to ask to leave."

Joey cringed internally. The show had seemed like something easy and fun to begin with, plus he had the added bonus of meeting sophisticated women he would otherwise never have met. The problem was, they were turning out just like Aimee predicted…unsuitable for station life. Two of them had already asked him how much the place was worth, and whether he'd consider selling.

"Ah, yeah, sure. Umm…I was thinking of taking Amber out to the ruins."

Justine straightened in her chair. "You're sure?"

"Uh, yeah. It's nice out there."

She nodded. "It is, but…isn't it more of a private place. Historical and, well…special."

Joey cocked his head. "Sally told you that's where the plane came down?"

Justine nodded.

He took a deep breath. *She was right.* Shame washed through him. He had all but ordered Aimee to take Justine out there, and on her birthday of all days. He sighed. *Maybe Aimee had a right to be pissed off right now.*

"You okay?" Justine asked.

"Yeah, just…" He looked over at the screen finding himself glaring and pointing at Aimee.

Justine followed his line of vision. "Aimee?"

"Umm…maybe the billabong out on Roper Creek will be a good place to take Amber."

Justine winced. "It's not going to be a repeat of your date with Brittney is it?"

Joey laughed. "No. I promise we'll avoid the bugs this time. The billabong has a raft and definitely requires daylight, so maybe we can go out there for a picnic lunch or something?" He looked down at the vinyl floor of the van, thinking about the days Tracey and himself would meet up there as teens.

"It sounds wonderful." Justine flipped a page in her notepad. "Where is it?"

"Southeast. There're no tracks out to it," Joey said, realising they'd have to use horses or bikes to reach it. The road had washed out a decade ago.

"How far?"

"About ten minutes on the bike."

Justine nodded and made notes. "Okay. I'll think of a few conversation starters, and maybe you could tell her a bit about your parents? An anecdote from the time you spent at the billabong with them perhaps?"

Joey nodded.

"Any chance of looking at the scene before lunch?"

Joey nodded again and scratched his head. "Only thing is, I'm going to be up at the yards with the shearers with most of the workers. Sal is heading into Roper Creek in the morning and Danny is out with the rest of the guys rounding up the next flock for shearing."

"Oh. Well, that's okay, maybe we can head out early or something. No big deal."

"Well…Aimee will be around. She works with the horses Thursdays."

"Oh?" Justine raised her eyebrows.

Joey grimaced. "Yeah, sorry, I know you and her don't really get along, and I can imagine you'd rather sue her for damages, but I promise, she'll look after you."

"I have no doubt. By, oh, I meant, she works with the horses?"

"Oh, right. Yes. She trains them and so forth, but tomorrow she's supposed to be trying to get the stallion on the fillies. That's if her bloody horse didn't completely ruin him."

Justine's eyes crinkled in question.

"Her horse, Kite, the one that trotted off on her the day you arrived?"

Justine nodded.

"Well, Handsome Boy, the stallion, mounted her and hasn't looked at any of the other horses since."

"Oh. I'm sorry."

Joey frowned. "For what? It was hardly your fault. Just another stellar Aimee moment." He huffed out a breath. "I'm sorry about her. I really am. She's not been herself this week. I've never seen her so riled up at someone like she is with you."

"I must agree. She has a way of getting under my skin also."

Joey nodded. "I'm going to send her away. That will make it easier on everyone involved."

Justine gasped. "What?"

He shrugged. "She asked for it."

"By doing what? Trying to have fun and protect everyone's welfare?"

"Protect everyone? She threw you from a water tower."

"I was strapped to her, I was safe."

Joey scoffed and pointed to the screen. "You don't look happy."

Justine shook her head. "That was simply fear and adrenaline. I believe her constant disputes have more to do with ensuring the people she loves remain safe while outsiders play pretend at fitting in."

"You've been talking to Sally." Joey huffed. *Bloody women, always sticking together.*

"No, but I have been talking to Aimee. She's worried about you."

Taken aback, Joey blinked. "Worried about me?" A larger realisation occurred to him. "Wait. You've been talking to Aimee? Civilly?"

Justine smiled. "Yes."

"Huh." Joey narrowed his eyes, trying to picture the two fiery women speaking without a healthy serving of snark. "Well…she's around tomorrow. If you want to go out to the billabong in the morning, ask her."

Justine nodded. "I'll have the film crew go with you and the contestants in the morning. I need more sound bites and captures of their reaction to the work." Putting down the notepad, she

115

looked at her watch. "For now, would you mind if I use your phone. I promised someone a call."

Joey smiled, reading between the lines. "A special someone, hey?"

Justine nodded and gave him a closed-lip smile. "Something like that."

"Well, right this way," he said, holding out the crook of his arm.

***

Tired of her self-isolation and her one-sided internal argument with Joey, Aimee finally finished picking up all the screws Mitsy managed to knock over the moment they entered the shed, and made her way out to find Justine. Walking into the large quadrangle between the station buildings, she saw Justine with her arm hooked around her brother's. *What the…?*

Following them, she remained in the shadows for the sole purpose of avoiding Joey as he led Justine to the door to the office.

"You can call him in here," Joey said, giving Justine a wink.

"Thanks," Justine said, smiling politely. "I promise I won't be long."

"Take all the time you need to talk to your special someone," Joey said, waving her off.

Special someone? Aimee took a deep breath and clenched her teeth.

"Hi, sweetheart," Justine's voice drifted from the open door.

Aimee sighed, planning to turn around and leave Justine in privacy. Unfortunately, the movement tugged at what she suspected was a cracked rib, and made her pause and grimace for a few moments.

"Aaron! Don't you dare," Justine said before giggling. "I'll tell your mother on you," she added.

Ugh. The playfulness was sickening. Aimee clutched at her torso and slowly moved away, wishing the wind would stop carrying the conversation in her direction.

"Yeah, I know honey, but I'm working. I'm not sure you'd be allowed to come out here. Yes, I know it's just for the weekend. Okay. Yes. I'll check."

Aimee stood up straight and almost cried out in pain. *She was going to ask to bring this mystery man out here?*

"Look, I said I'll ask okay, but I'm not promising anything. Can I call you back later?" A pause and Justine chuckled. "Good. Now get back to work, sweetheart, you can't afford to get fired. I love you."

Aimee's stomach sank and she slumped making her ribs complain again. Quickly hobbling out of sight, Aimee held back a hiss as Justine exited the study. Aimee rubbed the ache in her chest, blaming the battered ribs and not the muscle still beating below her hand.

Justine made her way along the verandah to the kitchen door as Aimee held vigil against the tall stone pillar at the other end of the house. Emerging a short while later, Justine waved goodbye to whoever was in the kitchen after presumably checking if the boyfriend could have a booty call. In two minds about discovering what Sally's answer might be, curiosity got the better of her and like a Band-Aid, it was best to rip it off fast.

"Hey, there you are," Sally said when Aimee walked in, finding Joey in the kitchen with her.

"Have you apologised to Justine yet?" Joey asked.

"Apologise for what?"

"For shoving her off the tower."

"I didn't shove her, she volunteered."

Joey scoffed. Giving him a glare, Aimee looked at Sally. "I accidentally overheard Justine talking to her *significant other*. Is he coming out here?"

"Oh, she told you about Aaron?" Sally said. "I was surprised, too. Should have guessed, though."

Aimee wished that didn't feel like a knife to the heart. She wished so hard she thought she might crack another rib.

Joey answered her previous question. "He's heading out here on Saturday, so please play nice."

"Whatever," Aimee muttered, grabbing some leftovers from the fridge and wishing she had thought to stock up her own pantry earlier.

"I'm not appreciating the attitude."

"And I'm not appreciating picking up your slack."

Joey stood so abruptly, Aimee's neck cracked when she looked up at her brother. "It's under control."

"What is?" Sally said, moving closer. "What is Aimee talking about?"

"Nothing."

"*Nothing?*" Aimee let out a bark of dry laughter. "Bullshit. Why don't you tell Sally about the bills that haven't been paid, or the fuel and equipment that wasn't ordered, or maybe about the lack of maintenance along the boundary fences. Last I checked, you and Danny had dibs on the dozers around here, but apparently neither of you could be bothered to use them."

"What?" Sally said.

"Look!" Joey yelled. "It's been busy, okay?" Joey ran a hand through his hair, and looked ready to continue defending himself when the three contestants entered the kitchen.

"There you are, handsome," Brittany said, hooking her arm in his. "Come for a swim?"

Aimee held back a look of displeasure as Tiffany took up a post on the other side of Joey and gave him a smile that rang false from miles away. She glanced at Amber to find the woman greeting Sally with a smile and a nod. Amber did the same to her, forcing Aimee to smile and nod back.

"How's the ribs?" Amber asked.

Aimee tensed. "What?"

Amber gestured to Aimee's chest. "I can have a look if you like?"

"Uh…"

"What's wrong with your ribs?" Sally asked, moving around the bench to Aimee as Joey distracted himself with the other two women.

"Nothing. They're fine," Aimee said, stepping back and covering the throb she could feel with a hand. Confused about why Amber was asking after her health, Aimee decided it was time to vacate the scene. Besides, hiding from the world was exactly what the doctor ordered, and after saying goodnight and shutting herself in her loft, she wondered if anyone would miss her if she stayed there for the rest of the week.

"There you are," Justine said, catching Aimee as she tried to flee to her loft.

"And here I go," Aimee said, moving past the woman and hating how her throat closed up.

"Hey! You okay?" Justine jogged to catch her. "I heard raised voices."

Aimee paused and clenched her teeth, shutting her eyes in the process and wishing this moment of her life was over. Turning around with a little more composure, she said, "Joey."

"You argued again?"

Aimee nodded in short, sharp movements. "Yeah."

"I told him that I jumped with you earlier. You didn't force me off the water tower."

"I know."

Justine frowned at her. "What's wrong?"

"Nothing. I'm beat. Goodnight." Aimee didn't enjoy the way Justine's face fell at being so callously dismissed, but at least it had been effective. Left in peace, she reached her sanctuary and let herself fall apart.

CHAPTER ELEVEN

Knock. Knock. Knock.

"Huh? What?" Aimee rolled over and dislodged the book on her chest before wincing. "Ow. Ow. Ow."

Someone knocked at her door again.

Aimee rubbed at her eyes and looked around, completely disorientated. The sun was streaming through the window, lighting up the loft and her position on the couch. She carefully rose and padded to the door, opening it to discover Justine on the other side.

Aimee's heart sank a little. "Oh. Hi."

Justine looked confused at the lacklustre tone in Aimee's voice. "Hi. Everything okay?"

"Yeah. It's just dandy." She turned and walked to her kitchen. *What time was it?* Picking up her heavy duty watch, she gasped. *Eight!* She overslept. She *never* overslept. "Ugh," she muttered as she splashed water on her face. Apparently having your ribs squashed coinciding with a little too much ale and pain killers wasn't great for early rising, thought Aimee.

"You okay?"

"Yeah. I'm awesome. What do you want?"

Justine stared at her, not convinced by the vague answer and clearly suspecting something was up. "Joey is having a date with Amber at the billabong. He said you'd be able to show me out there this morning if I asked."

"Are you asking?"

"Yes."

Aimee sighed. *The billabong. That was Tracey and Joey's special place. The idea of him taking a contestant there was bizarre.* She shook her head.

Justine frowned. "Aimee, what's going on?" Justine reached out to find Aimee move away from her touch.

"I can show you the billabong."

"Then why did you shake your head?"

Aimee ignored the question. "Are you ready to go now?"

Justine studied her for a moment. "If you are, yes."

"Fine. I'll meet you downstairs. Be there in a minute."

"Umm…sure."

Aimee changed out of yesterday's clothes and made a quick cup of coffee. Downing the strong black beverage as she brushed Kite, she felt the caffeine rid her body of the alcohol and painkillers from the night before. Her mind was clear, but apparently her ribs were still sore. Withholding most of her grunts of protest, saddling Kite was excruciating. Mounting her even more so.

"Come on, let's go. Daylight is wasting," Aimee said as she guided her horse out of the stables to greet Justine.

The gentle sway of Kite's gait tugged and pulled at what Aimee was now suspecting were broken ribs. Consciously riding slightly ahead of Justine, she concealed the arm that braced her torso to hold her side. It appears zip-lining in tandem was one of her poorer ideas. *Maybe I should stick with one night stands and beer drinking contests*, she mused to herself. The consequences were far less painful. *At least beer didn't cheat on people. At least one night stands left in the morning taking their emotional baggage with them.* Aimee sighed heavily, the effort of expelling her lungs making her wince again.

"Are you okay?" Justine asked from beside her.

"I'm fine. Here's the billabong," Aimee said, pointing to a stand of trees surrounded a pool of water.

Justine gave her a dubious look.

Averting her eyes, Aimee kept talking. "It's fed by an underground stream that forms part of Roper Creek. It's how the town got its name. There's a chain of billabongs along this section that tap into the water table until the river comes out of the ground and flows past town." Chancing a glance at Justine, she saw the woman looking at her with a raised eyebrow, clearly not accepting the diversion. "Just go find your perfect shot," Aimee snapped, clicking her tongue and trotting Kite to the water.

Bad move, she thought as she slipped off the saddle. *That hurt like a bitch.*

"That's it. Something's clearly wrong with you," Justine said, dismounting her horse and striding over to her.

Aimee simply scoffed. "Trust me, there's a whole lot wrong with me."

"Are you injured?"

"Injured?" Aimee frowned and shook her head. "Nope."

"Then why are you grimacing?"

"I'm not."

Justine poked her in the side making Aimee scream.

"Damn it! What'd you do that for?"

Justine hopped about looking devastated at the amount of pain she had caused. "Shit. Are you okay?"

"No!"

Clucking her tongue, Justine's panic subsided. "Oh, stop being a big baby." She grabbed the arm Aimee was using to brace her torso. "Show me your side."

"No."

Justine tugged at Aimee's shirt to lift it.

"What are you doing?" Aimee said, holding back her progress.

"Stop being stubborn for once, and let me look."

"I'm fine."

Justine put her hands on her hips back and fixed her with a glare. "You know, you say that an awful lot."

"Because it's true."

"Show me what's wrong." She made a grab for Aimee's shirt again, untucking it from her waistline.

"Stop it."

"Oh, come on. It's not like I haven't seen you naked before."

Aimee sneered at her. "Yeah, and I won't be making that mistake again."

Justine gasped and looked like she'd been slapped. "What did you say?"

"I said I'm done."

Justine's crestfallen face scrunched into a frown. "What?" Justine grabbed for her hands, looking desperately confused.

Aimee shook off the touch.

"Aimee, Jesus, I have no idea what's happened. Talk to me."

"What's the point? What could you possibly want from me?"

Justine reached for her again, finding herself successfully grabbing Aimee's hands. "*Want* from you? Aimee—"

Aimee yanked her hands from Justine's grip. "Forget it." Turning back to her task, she was yanked forcibly around again and she gasped in pain.

"Shit. I'm sorry, are you okay?"

"Leave me alone." Aimee turned again but Justine stilled her with a hand on her shoulder.

"No, you don't get to dismiss me like that. You brushed me off last night, I'm not letting you do it again. I don't understand what's going on."

"Well, I understand just fine. I'm a fling. A dirty little secret. I get that, but how dare you rub it in my face just how replaceable I am."

"What the hell are you talking about? I'm not replacing anybody."

"So, what, you're planning to bring him to our bed?"

"What?" Justine made a disgusted noise and threw her hands up in the air. "I have no idea what you're talking about. You're bloody insane."

"I'm talking about Aaron. I overheard you talking to him on the phone and Joey specifically told me to play nice with him when he comes up tomorrow."

"Aaron?" Justine tipped her head back in sudden understanding. The woman started to chuckle and reached out to grab Aimee by the shoulders, but Aimee shoved her roughly away just as Joey arrived on a quad bike followed by his entourage. Justine tripped on the uneven ground and her back thumped against the dirt. A spike of fear rippled through Aimee fearing she'd hurt Justine.

"Aimee! Enough!" Joey barked, skidding to a halt beside them. "Go pack your bags, missy, you're going to Armidale...*now!*"

Aimee screwed her face up at him ready to thump him square in the nose. *This was absolutely none of his business. He wasn't about to get his heartbroken by some city tramp.* "Piss off, Joey!"

"Hey, this is my fault. It's just a big misunderstanding," Justine said, dusting herself off and moving between the aggravated pair. "Aimee—"

"Misunderstanding?" Aimee scoffed. "Yeah, right, that's what this is." She laughed with a cruel hollow sound. "Why don't you and your little boyfriend shack up in my bed that I've just been turfed out of? Hell, I certainly won't be using it again. It's nothing better than kindling to me now." Aimee glared at Joey and shoved him out of her way as she stormed over to Kite, who had retreated with the argument.

"Aimee, it's not what you think!" Justine called out to her retreating back.

Aimee paused after mounting Kite, tears blurring her vision. "Oh, I'm pretty sure it's exactly what I think. But don't concern your pretty little head about it. I'm just a simple country girl. Give me a beer or two and I'm over it. Have a nice life."

Clicking her tongue, she urged Kite into a run to destinations unknown. Sobbing and barely able to ride, she found a sanctuary by pure instinct and crumbled completely. *What was the use of love when all it got you was a broken heart and the rejection of your brother?*

***

Glaring at the piece of horizon his sister disappeared over, Joey fumed. Willing to listen to reason about Aimee's protectiveness and emotional upset at this time of year, now she had done her dash. Physically assaulting someone was unacceptable. "Damn it," he growled.

"Don't send her away. It's my fault she's so angry," Justine said, brushing off her film crew who had surrounded her in concern.

Joey turned his brown eyes on the dusty looking woman. "It doesn't matter now. She knows the consequences of fighting on this station."

"But she's just confused. She thinks Aaron is my boyfriend," Justine said, pleading with him.

"Huh? What has that got to do with anything?"

"She…I…" Justine sighed.

"Look, Miss Cason, assaulting someone on my property is a sure-fire way to get fired or kicked off the station. Aimee knows that. The instant she shoved you to the ground, she broke her chances."

"I tripped and fell. It's not like she knocked me on my arse with a right jab to the nose."

"I don't have to explain myself to you. Need I remind you this is my property, and I run it as I see fit."

Justine took a deep breath. "Yeah, I've noticed."

Joey narrowed his eyes at her, trying to find the hidden meaning. About to interrogate her further, Justine called out to her crew and scoped out the scene, leaving him alone with Amber.

"Everything okay?" she asked him.

Joey painted a smile on his face and looked over. "Yeah. Sure."

Amber bit her lip. "So…ah…do you like kids?"

Joey blinked. "Yes."

"Woah, guys. Save that conversation for the camera," the lighting technician said as he collected gear from the bikes. "Justine will be pissed if she missed that juicy gossip."

Joey sighed as he watched the man walk away.

"This…show, is incredibly constricting."

Joey had nodded before realising Amber had used consecutive words with more than two syllables. "Ah…yeah, it is."

"It's worse than tax law," Amber said with a smile.

"Tax law?"

"Mmm."

Joey blinked at her. "You know about tax law?"

Amber shrugged and looked over at the set up the crew were piecing together at Justine's direction. "It's part of the job. Well, ex-job." She looked at Joey and said, "I was an accountant in a past life."

Joey was stunned. So far his picks had proved to be as shallow as their looks. Initially charmed by their buoyant outlook and attractive features, it hadn't been until he got them on the farm that he realised their redeeming qualities only went skin deep. Tiffany was looking for a free ride through life and only seemed interested in working on the perfect tan. Brittany had done nothing but complain about the dust, dirt, lack of a city skyline and about the prevalence of wildlife. "I have a ton of accounting to do, so if you ever get bored…"

Amber smiled, and Joey's insides squirmed. Of all the women he'd brought to the station, Amber was the one that scared him the most. She was quieter and less inclined to throw herself at him. While the other two contestants kept him busy with their constant need to touch and talk to him, he had been acutely aware of the quiet woman watching on with amusement. Shorter, dark-eyed, and with brunette hair just lower than her ears, she was nothing like the type he usually noticed. "Ah…" Smooth Joey. "So…what do you do now?"

"I'm three semesters away from completing my nursing degree."

Joey's jaw dropped.

"Okay, guys! Let's date!" Justine shouted out to them.

"Time to put on your TV face," Amber said, plastering that dazzling, yet plastic, smile on her face, erasing the intelligence she had just revealed.

God, dating was horrible enough as it was without two cameras in your face and a woman checking conversation points off her script. Joey's palms sweated and he kept smiling.

"Ask about wanting a family again," Justine prompted.

Amber cleared her throat and picked up her wine glass. Sipping it, she looked up at him over the rim of the cup and said, "Do you like kids?"

About to answer, Justine chimed in. "Try saying 'do you want a family?'"

Amber cleared her throat and repeated the process with the appropriately phrased question.

Joey felt like he was on a god damned soap opera. *Thank God this was the last date.* "Yes. I do."

"I just need the right woman," Justine whispered.

"I just need to find the right woman, you know? Someone that can handle the remote lifestyle. Be able to look after themselves and pitch in."

"Does it get lonely out here?" Amber asked, off-script.

Glancing at Justine, she seemed happy with the new direction of conversation, so he answered, "No." He put his glass down. "At least, not for me. My family is here. My sisters, their families. Life out here is what you make of it, you know? Yes, it's hard work, and yes it's isolated, but it's my passion. I couldn't imagine doing anything else." Joey trailed off and thought of Aimee. "My little sister, she's never left this place for more than three days at a time. Even then, it was only for gymkhana events or sheep sales."

Amber frowned. "Aimee? The one you just banished."

Joey exhaled roughly. "Yeah." He flicked his eyes to Justine and noticed she had completely zoned out. "She's..." he sighed, acutely aware of the cameras rolling. "She's not banished."

"Why Armidale?" Amber asked.

Joey fidgeted, disliking how brazen and loud he had been with his argument with Aimee. "She studies there."

"Doing what?"

Justine leaned forward from her perch off-camera.

"Agriculture. Masters actually. She graduated with honours a couple of years ago. Her…" he shook his head. "The knowledge she has, the instinct, it's incredible. Her professors have been asking her to study on-campus for years. I think they want her to teach."

"Wow," Joey heard Justine whisper.

Amber and Joey both glanced at her. Justine cleared her throat and waved her hand. "Continue."

"She didn't want to go?" Amber asked.

Joey laughed. "No. She told them to stick it where the sun doesn't shine."

Amber smiled. "She sounds like a real woman of the land."

He nodded. "Very much so. Believe it or not, they keep asking her back. They have a doctorate all lined up for her, too."

Amber's eyebrows rose. "She's that smart?"

Joey nodded. "But her life is this place. She was born here. She was raised here. She belongs here."

"Yet you just told her to leave," Justine said.

Joey averted his eyes. "She needs to grow up. Get some world experience, too."

"She's twenty-four, I think she's grown up enough, and the world is a cruel place."

"Why do you even care? You two have been at each other's throats since you got here, and don't forget, she just tossed your arse to the dirt and threw you off a water tower."

"She's angry, and I jumped with her."

"She's always angry." Joey sighed and stood up from the plaid picnic rug. "That's her flaw. She's abrasive. Always."

"There's a reason for that."

Joey's eyebrows arched and he put his hands on his hips. "Oh? You're suddenly an expert on my sister? You've known her for two seconds, what gives you the right to stick your nose into our family business."

"Exactly, she's your sister, so you should have known not to send a complete stranger with her to visit your parent's gravesite on the anniversary of their death!"

Joey clenched his jaw. Guilt made him defensive. "You know nothing about us."

"And apparently you know nothing about *her*. Don't you get it? She's trying to protect you from yourself. She's trying to stop you from taking risks with the lives of these women here…" Justine gestured at Amber. "And the lives of your family and workers. She's just trying to make sure no one gets hurt."

"She threw you off a water tower and pushed you into the dirt. Who exactly is she supposed to not be hurting?"

"Will you please listen for once. I jumped *with* her!" Justine took a breath. "And I hurt her first," Justine said quietly. Her eyes scanned the horizon for a moment. "In fact…" Throwing her notepads to the lighting man, Justine jogged to her horse. "Follow my notes and finish off the date," she instructed them. "I have someone to apologise to."

Joey, Amber and the film crew stood mouths agape watching Justine ride off.

"That was weird…right?" Amber asked him.

"Definitely." He furrowed his brows and cocked his head. Justine was obviously a glutton for punishment if she was prepared to walk into the bear cave. He scratched his head. *Women. He would never be able to understand them.*

***

Completing his date with Amber pleasantly surprised at her lack of air-headedness, he went to the office on his return to catch up with all the work Aimee had accused him of neglecting. Months had passed since he went to the city to seek new challenges and new women. Months of time where bills and paperwork had piled up at the property. Months of chores that he'd let slide as he tried to re-evaluate his life.

With a heavy sigh, he opened bills, bills and more bills. Thankful for the good rains last season that funded their investments, he piled the accounts he was grateful he could honour into a tray. Next came agriculture-related correspondence. Invites to open days, field days, and regional shows followed. Saving personal correspondence to last, he organised the letters in piles for Sally's family, Aimee and for him.

One letter caught his eye. Addressed with gold gel pen, he opened it and his heart sank.

Dear Mr Joseph Turner
You are cordially invited to celebrate
the marriage of
Mr Gregory Chambers
to
Miss Tracey Geraghty
on 4 December
at the sale yards, Roper Creek
Please RSVP by 8 November

"Damn it!" he growled, screwing up the invite and tossing it across the room, narrowly missing Sally, who was walking in with a mug in her hand.

"Jesus, Joe!"

"Sorry," he muttered.

"What was that in aid of?" she asked, putting the cup on the desk next to her brother and retrieving the crumpled ball. "Oh, Joey," she whispered when she read it. "I'm sorry."

He shrugged. "It's her life. She can marry who she likes."

"I know, but—"

"Save it, Sal."

"All right, all right," Sally said, raising her hands in defence. "Have you seen Aimee? She was supposed to collect Robbie to help with the horses, but I haven't seen hide nor hair of her."

Joey sighed and held his head in his hands as his elbows rested on the desk. "She's probably packing."

"Packing?"

"She's going to Armidale."

Sally's eyes widened. "What did you do, Joseph?"

"I did nothing, so back off. She assaulted Justine."

Sally gasped.

"She knows the consequences of violence on my property."

"*Your* property? Last I checked, we had equal shares."

"You know what I mean."

"No, Joseph, I don't. We accepted your will to be in this show, but ever since that lot have gotten here, you and Aimee have barely had a civil word to each other. It's got to stop."

"Armidale will do her good, Sal. She's got lots of opportunities there."

"You better hope that's the case because you'll be answering to me otherwise."

Joey shook his head and glared at the paperwork on his desk.

"Now, how was the date?"

Confused by the change in subject, he said, "Good. Amber is…surprising."

"Oh? The accountant?"

"Yeah. You knew?"

"Justine mentioned it the other day."

"She's doing nursing, too."

Sally nodded.

"She's…nice."

"Pretty too," Sally said with a smile.

"Yeah, but it's not just that, you know? After Justine went off on her Aimee-crusade, we just sat down and talked for ages about—"

"Wait. Aimee-crusade?"

"Yeah. She got all moody and took off to find Aimee."

"I thought you said Aimee assaulted her?"

"Aimee pushed her over."

Sally's hands went to her child-bearing hips. "You mean to say you banished your kid sister because she pushed someone over!"

"Yes, but—"

"What were they arguing about?"

Joey worked his jaw as he tried to catch up. "Umm…about Aaron."

"Aaron?"

"Yeah. Aimee seemed to think he was her boyfriend…I think." Joey scratched his chin as understanding dawned on his sister's face.

"I knew it. I knew it. I knew it."

"Knew what?"

Sally grinned. "I think our little sister is in love."

Joey scoffed before chuckling. "Yeah, right, whatever."

Sally just nodded at him.

"What? With Justine? No way, they can barely stand each other."

"Tell me one time Aimee has ever been jealous?"

"Jealous? Aimee?" Joey chuckled again. "She's made of stone, Sal. Nothing gets to her."

"Exactly." Sally shot him a wink and left the office, leaving him utterly confused.

"Bloody women," he muttered, shaking his head, having no idea what the point of that conversation was. Picking up the invite Sally had left on the desk, he sighed. *There was no way in hell he was attending that wedding*, so without further thought, he threw the invite in the bin.

***

She spotted the rider a kilometre out. Contemplating whether or not to stay or run, Aimee sighed. Having exhausted herself with tears she tried not to let out, she shivered in the fading light and decided she didn't care anymore.

The rider dismounted and walked cautiously over to her. "Mind if I sit down?"

She wanted to snap something snarky like 'do whatever you like, I don't give a rat's arse', but her throat had closed up and tears were threatening again, so all she could manage was a small shrug. She should have been furious that Justine had been wandering around the property alone, but seeing her offered an unfamiliar comfort that Aimee had only ever found in her siblings. She reminded herself that Justine was the reason she was sitting at the ruins falling apart. *Damn it. She was breaking her.*

Justine sat beside her and they watched the sun touch the horizon in silence. She rustled in her pocket and handed Aimee a picture. The photo was left hanging for a moment before Aimee exhaled roughly and snatched it from the persistent woman. She hesitated a moment, watching the sun disappear in full, and looked at it. A young boy in glasses and a smile looked back at her. He was wearing a school uniform and had short-cropped blonde hair.

"Aaron. My son," Justine said.

Aimee's lungs expelled in a violent shudder, and relief, hope and utter terror shivered through her along with a healthy serving of pain. "Your son?" she barely choked out before she had to turn her head away to scrub at more tears. She clamped her jaw together and squeezed her eyes shut as she tried to rein herself in.

Justine's hand touched her thigh and rubbed slowly. "He's nearly thirteen. He's smart, cute, stubborn and my whole world."

"I thought…"

Justine sighed and squeezed her leg. "I know. I haven't really had a chance to tell you about him. We got hot and heavy pretty fast and, well, it's busy out here. There hasn't really been a chance to talk about my life back in the city." Reaching over, she took Aimee's hand in hers. "I don't have any sort of significant other. Not since Aaron. You're the first person I've been with for a really long time. A *really* long time."

Aimee nibbled on her lower lip as she let that sink in.

"I, uh, don't have a lot of experience with…this." Justine gestured between them. "With, umm, women."

"You've never slept with a woman before?"

Justine shook her head.

"Well, if it helps, I couldn't tell. You're…" Aimee let out a breath. "Kind of amazing."

Justine smiled shyly. "I've had a lot of time to think about it."

Aimee gave her a curious look. "How is it you haven't dated anyone?"

"Being a single mum is rather time-consuming. Being a single mum and riding competitively even more so."

"Competitively?"

"Equestrian. Dressage. Cross Country. Jumping. I…competed for Australia for a few years."

Aimee blinked. "Wow."

"Yeah. I couldn't have done it without my mum's support, though. A few years ago I got out of the sport and moved into television. It's a job that makes me travel a lot, I'm afraid. I used to cover sports events but got a chance at this reality show. Aaron isn't too pleased that I'm away at the moment. My mother is apparently making him mop floors."

Aimee turned once again to face the sunset. "I, ah, accidentally overheard you talking to him."

"And jumped to conclusions?"

Aimee straightened her back. "We never really said this…whatever it is, was exclusive."

"It is to me."

Aimee pressed her lips together and nodded, looking down at the hand on her leg. She placed a hand over it and chewed her bottom lip, having no idea how to express the turmoil inside her. Meeting this woman, connecting with her on a physical and emotional level she hadn't allowed before, sharing the anniversary of her parent's death, and becoming insanely jealous over what turned out to be a boy, represented a connection she'd never experienced. She was in over her head, and if she was honest with herself, she was drowning a slow but pleasurable death. "So," Aimee started before clearing her throat. "You have a nearly thirteen-year-old son. How is that possible?" Aimee blinked, realising she didn't know how old Justine was. "Are you old enough for that?"

Justine nodded. "I had him young. *Very* young."

"How young?"

"I was sixteen."

So she's twenty-nine, Aimee thought to herself. "And he's coming to the station?"

"Yes. Mum is driving him out here as we speak." Justine laughed softly. "He's always wanted to play cowboy."

"Can he ride?"

Justine nodded. "Takes after his mother."

"He's pushy and annoying, too?"

Justine gave her an offended scoff before pinching her. "Says the most closed-off, difficult woman I've ever met." Justine poked at Aimee's stomach in jest making her gasp and flinch away. Justine grimaced. "God. Sorry."

"It's okay," Aimee said, rubbing at the bruise beneath her clothing.

"May I?" Justine asked, tugging at the shirt.

Aimee huffed out a breath and held her arm out, allowing Justine to tug the shirt free from its confines and lift it. Aimee watched her wince.

"That looks nasty," Justine said. She gently prodded at the bruise, pulling her hand back quickly when Aimee flinched. "I'm sorry."

Aimee looked at Justine and smiled. "It's okay."

"Maybe Amber should take a look at it."

"Amber? What on earth for?"

"She's a nurse…well…almost a nurse."

"You're shitting me?"

"Nope."

"Huh…" Aimee averted her eyes to the horizon. "I'll be fine. Besides, there's nothing you can do about ribs. They just have to heal."

"Sounds like you've hurt them before?"

"Once or twice." Giving Justine a wink, she looked back at the clouds catching the last of the sun's rays in a shade of brilliant orange.

Reaching over, Justine rubbed the back of her fingers against her cheek. "You don't always have to be so tough, you know?"

Aimee shrugged. "Who says I am?" Justine's fingers kept brushing her cheek and Aimee glanced over at her.

"I'd say everyone. You're very…defensive, I guess. Except when you're hitting on someone."

"I wasn't hitting on you."

Justine smirked at her. "Well, whatever it was you were doing, I saw a different side to the snarky, independent station woman…if only for a moment."

"I'm a soft touch for rocky road ice cream."

Justine arched her eyebrows.

"Not that nameless brand stuff. That's horrible. I mean that imported ice cream that comes in cardboard tubs. It's a rare treat, though, because, you know, no corner stores out here."

Justine smiled and shook her head. "So, if I ask Aaron to procure some of this ice cream you have a fondness for, will you forgive me?"

Aimee grinned at her. "That depends."

"On?"

"Whether I'm still here or not. If you hadn't heard, I'm being shipped to Armidale."

Justine nodded in understanding. "Uni."

"Yup."

"Agriculture, so I'm told."

"Yep."

"Apparently there's a brain under that hat, too," Justine said, tipping Aimee's wide-brimmed hat off-kilter.

"So they say. Surprised?"

"Pleasantly. Though, judging by the array of books on your shelf, I shouldn't be."

Aimee gasped in mock offence. "You looked through my stuff?"

Justine smiled. "We can't make love all the time, you know. I had to fill in time somehow, and snooping seemed like a good idea."

Aimee nibbled at her lower lip again. "We make love?" The question unintentionally acted like a loaded gun and the atmosphere charged itself. Light teasing moved over for serious and raw. Aimee nearly took the question back when Justine's smile faded.

"I think we do," Justine breathed, her eyes flicking to Aimee's mouth.

Aimee licked her lips. "I do, umm, too."

"I didn't mean to fall for you," Justine said, dragging her hands up to cup Aimee's face.

Aimee shook her head and leant her forehead against Justine's. "You're only here for one more week."

"I know." Justine's tongue slipped out to wet her lips.

"You're a city slicker," Aimee said after a swallow, and moving a hand to caress Justine's neck.

"Who knows how to ride and train horses."

Aimee gave her a wobbly smile before shaking her head slightly. "Our worlds are vastly different."

"I don't care."

"I don't know how to do relationships," Aimee said.

"And my son will make this complicated, but Aimee, those things don't matter. At least, not to me. I'm..." Justine rushed out a breath. "I think that I may have fallen for you. I don't want to give this up just yet."

Unable to resist the pull any longer, Aimee closed the gap with a grunt and kissed the woman who altered her senses. Mouth's moulding against one another as though they were made to fit together, the women kissed away the remainder of the daylight, leaving all the difficult questions to dissolve under the stars.

CHAPTER TWELVE

Aimee woke with a smile on her face and a welcome warmth at her side.

"Morning," Justine whispered to her.

"Morning." Moving to drop a kiss on the head of the woman snuggling into her neck, Aimee gasped instead. "Shit."

"Sore?" Justine asked, raising herself up on her elbow.

"Yeah. Some sexy woman accosted me last night. Forced me to make love to her."

"Poor dear."

Aimee grinned. "I know. My life sucks."

"Can I suggest a pain killer?"

Frowning, Aimee said, "I don't think pills will fix my ribs."

"Oh, honey," Justine said in a deep voice. "I wasn't talking about your ribs." Running her hand down Aimee's naked length, she teased at the curls of her sex. "I was thinking of something like a pleasure pill."

Aimee gasped as Justine disappeared beneath the sheets. *Oh, God. This is how people should wake up in the morning.* Thoughts vanishing as Justine touched her, she let the pleasure override the ache in her chest. Groaning and panting, she frowned at a noise intruding on their love-making before Justine pushed her off the brink of sanity.

"Oh, God!"

***

A steady thumping pulled Aimee from her bed and from the repayment of Justine's wake up call. Throwing on a robe, she washed her face and yanked the door open.

"What!" she barked at Sally.

"Umm...you two finished?"

Aimee's face dropped. "What?"

"I, uh..." Sally cleared her throat. "Tell Justine her mother and son are here."

"Justine isn't here."

"Yes, Aimee, she is. Please pass on the message."

Aimee frowned. "How do you know?"

Sally looked everywhere but at her sister. "Because...ah...I came by earlier."

Aimee's eyes widened and she blushed. "Oh...I see."

"Well, thankfully, I didn't, but I certainly *heard* enough."

"God, Sal, just don't," Aimee covered her eyes with her hand. "We'll be down soon."

"Okay. Good. Right. I'm going to go."

"Please do." Aimee shut the door and leant her forehead against it. Walking back to her bed, Justine lay there breathing deeply.

"What is it?"

"Your mum and son are here."

Justine frowned. "Okay. Make this quick then."

"What? You still want me to... Jesus. Sally was up here before and heard us."

"Aimee, I don't give a shit who's doing what. You're not leaving me like this."

"But I—"

"Fine." Justine closed her eyes and ran her own hand down her body, instantly rendering Aimee's mouth dry.

Watching for a brief moment, Aimee shook her head at her own stupidity. Throwing off her robe, she knelt down and worked around Justine's probing fingers to help her climb that peak. And, hell, how she climbed it.

***

"You've, ah, got a little something..." Aimee pointed out to Justine as they hurried across the yards.

"What? Where? Shit. Fix it."

Aimee smiled as she tucked Justine's collar over the accidental mark she left on her neck. "You know, for someone that was just begging me to finish her off before literally taking the task in her own hands, you're awfully nervous."

"They're two different things. Wanting you to make love to me in the privacy of the bedroom, and facing my family with the woman I lo—" Justine stopped walking and threw her hand over her mouth.

The accidental confession stunned them both.

"I'm sorry."

"For what?" Aimee asked, stepping back to the woman who had halted two steps sooner than herself.

"It's too soon."

"Maybe."

"Maybe?"

Aimee cleared her throat. "Or maybe not."

"Really?"

Aimee lifted her shoulders to her ears and felt giddy and completely exposed. Love had to be what she felt for this woman, and it wasn't until Justine nearly said the words that she let herself admit that. "I—umm…" she started quietly, before reaching out to pull Justine to her by the back of the neck.

"Mum!"

The women sprung apart.

"Aaron." Justine smiled and embraced her son who had run across the yard. "Aaron, I'd like you to meet someone. This is Aimee," she said, letting go of her son and swinging him around. "Aimee, this is my son, Aaron."

"Hi," Aaron said, thrusting out his hand.

"Hi," Aimee greeted, taking the young man's hand in hers. His grip was firm and he shook with vigour. Wearing glasses like his mother, and wondering if it was a hereditary thing, Aimee looked him over. As tall as Justine, which wasn't saying much, the boy was lanky with rapid growth and sported a hair colour in complete contrast to the brunette woman at his side. His eyes were the same amber shade and the freckles Justine usually covered up were visible on her son. "I hear you want to be a cowboy?" Aimee asked, making Aaron look at his mother in mortification.

"Mum," the boy whined.

Justine shrugged. "Mum," she greeted the greying woman who had followed Aaron. "This is Aimee," she said, introducing them. "Aimee, my mother, Dawn."

The women smiled at each other and inclined their heads politely. Aimee got the distinct impression she was being sized up. Especially when she saw Sally knowingly smile from the porch.

Justine cleared her throat. "Mother?"

"Yes, dear?"

Justine shook her head slightly and widened her eyes with warning.

Dawn clucked her tongue. "A pleasure to meet you, Aimee. I'm going to have a cup of tea. Why don't you three ride the horsies or something?" she said, dismissing them with a wave of her hand.

"*Horsies?*" Aimee mouthed to Justine.

Justine shook her head begging her not to ask, and snagged Aaron's hand. "Honey, I've got to go over the footage from yesterday and plan the filming schedule tonight. Would you mind hanging with Grandma for a couple of hours? I won't be long, I promise."

Aaron groaned in typical teenage fashion.

"I promise I won't be—"

"Wanna ride?" Aimee asked the boy.

"Yes!"

"Aimee…"

Aimee held up a hand to Justine. "How about I take you up to the shearing sheds and introduce you to my nephew. He's about your age and I bet, far more fun than sitting around here with your grandma."

"Can I, Mum?" Aaron turned his excited eyes on his mother, who looked doubtful.

"I…uh…it's a big property," she said, giving Aimee a poignant look.

"And I'll be with him the whole time."

"Really?"

Aimee nodded.

Justine sighed and looked back to Aaron. "You must do everything Aimee tells you to do."

"Yes, Mum," he whined.

"I'm not kidding, Aaron. It's important."

"Geez, Mum. I get it. Behave and do what I'm told. Now, where are the stables? Is that them?" The boy ran off before either woman could confirm.

"Energetic."

"Too energetic."

"He'll get on with Robbie well."

Justine heaved out a breath. "You'll look after him?"

Aimee smiled, turning to face the woman and take her hands. "You know I will."

Scanning the area for observers, Justine spotted Sally smirking at them from the verandah. "I know. You look after me so well." With a wink that left Aimee wishing they were somewhere private and preferably naked, she watched the woman go, not noticing her sister sidle up beside her.

"Ah, such sweet, innocent love."

Aimee jumped with a curse word slipping unbidden from her mouth.

"Language."

"Bugger off."

"So…is it?"

"Is it what?" Aimee snapped at her sister and stalked off towards the stables.

"Love."

"I don't know what you're talking about," Aimee said over her shoulder.

"I'm going to find out, you know. One way or another."

"Whatever," she yelled back before ducking inside the sanctuary of the stables.

"Are you my mum's girlfriend?"

Or so she thought. Gaping at Aaron and feeling herself blush from head to toe, she ignored him and walked over to River. "You can ride him. Do you know how to saddle a horse?"

"Of course," he said with a voice that screamed 'duh.'

"Definitely your mother's child," she muttered and left him to it. Saddling Kite, she kept a wary eye on Aaron's ability with a horse and found herself pleasantly surprised. "You ride?"

"Only every weekend."

"Do you compete like your mum did?"

"Yeah. I'm reigning show jump champion for my region and division."

"Huh," Aimee said. The boy wasn't the most modest person she'd met, but then again, he was a teenager. *Robbie boasted about anything he won for a solid three months*, thought Aimee.

"Did you know Mum won silver in the games?"

Aimee's eyebrows rose. "No, I didn't. Silver, huh?"

"Yeah. So awesome."

They mounted their horses and headed for the cottage.

Aimee nibbled at her lower lip, wondering how she was going to approach Joey to relieve Robbie early. Robbie acted as an apprentice during the shear, and spent the entire day fleece skirting, fetching water, helping change shearing blades, and putting antiseptic on nicks the sheep may have suffered. In short, he was an invaluable part of the process. Talking to Joey wasn't high on her list of things to do, either.

Watching Aaron for a while, Aimee frowned.

"Ease up on the reins a little. Let your knees guide the horse."

Aaron frowned. "I know how to ride."

"I agree, but see how River is tossing his head? The bit is a little tight."

Aaron pouted and looked to what Aimee was talking about. "I'm controlling the horses head. That's Jeremy's number one rule. Control the head, control the jump."

Aimee bounced her head in understanding. The boy knew how to ride jumps and tight circles in an arena, but out here…she shook her head slightly. "Do you ever get to just ride, or is it only when competing?"

"Just jumping. I keep asking Mum to take us on some trails, but there's never time. Life's busy, you know?" Aaron shrugged and averted his eyes to stare out at the horizon.

Aimee felt her heart break a little for him. "Well, when you get a chance to ride out here, you can be more relaxed. The horse can take the lead a little more and enjoy just being out walking, or trotting or whatever. There's no corners, no rails, just open space. Do you see what I mean?"

"But how do you make them go straight?"

Aimee inclined her head to her reins. "I trust Kite to know where she's going. These are station horses, they know this land inside and out. Besides, I can still direct her, but she doesn't need to be constricted by the reins to do that."

Aaron looked at her style and compared it with his. He let some slack out on the reins and River immediately settled. Letting him get used to the new way of riding for a while, and coming out of a rough patch of country, Aimee said, "So…" Aimee smiled. "Wanna race?"

Aaron's eyes lit up and with a click of their tongues and a flick of their reins, they took off over the gentle swell of hills.

***

"So…Aimee's rather charming," Dawn said to Sally as she accepted the cup of coffee that was on offer.

"She can be when she puts her mind to it."

"Something's going on between her and Justine, isn't there? Something big?"

Sally could have launched across the bench and kissed Dawn. "You think so, too," she said emphatically. "Wait. Is Justine…" Sally checked for eavesdroppers while she tried to find a diplomatic way to ask Justine's mother if she was a lesbian. "Umm…Justine has a son."

"Yes, she does."

"And the dad?"

Dawn's lips tipped up at the corners. "The dad is not a significant part of their life. Justine isn't seeing anyone, male or female, and hasn't done so since Aaron was born." Dawn looked at the kitchen door before leaning closer to Sally. "There was a rumour a while back about her and a woman at the stables when she used to compete."

"Compete?"

Dawn sat up straight and proud. "My daughter is an Olympic athlete. A silver medallist, actually. She competed in the Sydney Olympics for Australia."

"What discipline?"

"Eventing."

Sally was impressed. Dressage, show jumping and cross country were tough enough disciplines on their own, let alone combining them into one event.

Time went by in a rush as Sally and Dawn discussed the ins and outs of international equestrian events, the trials of travelling with horses, and had just begun on the topic of raising daughters when Justine and Amber joined them.

"She was hopeless," Sally said with a laugh as Justine swung the kitchen door closed. Answering Justine's questioning look, she said, "Aimee. She tried to be different one night and wore a dress to the local dance. She ended up punching someone in the face for asking to buy her a drink, and was arrested in the name of public safety when a group of men wolf-whistled her." Sally chuckled to herself.

"She was arrested?" Justine said, looking shocked.

"Sort of. The sergeant escorted her out and suggested she go home before she decked everyone."

Justine shook her head, and in the silence that followed, Amber said, "Umm…want a hand?"

Sally looked at her with surprise. "You want to help prepare dinner?"

"Justine said it'd be good if we helped out. I can't cook worth a damn, but I'm willing to try. Is that okay?"

"Of course, it is." Sally walked over to Amber and took her by the shoulders to direct her to the chicken she had just taken from the fridge. "I need that stuffed."

"Excuse me?"

"Cut up some lemons, garlic and thyme, and shove them into the chicken."

"I…okay."

Sally watched over Amber for a moment before giving Dawn a wink and gestured to Justine. Dawn grinned in response. "Where was I?" she said to Dawn. "Oh! Aimee." Sally chuckled again. "She's always known her own mind, that one."

"Has she ever been interested in men?" Dawn asked, earning a surprised look from her daughter as Justine turned on the kettle.

"Mum, that's not—"

"Never." Sally caught Dawn's eye and winked. "Aimee's always been a lady's lady. Joey used to have an issue with it, but wisely chose to get on with his life."

"Oh?" Justine said.

Sally looked at Amber while Justine frowned at the kettle.

"So, she's had girlfriends before?" Justine asked, busying herself with preparing coffee. "Anyone else want one?"

"No thanks, dear. And no. Aimee's always been a love 'em and leave 'em kinda girl. She's good at it, too."

Justine choked down her first sip of coffee. "Sorry? Good at it?"

"Well, yeah. She's a beautiful woman," Sally said, wondering if Justine realised she was nodding. "She's charming, good-looking, and knows exactly how to sweet talk any conquest she takes a fancy to."

"Sorry, conquest?"

"A regular Casanova," Sally said, before giving Amber a quick tip on how to cut the lemon. "See girl, like girl, bed girl." Sally smiled to herself when she heard Justine's cup hit the granite bench top with a clatter.

"I see."

"My sister had an affair with a girl once," Amber said. "It didn't take."

Everyone considered that information for a moment. Sally, however, found the perfect opening. "Well, if your sister is, sorry for sounding crude, is as well-endowed as you, then Aimee would definitely have tried it on."

"She's not," Amber said, looking confused. Amber narrowed her eyes. "She likes large breasts?"

Sally shrugged. "Everyone has a type." Noticing Justine look down at her chest, Sally continued. "She did give you a smile and a wink when you arrived."

Amber's mouth dropped open. "Oh, my gosh, she did."

"She did what?" Justine said.

Sally raised her hands. "Don't worry, I told her she's not allowed to hit on the contestants. She was told they were out of bounds."

"And so they bloody should be," Justine said. "Don't tell me she makes a habit of hitting on any eligible woman that comes out here?"

Sally shrugged.

"What is she? A Neanderthal?"

Aimee chose that moment to enter the kitchen. Everyone was staring at her. "Uh…hi?" Getting an odd glare from Justine, Aimee said, "Aaron is fine. He's up at the shearing sheds with Robbie and Joey learning the ropes. I promise he's in safe hands." Justine narrowed her eyes but didn't say anything. Looking around the kitchen, Aimee stared for a moment when she noticed Amber in the kitchen wrist deep inside a raw chicken.

"See something you like?" Justine said, snapping her out of her stare.

"I'm sorry?"

Justine gestured to Amber, prompting Aimee to give her the once-over in case she had missed something beyond finding the woman with a chicken on her hand. The red in Justine's face when she looked back at her was intriguing. Aimee cocked her head. "Maybe," she said. Walking across the kitchen, she purposely bumped Amber, apologising with a hand to the small of her back. Smirking at Justine's explosive expression and congratulating herself for accurately reading Justine's mood, she snagged a drink from the fridge and went back to Amber. *Jealousy was an interesting colour on Justine.*

"What are you making?"

Amber stood up straight and blinked. Looking around briefly, she pointed at herself. "Me?"

Was this woman intellectually challenged? "Ah…yes?"

"Oh. Umm…" Amber looked at the chicken she had just stuffed. "Roast chicken with—Sally, what is this again?" she asked Sally, who had been quietly chuckling in the corner. Something that put Aimee on high alert.

"Huh? Oh…thyme and lemon stuffing."

Amber smiled at Aimee. "Roast chicken with thyme and lemon stuffing."

"My favourite," Aimee said with a smile that flustered Amber. Curious about the reaction, coupled with Justine's constant glare, Aimee glanced around the kitchen to find Sally smiling to herself and Dawn pursing her lips in an effort not to smile. Shrugging it off, she sipped at her drink. "So, where are your competitors?"

"Oh, well, Brittany is sobbing and Tiffany is doing her nails."

"Sobbing?"

"She's been let go," Sally said as she handed Amber a tray. "Put the chicken on this, then in the oven for forty-five minutes at one-eighty."

Amber's jaw dropped. "Ah…say that again."

"Here, I'll show you," Aimee said, picking up the tray and putting it in the over. "Timer," she said, pointing to a dial which she then turned to forty. "Temperature." Adjusting the second knob to the correct setting, she stood and smiled at Amber. "Voila."

"Oh, you speak French?"

"Yeah…nuh." Aimee laughed. "I speak fluent sheep, though."

Generating the response she was aiming for, Amber laughed in a dainty fashion and touched Aimee's forearm. Seeing Justine stride across the kitchen, she gave Amber a wave before she was predictably hauled off somewhere private under the guise of working out where to set up next week's dates.

"What the hell!" Justine snapped when they reached the study.

"Good question. What's with the weirdness in the kitchen? And, by the way, jealousy doesn't suit you."

"I'm not jealous!"

"Says the woman who just dragged me from the kitchen when Amber touched my arm."

"Oh, please. You were fawning all over her. I'm surprised she didn't faint with the amount of attention you put on her."

"Attention? I asked her about the chicken and showed her the oven."

"Exactly!"

Aimee threw her hands up in the air and paced the office. "You're nuts."

"Sally told us all about you."

Aimee's hands dropped. "Oh, did she just. Tell me, what did she say?"

"For starters, she said you hit on women possessing certain qualities."

"Qualities?"

"Pretty girls with big…big…" Justine held her hands out before dropping them with disgust.

"Okay. What else did she say?"

"You like conquests."

Aimee blinked rapidly. *She liked what now?* "Conquests?"

"Apparently no single woman within two hundred square kilometres is safe from you."

"What?" Aimee raised her eyebrows. *What the hell was Sally playing at?*

Justine began to pace around in circles, her movements erratic and arms flailing. "Is that what I am? A conquest? An eligible woman you wanted to bed? A challenge to get you off?"

"Ah…no?" Aimee cocked her head, recalling the way Sally was chuckling and smiling in the kitchen. Her eyes widened in understanding. *The bitch!*

"Sally was telling us how you were sizing up the contestants the moment they got here and apparently thought Amber's assets were worth checking out."

Smiling, Aimee said, "They are." Aimee cupped her hands at her chest. "She's—"

"Don't finish that sentence."

Aimee began to chuckle.

"Why are you laughing?"

"Justine, come on. Sally is baiting you."

"To achieve what? I thought this was real!"

Aimee snagged the woman's arms before they struck her and pulled her close. "It is. Very real."

Justine breathed heavily in her arms.

"Sally did a number on you."

"She what?"

"She promised me she was going to find out what was going on between us this morning after I refused to tell her. She stirred you up deliberately."

Justine frowned and let that sink in. "So…the women she told us about?"

Aimee sighed. "Yes, I've tried to hit on women with that cocktail you hate. No, I don't do it with every eligible female I come across, and no, I'm not into conquests. Before you, the relationships I had were brief, meaningless and easy. They got what they wanted, and so did I." Aimee cupped Justine's face. "I haven't been with anyone longer than a night. Ever."

"Really?"

Aimee nodded and rested her forehead on Justine's. "Which is why you scare the shit out of me."

"Oh, don't worry. I'm equally as terrified."

Closing their eyes and breathing each other's air for a long moment, their peace was interrupted by Sally's sigh. "I knew it."

Jerking back, Aimee glared at her sister. Dawn was right beside her. "Knew what?"

"This. You two." She gestured between them. "It's more than just sex."

"Oh, my God," Justine said, blushing and hiding her face against Aimee's chest.

Aimee clenched her jaw. "It's also none of your God damn business."

"Yeah, yeah." Sally waved her off. "It's about time," she said, leaving the office and high-fiving Dawn.

"Do you have siblings?" Aimee asked Justine after they finished staring at the doorway.

"No."

"Lucky."

"Seems that way."

Aimee took a deep breath. "So are we okay?"

Justine nodded and rested her forehead on Aimee's chest. "I'm sorry for acting like a lunatic."

"It was rather cute."

"Cute?"

"Yeah, you looked all crazy and frazzled." Aimee gave her a crooked smile. "Cute."

Justine shook her head. "You have a skewed perception. I'm sure I looked like I needed institutionalising."

"Maybe a little." Smiling at each other, Aimee dropped a kiss on Justine's temple. "You're okay with this?"

"Okay with just being outed in front of my mother? Yeah, sure, why not?"

"Good." Aimee lowered her head and gave Justine the kind of kiss that promised more.

"Oh, wow," Justine whispered when they parted. "Do we really have to go back out there?"

"Not if you don't want to."

Justine shook her head. "I really don't."

"Neither do I." Kissing Justine again, and making sure Justine's temporary bedroom was private and secure, Aimee showed Justine exactly why she didn't need to be jealous. Nothing had enraptured her more than the woman arching and moaning in her arms, and Aimee doubted anything ever could.

***

Sitting on the side verandah lost in thought, Joey sighed. *What a mess.* Brittany left with a bang, even taking the time to slap Joey across the face for leading her on. Joey scoffed and sipped at his beer. *Leading her on? Seriously? It was a reality TV show! Surely she understood the premise behind it?*

Shaking his head, he sighed and looked up at the stars. "Don't suppose you have any advice," he said softly, hoping his parents could answer.

"No. I don't."

"Aimee!" Joey sat up straight. "Where'd you come from?" he said.

"The office. Talking to them again?" she said, joining him on the swinging chair.

"Talking to who?"

"Come on, Joey, we used to do it all the time as kids." Aimee stared up at the stars and smiled softly. "I do it all the time."

Joey gave her a sad smile and squeezed her leg. "How you sleeping?"

"Fine," Aimee said, bouncing her head.

"No nightmares?"

She shook her head. "Not this year." Her eyes glazed over and a tiny smile tugged at the corner of her lips. Joey blinked. His sister almost looked happy. Eternally closed-off and sparse with her affection, he realised how different she had been in the past few days. Numerous times he had seen her guiding Justine around by the hand. Sally had received a couple of hugs and her smile had been easier to come by. Joey had been the only one that had earned her scorn. *How did I miss this?*

"You look happy," he said, echoing his thoughts.

Aimee shrugged. "I guess." With a deep breath, she turned to him. "I'm going to Armidale."

Joey's blood chilled. Aimee volunteering to leave the station for a good month or more was unheard of. "What? No, you don't have to—"

"I've made up my mind. I leave next week. I've already contacted the uni and asked Maggie to open up the apartment."

"But—"

"It's okay, Joe." She reached out and took his forearm. "I want to go. You're right, I need to get away for a while. Open up my horizons and all that."

"Oh, Aims, are you sure?"

She nodded to him. "Very. Besides, I've only got a semester left to complete my master's degree. I'll be back by Christmas."

Joey really hoped that was true because Sally would never forgive him if Aimee didn't come back. "Does Sal know?"

She shook her head. "Not yet. I'm telling her tomorrow."

Joey nodded and leant back into the seat, looking up at the stars for guidance again. Silently they sat side-by-side and watched the moon rise from its hideout in the eastern sky.

"Tracey is getting married," Joey said after a sip of beer.

"What? Really? When?"

Exhaling roughly, he said, "December. I got the invite a couple of days ago."

Aimee squeezed his forearm.

He shrugged. "It's okay."

"Yeah, but…"

Rubbing a hand through his hair, he said, "I had my chance. I blew it. Shit happens."

Aimee squeezed again. "Maybe one of those girls will be the one?"

They looked at each other and laughed.

"You never know," Joey said as they caught their breath.

"I like Amber if that helps."

"Depends."

"On?"

"Do you like her breasts or her mind?"

Aimee smirked. "Both." Leaning over, she whispered. "But don't tell Justine that."

"Justine?"

Aimee looked away shyly and nodded. "We've, umm…kind of being seeing each other."

"*What?* You and Justine?"

"Yeah."

"Seeing each other? As in…" he raised his eyebrows.

"Yeah."

Joey studied his sister for a heartbeat. "She's a single mum."

"I know."

"Who lives in Sydney."

"I know."

"Who is leaving next week and not coming back."

"Yes, I know, Joe."

"Sorry, but, I'm trying to figure this out." Joey sighed and shook his head. He knew his sister specialised in one-night stands, and finding out she'd been sleeping with a woman with a child was unsettling. People like that look for more than a night to scratch their itch. "She's a mum, Aims. You can't just do your old trick of wham bam thank you ma'am, and send her off satisfied."

"Don't you think I realise that?"

Joey shook his head. "Since when do you know how to do relationships?"

She glared at him. "You are in no position to dish out advice."

"At least I've been in a relationship, and that was without the complications of children and distance. How the hell do you expect to maintain one with Justine? It's unfair to her and to Aaron."

"So what would you have me do? Break it off with her because it all seems too hard?"

Joey stared at his sister for a moment and quietly said, "Yes."

Aimee stood angrily. "Well, news flash, Joseph. I'm not you. I don't run when things get difficult. I'm not leaving Justine, what we have is…is…Christ, I have no idea, but it's something. It's bloody terrifying, but it's worth it. Just because you made a miserable choice, doesn't mean you have the right to tell others how to follow their hearts. Stick with bimbos. It's all you deserve." Aimee stormed off into the yard leaving Joey's mouth gaping and more than a little pissed off.

"Bugger you!" he screamed at her retreating back and threw his beer can after her. The empty can rattled about uselessly in the dirt. "Shit," he muttered as he stood and made for his room.

"Woah!" came a female voice as he rounded the corner and slammed into someone. It was Amber.

"Hell, sorry." He bent down and picked up the books and paper he had inadvertently knocked from her hands. He studied the title of one book. *Anatomy*. "Studying?" he asked, handing back the text.

"Yeah, I have exams in a couple of weeks."

"Oh."

"You okay?" Amber asked him. "I heard shouting."

He wiped at his face. "Nah. It's all good."

"Was it Aimee?" Frowning at him, Amber said, "I recognised the voice."

"Yeah. Aimee, she's…making a big mistake…I think."

"Wanna talk about it?"

Joey narrowed his eyes with thought. "No. Want to join me for a drink and a swim?"

Amber smiled. "Sure."

***

Waking with a groan the next morning, Joey tried to roll but found his progress hindered by a warm body. "Shit," he whispered to himself when he found Amber stark naked against his equally disrobed body. Sliding his arm out from under Amber, he climbed out of bed and stared at the company on his sheets. Amber was attractive, there was no doubt about that. His eyes roamed her features. *Very attractive and also very naked.* Pulling the sheet over her, he sat in his chair and tried to clear his head. *What happened last night?*

Aimee. Fighting. Amber. Drinking lots of scotch and swimming. Sex in the pool. *Really* good sex. Sex in the bed. Sex that he'd gladly repeat again. Joey smiled at Amber's sleeping form. Even intoxicated, the woman had managed to make him feel the stir of something. That hadn't happened in a long time, and if he was honest with himself, that feeling had faded long before he broke up with Tracey. He'd been searching for it ever since.

In retrospect, he never assumed *Romancing the Farmer* would help him find a wife, or even a girlfriend, but with Amber lying in his bed looking as though she belonged there gave him a lot to think about. *Could he love her? Could she deal with living on the station? Could they make a life together?*

Amber rolled over and exposed her bare chest, encouraging his libido to awaken. Wondering whether Amber would be interested in continuing the morning where the night left off, a realisation struck him. They had shared really good *unprotected* sex.

Joey cringed. *You stupid bloody idiot!*

***

"And that's a wrap. Thank you, everyone." Justine shook Joey's hand and Amber pulled her in for a hug. Conversing with her film crew for a moment, a smiling Justine walked over to Aimee, who was resting her body against the side of Kite's stall.

"Is it just me, or do they look really awkward?" Aimee asked her as she approached.

"They do, don't they."

Staring at the new 'couple' they both cocked their heads. Since the night of their argument, Aimee had been avoiding her brother but had still managed to notice something was off with him. Amber, who she had seen more than once, had been just as unsettled.

"Are you ready to go?" Aimee asked leaning slightly into Justine as the film crew loaded their vehicle and hitched the trailer to it.

"Yeah."

"Come up for a sec?"

Justine nodded and together they climbed the stairs to the loft.

"Here," Justine said as soon as the door was closed, handing Aimee a piece of paper. "My mobile number. Call me?"

"I, uh, don't have a phone."

Justine blinked for a moment. "You don't have a mobile?"

Shaking her head, Aimee said, "They don't work out here."

"Oh. Right. Of course."

"But I'll get one," Aimee said, pulling Justine to her by the hands before wrapping her arms around her waist.

Justine smiled, and for a long time, Aimee let herself get lost in those light brown eyes. This was hands down, the hardest thing she'd ever done. Letting Justine walk away not knowing when she was going to see her again. *Maybe Joey was right. Maybe it was easier to rip the Band-Aid off and call it a day. Her heart clenched at the thought. No, whatever this was with Justine, it was something that could never be walked away from.* She squeezed tighter.

"Hey," Justine whispered. "It's going to be okay."

Ever the mind reader, Aimee thought wryly to herself. Since Aaron had left last Sunday, the pair had spent every spare minute together. Falling asleep in one another's arms, making love to all hours, and just sharing quiet moments, all of it adding up to an inescapable truth in Aimee's heart. She was head over heels for this petite city girl.

"Shh," Justine said, wiping at the moisture gathering on Aimee's lashes. "Farm girls don't cry."

"It's dust. I have allergies." Aimee scrubbed at her eyes quickly.

"Mmhmm."

Aimee rested her head against Justine's forehead. "I…this…" she breathed out heavily.

"I know." Justine caressed her neck sending shudders down her spine.

Aimee tilted her head and took Justine's lips in a slow, burning kiss. She didn't know how to voice what was going on inside her, but she could sure as hell show the woman before she drove off in a cloud of dust.

CHAPTER THIRTEEN

Armidale. Situated in the Northern Tablelands of New South Wales, it was five and a half hours northeast of the station. It was also grey, cold, and desperately lonely. Aimee opened the door to the cottage that had been in her family for a century. Utilised as a townhouse for various family members attending the University of New England in Armidale, it had been vacant for years. Despite Maggie, an old family friend, and her efforts at bringing fresh air to the place, it still smelled musty and disused. Quickly building a fire to offset the chill and setting it alight, Aimee stared unfocused into the flames until they required stoking again.

She'd always been independent, enjoyed her own company, and prided herself on being tough. Learning how to cope as a young grieving child had taken years of counselling and learning how to get through each day. She had discovered at a young age that spending every spare minute being busy made life that much easier to live with. Time helped. Time and a love for the land she grew up on. A property she would spend days exploring on her own with no one but her dog for company.

Now, sitting in a dark room, staring at flames that should be familiar and comforting, she had never felt more isolated. More hollow.

With a sigh, she urged herself to move further into the cottage than the living room. So full of images of Justine and their heart-wrenching goodbye, she unpacked in a daze. *How was it possible that after a two-week affair, she felt so lost without Justine?* She shook her head. It didn't make any sense to her.

Fingering the slip of paper in her pocket, she snatched up her car keys and headed to the main street. *Time to fill the fridge and find a pay phone.* Talking to Justine would go a long way to easing her mind.

Forced to leave a message, Aimee returned to the townhouse and moved through the motions. She prepared dinner, slept, and drove into the university at eight Monday morning. A sprawling university situated on the hilly outskirts of Armidale and filled with promise of higher learning, Aimee organised a parking permit and found her lecture room. For the first week, she listened intently, appreciated the welcome from professors she'd had many discussions with on the phone, and went home each evening feeling hollow and restless…and sore. Knitting ribs and the ache in her left side kept Aimee's nights restless.

***

A week later, and four days of classes behind her, Aimee finished her morning coffee and sighed. Friday. She had no classes on Friday, though the professor of the agricultural course was trying to encourage her to come along on a field trip for the undergrad students. She was tempted. The house had become a symbol of loneliness and it was here she felt most uncomfortable.

I should have brought Mitsy with me.

Aimee sighed again and fingered the battered slip of paper she constantly kept in her pocket. Staring down at Justine's looping numbers and the words listing her address, Aimee sighed. Not being able to reach Justine all week had left her nervous and wondering if she'd dreamt the week they had spent together at the station. She'd left messages, but with no way of contacting Aimee, Aimee had to assume Justine received them and was feeling just as frustrated about the lack of communication. Now, with the prospect of three days alone with little to do, she felt anxious. Life on the station was constant and hectic. There was never an idle moment. Urban life was full of pace and stretches of boredom.

"Stuff this," Aimee said, shoving back her chair. Grabbing a jacket, ensuring the fire was out and tucking her wallet into her pocket, she left the cottage and Armidale behind her in favour of the big smoke.

A decision that had her white knuckling the steering wheel five and a half hours later as she drove from the quiet township of Armidale into the throng of Sydney.

"What the hell is wrong with you people!" she screamed at her windshield. *City drivers are bloody insane.* "Oh, God. Oh, God," she said as she realised she had to change lanes again. Earning herself a beep of a horn, she swore to herself and finally took an exit off the highway. Pulling over at her first opportunity, she huffed out a breath and let her head fall back against the headrest. "Chaos. Pure bloody crazy chaos."

After letting her heart rate drop, she looked at her watch. One o'clock. *Justine surely would still be at work.* "Damn."

Stomach grumbling, Aimee looked around for a source of food. Not far up the road was a massive tower declaring the inclusion of a number of chain stores in what she presumed was a shopping mall. Grimacing, she bit the bullet, merged back into crazy traffic and then nearly sideswiped a tiny car with her bull-barred Landcruiser as she attempted to fit into a teeny parking spot.

"Oops," she muttered as her door hit the tiny car when she opened it. Wiping at the little car, she couldn't see any lingering damage and made her way into the shopping centre.

The shopping centre overflowed with people, most of whom were on their phones and paying very little attention to what was going on around them. Hitting a few because of their erratic walking paths, Aimee stuck with the outer wall and moved towards the sign pointing to a food court.

It was manic.

Business suits and skirts hurried about with coffee and some rice contraption wrapped in a dark green layer. Finding them in a window a few moments later, she realised they were sushi rolls. She grimaced.

Spotting a carvery store, she ordered a roast beef meal and a fizzy drink.

Stomach sated, she figured her next step would be finding a mobile phone.

"Hi there, can I help you today?"

"Hi. Yeah, I need a phone."

"Wonderful. Are you currently using our service?"

Aimee shook her head. "No."

"That's not a problem. We can transfer your number across automatically."

"I don't have a number to transfer."

The woman with a very tight ponytail stared at her for a heartbeat. "You don't have a mobile service?"

Aimee shrugged. "Nope."

The city woman blinked for a moment. "Oh…okay. Well, let me show you some of the phones and plans we have."

"Great."

An hour later, Aimee had a headache. The woman banged on about data plans, call plans, SMS plans, and all the available smartphones and their monthly payment options. Once she was done with phones, she rambled on about broadband plans in the home, tablet and mobile broadband options and somewhere after the first five minutes, Aimee had zoned out with absolutely no idea what the woman was talking about.

"So, which one do you think will suit you?"

"Ah…I just want to be able to ring my girlfriend."

The woman raked her eyes over Aimee's jeans, flannel shirt and work boots before giving her a smile. "Do you know what service company she's with?"

Aimee shook her head.

"If she's with us, you can get an added one hundred free call minutes."

"Ah…that's good, but…" Aimee gnawed at her lip. "I might come back later if that's okay? I need to think about it all for a bit."

"Of course." The woman then gave her a bag with an absurd amount of pamphlets and sent her on her way.

Checking her watch and assuming she had hours to spend before she'd be able to see Justine, Aimee whiled away the remainder of the afternoon wandering the mall. Slowly becoming accustomed to the bustle of the place, she ate a donut and sipped at her coffee, and watched the city people rush past, finding their antics amusing.

They reminded her of chaotic ants. Heads down, they pushed past one another and stopped and started in random jams of bodies. Aimee chuckled as an elderly man on an electric cart started mowing down the pedestrians. *Madness.*

Deciding she'd had enough, Aimee picked up her bag of books purchased at the bookstore and her bag of pamphlets and headed for the exit. Fifteen minutes later, after searching for her four-wheel drive, she aimed for Justine's place, intending to stalk the driveway until Justine returned from work.

Double-checking the address, Aimee stared at the house. It was a two-level, brick home with a steep tiled roof that looked like it'd be at home in Switzerland. The short picket fence guarded an immaculately landscaped garden complete with water fountain. It looked like something from a TV show. Cocking her head, Aimee noticed two cars in the driveway. One a late model Toyota Prado and the other a fancy sports car. Having no idea if Justine owned either, Aimee climbed from her dusty vehicle, patted down her jeans to remove any excess dust, and decided to find out if she was home. In this suburb, surrounded by rather stately homes, she felt every bit the simple farm girl Justine once accused her of being. Head down, she entered the property and knocked on the door with her breath held fast.

"Aaron! We're leaving in five, so get your stuff together. Now!" Aimee heard Justine's voice call out from inside. The doorknob turned and the beige wood swung inwards. "Oh!" Justine said on a gasp. "Aimee?"

Aimee gave a dainty finger wave, instantly feeling foolish and like she'd imposed on Justine. "Hi."

Justine stared at her a blinked for a while. "You're *here*."

Scuffing her boots on the tiled step, Aimee looked down at them. "Yeah, sorry, I, uh…didn't mean to intrude."

"Intrude? No." Justine reached out and took her hands. "I was about to drop Aaron off and head to Armidale."

"What?" Aimee's eyes snapped up.

"I was coming up to surprise you."

"*Really?*"

Justine nodded. "Yes. Really."

They grinned at each other for a few heartbeats before Justine breathed out, "I've missed you."

Missing this woman intensely the past week, Aimee flew forward and smashed her lips against Justine's. Meeting her with a grunt, Justine spun them and pushed Aimee against the doorframe as she gave back as good as she was given.

Aimee grunted in pain.

"Oh! Sorry," Justine said, pulling away quickly and looking down at Aimee's side. "Are you okay?"

"I'm fine," Aimee said, rubbing her ribs. "It's healing." Leaning in with less physical impact, Aimee kissed the breath from Justine's lungs.

"Mum, I—*gross*."

The women pulled apart slowly with a smile on their faces. "Have you got your bag?" Justine asked Aaron without taking her eyes off of Aimee.

"Uh, yeah. Umm…Aimee?"

Aimee cleared her throat and looked at the boy stuck halfway down the stairs. "Hi, mate."

"Mum?"

Justine nodded. "Yes, I know." Smiling back at Aimee. "I was beaten to the punch."

"Sorry," Aimee said, feeling the beginnings of a blush.

"Don't be," Justine assured Aimee. "However, I still need to get Aaron to his grandparents. Come for a drive?"

"Sure."

Justine smiled and gave her a quick kiss on the lips.

"Geez, Mum. Save it for when you're alone," Aaron complained, sounding extremely embarrassed.

Justine chuckled in response. "Put your bags in the boot. Aimee, this way." Justine led them to the BMW and they soon headed west. Clutching at the seat because of Justine's city driving style, Aimee forced herself to relax.

"So, are you two like a couple now?" Aaron asked as the traffic thinned out.

The two women glanced at each other. Aimee floundered, wanting to say yes, but unsure of the protocol for dealing with the children of potential girlfriends. Justine smiled at her warmly and reached across for her hand.

"Yes, honey, we are."

Something warm burst in Aimee's chest.

"Okay," Aaron said matter-of-factly. "Is Aimee moving in? No! Wait! Mum! Can we live on the station?"

Both women tensed.

"We haven't really talked about that yet, honey. It's still pretty early for those kinds of conversations."

"Oh…right…but if it does come up, I'm all in for the country."

"Thanks, sweetheart," Justine said, a smile on her face.

In amicable silence, forty minutes passed and Justine soon pulled into the driveway of a cottage set in one of the outlying communities of north-west Sydney.

"Who lives here?" Aimee asked after Aaron bolted from the car.

"His paternal grandparents," Justine said, popping the boot and lifting it. "They wanted to be a part of his life from the get-go, and are really quite wonderful." Shutting the boot lid, she said, "This is where we keep our horses. They've got two acres out the back and we're up here most weekends. Aaron, however, comes out on his own once a month. Ed and Penny usually come and get him, but because I was planning to surprise you, well…" Justine shrugged.

Aimee smiled and placed a kiss on her lips.

"Oh…what's this then?" a female voice said.

Aimee blushed and gave Justine a significant amount of personal space. *Damn it, she really needed to hold back her urges.*

Justine laughed softly to herself. "Penny, this is my girlfriend, Aimee."

"Girlfriend?" Penny raised her thin, grey eyebrows and gave Aimee the once over. "Country girl?" she asked.

Justine looked at Aimee to answer. Clearing her throat, she said, "Uh, yeah. I'm from a property out west."

"Oh, Yarrabee Station, right?"

Aimee blinked. *How did she know that?*

"Yes," Justine said.

"Dawn said something was going on out there. Now I know what." She gave them both a wink and took Aaron's pillow from Justine's hands. "Come on, girls. Say bye to the boy so you can go have a weekend to yourselves."

"She's friends with your mum?" Aimee whispered.

"Well, yes. They were friends before Aaron's father and I were ever together."

"Oh…right." Aimee looked around furtively. "And Aaron's father…?"

"Lives overseas. An engineer. He's in Australia maybe once a year at most."

"Do they, uh, get along?"

Justine bounced her head. "We all do." Stopping Aimee with a hand on her forearm, she said, "We were teenagers when we had Aaron. Our relationship was never strong and was never going to last. We knew that from the start. We're still friends, but that shipped sailed a week or so before we found I was pregnant."

Aimee nodded her reply.

"Come on, Aaron's probably with Friar Tuck."

"Huh?"

"His horse."

161

Guiding Aimee to the back of the house, Justine took her to the small stable and shed. There, Aaron was feeding his brown and white horse sugar cubes, and a magnificent black horse was pushing his nose against his shoulder looking for attention.

"He's beautiful," Aimee said in wonder at the thoroughbred nuzzling for treats.

"That's Dreamer. I've had him for ten years." Justine grabbed some sugar from a container on a bench and walked to her magnificent beast. "Hey my boy, how are you?" Dreamer snuffled and sniffed at her outstretched hand. "I've missed you," she said, rubbing his nose affectionately.

"You rode him in the Games?" Aimee asked, putting a reverent hand on the horse's neck.

"I did. We did well, didn't we Dreamer?" Justine kissed him on the nose.

Aimee inspected the animal. "He's a stallion."

Justine nodded.

"A stud?"

Shrugging, Justine said, "I've never bred him, but he'd make beautiful foals."

Aimee nodded, thinking of the disaster it had been to try and get the stud horse Joey had hired to cover the young mares at the station. *Dreamer would be perfect for the job.*

Satisfied with his treats, Dreamer trotted back out into the paddock he came from and Justine said her goodbyes to her son. "See you Sunday," she said.

"Okay. Bye. Bye, Aimee," Aaron said with a wave.

"See ya, mate."

Alone with Justine at last, the two women came together with a crack the moment they finished the long drive, picked up drinks and tea, and shut Justine's front door.

"I've missed you so much," Justine said as Aimee lathered her neck with affection.

With a growl, Aimee took Justine's hand and started climbing the stairs. With a few words of direction to the bedroom, they spent very little time talking for the rest of the night.

***

Each weekend followed with much the same routine. After helping Aimee buy a mobile phone, they spent their spare time talking or messaging, and every weekend together. Aimee's loneliness subsided with the instant and convenient access she had to Justine's day, and her ribs healed without issue. Aimee travelled to Sydney two weekends a month, and Justine visited Armidale when Aaron was with his grandparents.

Aimee fit seamlessly into the small mother-son unit, and discovered they both had a fierce competitive streak when it came to Monopoly or any form of board game. More than once, Aimee was forced to referee the pair, and on nights Dawn came over, they decided to leave Aaron and Justine debating the finite details of their game and adjourn to the back patio.

"They get that from Justine's paternal side," Dawn said one night as they shut the sliding door on bickering mother and son.

"Yeah?"

"Playing Monopoly with him was taking your life in your hands." Dawn shook her head. "Bless his soul, but he was a terrible sportsman."

"Fine!"

"Fine!"

They heard Justine and Aaron snap at each other. Aaron could be heard clomping up the stairs and Justine flung open the sliding door and joined them on the patio. "I totally bought that apartment before he landed on my property. He owes me a hundred dollars."

Dawn looked at Aimee with her eyebrows raised. "Apple didn't fall far from the tree."

Justine narrowed her eyes at her mother. "I am not as bad as Dad."

"Yes, dear."

Justine crossed her arms and scowled. "I'm *not.*"

Aimee patted the seat beside her and Justine took the invitation. Aimee wrapped her arm over her shoulders and gave her a squeeze. A few minutes later, Dawn retired to bed, and Aimee and Justine spent the night chatting quietly on the outdoor sofa, wisely avoiding the subject of the board game abandoned on the dining table inside.

***

Every fourth weekend saw the three-person unit travelling to country towns so Aaron could compete on the show jumping circuit.

In late October, they travelled to Camden for the Australian Youth Show Jumping Festival; the last event on Aaron's calendar for the year. If he did well, he made the Australian youth squad. A fact that had Aaron excited and Justine a nervous wreck for the entire trip.

"I can't watch," Justine said, gripping Aimee's hand like a vice while burying her face against Aimee's shoulder.

Aimee patted her on her cap and chuckled. Justine went through this trauma at every event. They'd find a spot in the stands and Justine would mumble advice for each contestant, but when Aaron came up, she spent the entire time cringing and nervous for her son.

Aimee watched him start his run and smiled at his seamless form in the saddle. He truly was his mother's son. Justine's head shifted slightly and she knew from experience that she was watching out of one eye.

"Did you watch the show on Monday night?" Justine mumbled into her shoulder.

"Huh?" Aimee turned her head but kept her eyes on Aaron's progress. "Romancing the Farmer?"

"Yes. Did you watch?"

"I did." Aimee shook her head. It was the most misspent hour of her life watching all these desperate farmers meeting a line-up of twits from the city. Catch phrases like 'I'm ready to find love', and 'I'm looking for the man of my dreams' came to mind. Watching Joey meeting and selecting the three women that eventually came to the farm was cringe-worthy.

"What did you think?"

Aimee bit her lip.

"Aimee?" Justine said, lifting her head at the silence.

"Shh…Aaron's on his last jump."

He cleared the triple and earned himself a clean round. Justine let go of Aimee and stood, cheering and whistling loudly. "That's my boy!"

They waited for the results to come on the scoreboard and Justine squealed and grabbed Aimee when Aaron's name came first.

Being tossed around like a tumble drier, Aimee grinned as Justine simultaneously hugged her and bounced.

"He made it! Aimee, look! He made it!"

Laughing, Aimee nodded. "I can see, Jac, I can see."

Justine hugged her tight, for once not rolling her eyes for the use of the nickname Aimee bestowed upon her the moment she discovered her middle name was Anne. Justine Anne Cason. JAC.

The couple soon linked up with an excited Aaron, and mother and son bounced around again with joy.

"Ah, Justine?" a man said, coming over to them and looking tremendously uncomfortable.

Justine stilled in an instant. "Greg."

"Ah, so, umm…Aaron here has made the squad after today's results, and…well, I'm coaching the team next year."

Justine blinked. "Oh. Okay."

"Okay." Greg nodded at them all and walked off.

"I'm going to the ladies," Justine announced and left abruptly.

Aimee frowned at Aaron. "That was weird, right?"

"Totes."

"Totes? What is that?"

"Totally." Aaron rolled his eyes before giving her a mischievous grin. "Seriously, you gotta get with the slang sister."

Aimee arched her eyebrows. "Sister?"

"Ugh. Adults. So unchilled."

"Unchilled? What?"

Aaron gave her a friendly tap against her arm. "I'm messing with you."

"Oh." Aimee was left standing and shaking her head while Aaron walked away giggling and informed her he'd get his horse to the float. "What the hell is unchilled?" she asked Justine when she returned.

"Uncool."

"Oh."

"You know, your son needs to come with a translator."

"Totes." Justine chuckled and linked her arm with Aimee's, guiding them to the car and the float where Aaron was headed.

***

"What's up with Greg?" Aimee asked Justine after arriving at Aaron's grandparent's place that evening to return the horses to their yard.

Justine went bright red. "Umm…"

"Umm?"

Justine sighed and slumped her shoulders. "Greg used to coach the Australian team for the games. He's a bit of a womaniser, and when I was nineteen, he tried hitting on me."

Aimee's eyebrows shot up in the dim light. "And?"

"Well…" Justine fiddled with her earring. "I was more interested in his wife."

Aimee's eyes widened. "No!" she gasped. "You didn't?"

"No! Of course not! But…well…that's around the time I realised my sexuality. Greg is hot enough, but Helen…" Justine blew out a long breath. "Hotter. Much, much hotter." Justine smiled in thought. "Oh, but nothing happened. I'm not into married women."

"No? What about simple farm girls," Aimee asked, wrapping her arms around Justine's waist.

"I'm definitely into them." Drawing Aimee down for a kiss, they lost themselves in each other until a throat cleared behind them.

"Dinner's ready ladies," Penny said from a few metres away.

Aimee flushed. "God, that's so embarrassing."

Laughing to herself, Justine nodded. "Completely."

"So, Justine, have you decided what you're doing this Christmas? I know Dawn wanted you at the beach house, but we thought maybe you could all come here. Tony is going to be home."

Justine blinked at her son's grandmother. "I, ah… Sally…" Justine paused when Aimee's head shot up. "…offered to have us at the station."

"She did?" Aimee asked in wonder.

"Surely Christmas time is for being with family, dear?" Penny insisted.

"Yes, and they're Aimee's family. Besides, I have to take Dreamer out there at some point."

Penny nodded, barely hiding her disappointed scowl.

"Dreamer?"

Justine smiled at Aimee. "I spoke to Sally last week to organise a follow-up visit on your brother and his chosen woman. She mentioned that Kite was with foal and that no other mares fell pregnant. One thing led to another and I offered Dreamer out to stud for them. She suggested Christmas may be a good time to bring him out."

Aimee, acutely aware that Kite was pregnant to the downfall of the younger, stronger mares, also knew her brother was livid because of that fact. Justine's offer would save them thousands of dollars and potentially make them more. Dreamer was a genuine thoroughbred with a championship record. His foals would be worth a lot. "But we usually cover our mares in August. Joey agreed to this?"

"I have no idea but Sally certainly did."

Aimee smiled to herself. "You didn't have to do that," Aimee said at her girlfriend's overwhelming generosity.

"I know." Justine smiled and squeezed Aimee's thigh under the table.

"So, Christmas, huh?"

Justine nodded. "Christmas."

With a deep breath, Aimee inclined her head in return. They had spoken about telling Aimee's family about the depth of their relationship for over a month. Aimee, still angry with Joey, didn't think the man deserved another go at trying to convince her that dating Justine was a bad idea. Justine had assured her that this time she'd be standing right next to her explaining to Aimee's brother just how serious their relationship was, and how accepting Aaron had been. Sally, Aimee knew, would be thrilled, and had been constantly asking her how Justine was. Playing it down, Aimee was certain Sally was unaware of how much they saw each other.

Christmas…that would be their official 'we're in love' announcement.

Aimee struggled to swallow down the food in her mouth as she wiped her sweating palms on her jeans.

CHAPTER FOURTEEN

It was November and Aimee drove to the city with a specific plan in mind. This was the last weekend of the university semester, meaning she was going to return to the station come Monday morning. Now was her last chance to follow through on the plan she had in mind. Knocking on the door of the Killara home, Aimee waited a moment before Justine opened it with a smile.

"You have a key, you know?"

"I know." Leaning in, she gave Justine a thorough and dizzying kiss. "Where's Aaron?" she asked after pulling back breathlessly.

"Aaron?"

"I'm ready!" the boy said, rushing out the front door.

"Back in a few hours," Aimee said, kissing Justine again.

"Wait. What? Where are you two going?"

"Secret stuff, Mum." Aaron brought his finger to his lips.

"Secret stuff? Aimee, what—"

"Bye, Jac."

"But…"

Aimee grinned and hopped into her car where Aaron was already buckling himself in.

Following the boy's directions after giving him a map to the property they were headed for, an hour later, and after receiving several text messages on her phone she assumed were from Justine, they were at their destination.

"This is awesome!" he said, eyes round as they entered a renowned horse stud property.

"I know," Aimee said, giving him a wink.

The yards were immaculate and horses with breeding histories centuries old trotted about importantly. Known for breeding competition quality horses, Kevin also specialised in stock horses. Sending Justine a quick text that they wouldn't be too much longer, she led Aaron into the stables to meet an old family friend.

"Kevin," Aimee said, striding over to the sixty-year-old man and shaking his hand.

"Aimee. Well, look at you. No longer a snotty-nosed teenager." He grinned and crushed her hand. "But, it seems you brought one with you," he said, sending Aaron a wink.

"This is Aaron, my girlfriend's son."

"Pleased to meet you, sir," he said, shaking the man's hand.

"Oh, manners. It's more than I can say for you, Aims."

"Yeah, yeah."

With a deep chuckle, Kevin said, "So, you're after a yearling?"

Aimee nodded. "It's for my girlfriend. I want to keep it out at the property."

"This girlfriend of yours, can she ride?"

Aimee grinned. "Know a horse called Dreamer?"

Blinking, Kevin tilted his head. "Justine Cason's horse?"

Aimee smiled, knowing full well the remarkable memory of the horses the man bred. Dreamer's glory at the games help plant his place in Kevin's mind. "That's my girlfriend's horse."

"Christ! You hooked up with Justine?" Kevin looked at Aaron with renewed recognition. "My, you've certainly shot up since you were a grubby-faced toddler."

"Thanks," Aaron said. "I think."

Kevin turned back to Aimee. "So you want a station horse for her?"

"Yeah. She's taking Dreamer out there over Christmas to cover the mares."

Kevin laughed. "I heard about what happened with Handsome Boy," Kevin said, obviously having spoken to Joey about the disaster. Handsome Boy, the stud they hired, belonged to Kevin's son.

"Yeah, yeah. Show me what you've got."

Leaving Aaron and Aimee to it after showing them the horses for sale, they pair spent their time studying each animal.

"What about her?" Aaron asked of a particularly beautiful horse. Black mane and brown coat, she was truly a stunning specimen.

"Look at her ears and the tension in her back legs." Aaron did. "She's nervous." She pointed to a similar coloured horse. "She's a loner. See how she's keeping her distance from the rest?"

Aaron nodded. "So they're bad horses?"

Aimee shook her head quickly. "Not at all. That one at the back simply needs to be bribed to stay focused, and will need a lot of interaction. On a station, that's not always ideal. This nervous one can be calmed with a soft touch and a foundation of trust. She'll probably be a one-rider horse."

"And that's bad?"

Aimee sighed. "It depends. They're young and they could probably be handled by a couple of people."

"Like you and Mum?"

Aimee nodded. "Yeah, but even then, if she's not around a lot, they might change allegiances."

"So we move to the station then," Aaron said as if the solution was that simple.

Aimee wished it was. It was something she had been thinking about as her return home approached. Monday morning, she'd be driving back to Yarrabee Station with no idea how often she'd be able to see Justine from then on. *Would Justine want to become a station wife? Would Aaron want to live there? Would he still get all the opportunities he was offered in the city? Lastly, where would they live?*

"It's pretty isolated," Aimee said.

"Yeah, it's in the middle of nowhere," Aaron said in agreement. "But it's really cool, you know?"

"How so?" Aimee asked as they walked over to some other horses.

"Because everyone's there. Like, your whole family is right there. No travel, no planes, no passports. You have so much space to explore. Robbie is pretty cool, too."

Aimee smiled. She knew the boys had kept in touch via email. "What about school?"

"Gran has me fully paid for in a boys' college in the city. Pop used to go there. I'm boarding there from next year."

"What? You're going to boarding school?"

"Yup. Mum's not happy, but you know, its good education and stuff."

Aimee dropped her head and frowned wondering how Justine was going to cope with sending her son away to boarding school a mere hour from where she lived. "Robbie studies via distance education," she said absent-mindedly.

"Yeah, I know. That's so cool. A couple of hours in the morning and the afternoon is free time."

"Not really. He works."

"Yeah, but still better than school."

"True." Aimee recounted her days doing the same thing. A morning worth of study, and an afternoon to ride fences, herd sheep, and do station jobs. It had been a wonderful childhood. So free. Her heart broke for Aaron having to reside within a confined space to eat, sleep and learn. "What subjects are you interested in?"

"Maths. Computing."

Aimee grimaced slightly. Those two subjects were her least favourite, preferring to stick with biological sciences. "So you're smart then?"

Aaron shrugged.

"What do you want to do after school?"

"Like at uni and stuff?"

"Yeah."

"Engineering. I'm thinking aeronautical, but chemical engineering seems kinda cool too."

"Yeah," Aimee said, trailing off and feeling as smart as a log. "So, which horse?"

"What? From the skittish one and the hermit?"

"Yeah."

"Seriously?"

"Seriously."

"But what about that one?" Aaron pointed to a horse that was practically glaring at them from across the stall.

"He's cranky, and a colt. I'm looking for a horse that can breed with Dreamer in the future."

"Ah…" Aaron studied the two female foals. "Her." He pointed to the closest one that seemed to panic at the finger singling her out.

Aimee smiled, liking his choice. "Why?"

"Well, after we move to the station, Mum and her can bond."

Unable to hold down a grin, Aimee ruffled Aaron's hair and said, "I like your enthusiasm. Come on, let's find Kevin and see how much he's going to rob us."

***

"You're back. Where were you?" Justine said as she opened the door before Aaron or Aimee had a chance to get within a metre of the door.

Aaron grinned. "Secret stuff." He pushed past his mother and headed for the kitchen.

Aimee smiled at Justine's dubious expression.

"Secret stuff?"

"Yep." Aimee stepped over to her girlfriend and kissed her. "Patience little one."

"I'm only three inches shorter than you, I'll have you know." Justine closed the door behind Aimee and followed her to the kitchen where Aaron was devouring what was left of a cold roast chicken.

"Your pool isn't green," Aimee said, staring at the pale blue water through the large windows along the back wall of the house. Last time she saw the pool, it had a family of ducks living in it, which had coincidentally been the reason Justine didn't want to clean the water.

"Summer is coming," Justine said, offering no further explanation. "Cuppa?"

"Yeah." Aimee continued staring through the back windows over the pool deck and the landscaped gardens. She cocked her head and wondered where the eight-duck family had been relocated.

"Nana told her she refused to look after the gardens unless she evicted the ducks," Aaron said between mouthfuls. "They started attacking her ankles when she watered the flower bed." The teenager broke into a fit of giggles at the thought.

"They were simply protecting their young," Justine snapped.

Aimee suppressed a grin, realising this was a sore subject.

"Mum, they've been living in the pool all year. The ducklings were huge."

"They were six months old. How would you like it if I evicted you out of your home at that age?"

Aaron rolled his eyes. "As if."

"There, there, my little activist," Aimee said, pulling Justine into a hug from behind. "The little duckies will be okay."

"I can't see why Mum couldn't just wear boots like the rest of the pensioner gardeners do." She glared at the mugs on the bench as she tipped milk into them. "I mean, Penny isn't precious about it. She wears gumboots all the time."

Aimee hugged Justine feeling the tension in her shoulders. "With the pool clean, we can go swimming tonight. Maybe…" she looked at Aaron to see if he was distracted and whispered in Justine's ear. "… naked." Justine relaxed instantly and sighed.

Aaron looked at them suspiciously. Narrowing his eyes suddenly, he said, "No. Gross! My room is right over the pool! If I see boobs—"

"Aaron Timothy!"

"—or butts, I'm moving out!"

Aimee chuckled and let Justine go. "You going to live with the ducks?" she asked him.

"Nope. I'll move to Yarrabee. Aimee already said I could."

The progress of Justine's coffee cup stalled halfway to her mouth. "What?" Justine's eyes flicked to Aimee briefly. "You want to live on the station."

"Hell yes."

"Language."

Aaron huffed in a typical teenage fashion. "Yes. I do. It'd be so cool!"

"But…" Justine shook her head slightly. "We haven't really discussed—"

"But Aimee and I have. She said I can do distance education and work around the station. I can be with you instead of going to boarding school. We can live in the loft and—"

Justine held up her hand and glared at Aimee. "You've discussed this with my son without consulting me first?"

"What? No!" Aimee's eyes were wide and her breathing shallowed. Guilt at how easy and wonderful Aaron was making it sound invaded her chest.

"You think you can just come in here and spring this on me?" Justine continued. "You stole my son away this morning to parts unknown, I might point out. I trusted you with him, and this is how you repay me?"

"But—"

"You don't have the right to build up his hopes like that."

Aimee rapidly shook her head. "I didn't, he—"

"Is a thirteen-year-old impressionable child, who—"

"Enough!" Aimee said, slapping her hand on the counter. "Yes, Aaron is keen to move to the station, but no, I didn't discuss it with him. Like you said, he's thirteen. He's a teenager and they dream big. You need to remind yourself that he talks to Robbie all the time, who has obviously told him about what it's like living out there. I would never encourage him like that. He's *your* son, Justine. I would never interfere with that." Aimee filled her lungs and stepped back after having her say. Aaron looked stunned but impressed, and Justine just looked angry. Aimee snatched her car keys from the end of the counter. "I know your life is here, and I also know mine isn't." Aimee heaved out an exhale.

"Aimee…" Justine said, raising a hand towards her, but quickly letting it drop to her side.

"I'm sorry," Aimee said, and walked out of Justine's house feeling as though her dreams had just died. Needing space, Aimee climbed into her car and left. With nowhere to go but Yarrabee Station or Armidale, she headed west out of the city. Pulling over for fuel at Richmond before traversing the mountains guarding the city's western flanks, her phone beeped. It was a message from Justine.

I'm sorry :(

Aimee huffed out a breath and dialled her number.

"*Aimee?*"

"Hi."

"*Where are you?*"

"Richmond."

"*You're heading home?*"

Aimee shut her eyes and brushed a hand through her hair. "Yeah."

Justine sighed at the other end. "*I'm sorry. I didn't mean to…I…I'm just sorry.*"

"It's fine. It was bound to come up sometime, right? You have a job and a home in Sydney, and I belong at Yarrabee."

"*And none of that matters to me. You matter.*"

"So, what, you plan to catch up every other weekend? I'm not going to be in Armidale anymore. This was the last weekend we really had. I can't just take off at the drop of a hat."

"*I was never going to ask you to.*"

It was Aimee's turned to sigh.

"*Will you please come back?*"

Aimee rubbed her hand down her face. She had more than five hours in front of her to reach Yarrabee in the state's central west, and Justine's place was only an hour back. The afternoon sun glared at her through the front windscreen. "I never told Aaron you should move to the station."

"I know." Justine sighed softly. *"He told me rather frankly about what you talked about after you left. He's not very happy with me at the moment."* She sighed again. *"Please come back and talk to me? We still have tomorrow before you have to go back. I don't want to waste it."*

Pinching the bridge of her nose, Aimee relented. "Okay. I'll be an hour or so."

"Thank you, Aimee. I…see you soon?"

"Yeah."

***

She felt like a naughty dog walking back up the front path to Justine's door. With a figurative tail wedged firmly between her legs, she knocked and waited.

"Hi," Justine said, smiling and holding the door open.

"Hi."

"Come in."

"Thanks."

Uncomfortable with the formalities, Aimee crossed the threshold and waited for further instruction.

"Wine?" Justine asked.

"Something stronger, I think."

"Good call."

Walking to the kitchen, Aimee looked again at the cleaned pool now glowing under the spotlight.

"Here." Justine handed her a rum and coke and led them to the kitchen table. "Aaron went to a friend's place for the night."

"Okay."

They gave each other a shy smile and sipped at their glasses, and Aimee grimaced at the burn of the strong liquor on her tongue. Silence surrounded them for a while before Justine huffed and slammed her glass to the table top. "This is ridiculous. We've argued before. In fact, today was tame in comparison. Why does this feel so hard?" Justine's frustration tapered off at the end and her voice sounded dejected.

"I don't know."

Justine put her elbows on the table and shoved her head into her hands, covering her face and sighing. "I don't know what to do."

Aimee shifted to the chair closest to Justine and wrapped an arm around her shoulders. "Neither do I."

"We knew this was coming."

"I know."

Lifting her head, Justine looked at Aimee, making Aimee's insides squirm with the intensity of it. "I'm in love with you, Aimee."

The oxygen evaporated from Aimee's lungs and a strange burning replaced it. Eyes flicking back and forth between Justine's, she had no idea how to respond. She had never said those words before. Not to anyone that wasn't family. Feelings exploded within her, but she couldn't make hide nor hair of them. She didn't know what the protocol was but figured she needed to at least say something. Sucking in some air and about to respond, Justine stilled her lips with a finger.

"It's okay." Justine shook her head slowly. "You don't need to say anything."

Aimee's gut twisted. She didn't have the words, but she sure as hell had the feelings. Lurching forward, she pulled Justine to her and kissed the breath from her lungs. With an urgent need for oxygen, Aimee was forced to pull back a short while later. "We'll figure it out, okay?"

"Okay," Justine said, nodding against Aimee.

"Together?"

Justine nodded again.

Taking a deep breath, Aimee studied Justine's face. Tucking her hair behind her ear without being hindered by the glasses she was so used to seeing now, Aimee let out a long sigh. "Christmas is just around the corner. We'll see each other in a couple of weeks."

"I know." Justine put a hand over the one Aimee left resting on her cheek. "And after that?"

"After that, we make do. We figure it out as we go along. I…umm…I…" Aimee huffed, frustrated that the words she wanted to say remained on the tip of her tongue.

Justine smiled at her. "I know, honey," she whispered. Leaning over, she kissed Aimee. "I know."

Aimee shook her head. She was determined to get the words out this time. Cupping Justine's cheeks, she made those amber eyes the focus of her attention. "I love you."

Justine seemed to melt beneath Aimee's hands and they stopped wasting what was left of the weekend.

CHAPTER FIFTEEN

Summer apparently came early at Yarrabee Station. The green blush of the fields that Aimee had left behind a few months earlier had wilted and softened into a yellow dry blanket. Sheep and lambs dotted the hills happily grazing on the drying vegetation. Travelling over the dirt roads that took her home, she rolled down the window, inviting the smell of fresh air into the air-conditioned cab. Breathing deeply, she inhaled the comfortable heat and the fragrance of home.

The familiar scents gave her hope. She was coming home, and here she would be able to cope with the loss of Justine's company. Her mouth twitched up in a smile as she remembered their morning. Wrapped safe in each other's arms, they had woken lazily and came together tenderly before Aimee reluctantly left their bed.

As soon as Aaron finished the school term, they were coming to the station. "Just a few more weeks," she told herself.

Arriving at the homestead mid-Monday afternoon with the new filly behind her in the horse float, Aimee emerged from her car and puffed out a breath of air. She was instantly set upon by a brown and white wiggling mass of fur.

"Hello, girl. Miss me?" Aimee said, giving her dog an enthusiastic welcome. "Hey, girl? Miss me, did ya?" she said, rubbing the dog vigorously on the stomach when Mitsy rolled to her side and threw her legs into the air.

"Aimee!" Sally said a second before enveloping her sister in a bone-crushing hug. "We've missed you!"

"Aunty Mee! Aunty Mee!" Caroline called as she ran across the dusty yard.

Laughing, she returned the hug to her sister then swung her niece high in the air. "Hi, Rolly."

"Did you bring presents?" the girl asked seriously when she was returned to the ground.

Sally rolled her eyes. "I swear, manners and my children are like oil and water."

Chuckling, Aimee reached into the car and pulled out a wrapped box. Reading the tag, she said, "This is addressed to a Miss Caroline Higson. Sally, do you know who that is?"

"Me! Me! Me!" Caroline cried.

"Oh, but I thought your name was Rolly?"

"No, silly! It's Caroline Rolly Higson."

"Ah. Well, then. I think this is yours."

Taking the gift, Caroline tore into it and squealed when a new doll was revealed. She sprinted across the yard, eager to introduce it to her collection.

"You spoil her," Sally said as she watched her daughter.

"Nah." Wrapping an arm around Sally, Aimee pulled her against her. "It's good to be back."

"It's good to have you back. It's been…unusual without you around."

Smiling at her sister, Aimee let her go and attended to the horse float.

"Who have we here?" Sally asked when the black-brown filly was revealed in all its skittish glory.

"This…" Aimee said, struggling as the filly bucked and shied away from them. "Is Nameless."

"Nameless?" Sally crossed her arms and raised an eyebrow. "And why is does the horse that doesn't have a name here?"

"She's my new horse…sort of."

Sally's arms dropped to her sides. "You bought a horse?"

"Ah…obviously." Aimee shook her head at Sally and gently guided Nameless to the stables.

"Does Joey know?" Sally called out.

"Nope."

Grinning, Aimee entered the stables. The darkened interior spooking the filly even more than the long, bumpy ride in the float. "Hey…shh…" Aimee said softly, trying to rub the young horse's nose. It flinched its head away and Aimee dropped her arm, but continued to soothe the animal with her voice until it stopped shuffling about in panic.

"This is Kite. She's old, a bit of a know-it-all and currently pregnant with her third foal," Aimee said, introducing the young horse to her neighbour when she was finally able to coax her inside. "She's a hussy, and I suggest you don't take any romantic advice from her."

Kite walked over curiously, sticking her head over the front stall wall, and sniffed at the air filled with the scent of the new horse.

The yearling reared back slightly, nervous that a large grey mare just snorted at the air around her.

Chuckling, Aimee settled the horse into her stall and went to find Sally.

"Here," Sally said, handing Aimee a steaming cup of coffee as soon as she came into the kitchen.

"Thanks."

"Come on, let's sit," Sally said, walking out to the side verandah. The south side was protected from the heat of the sun and afforded them a view over the rolling valley. As far as the eye could see was tall yellow grass, dark green trees and shrubs marking the lines of the valleys and watercourses, and a deep blue sky watching over them all. Throughout the day, the picture would saturate with colour, before being washed out by the brilliance of the midday sun, only to deepen once again into rich gold and green hues only the setting sun could supply. Their family had purposely avoided erecting sheds or fences on this side of the house so the beauty of the landscape could be appreciated on idle afternoons. With a sigh, Aimee soaked it in.

"Where is everyone?" she asked her sister after taking a sip of coffee.

"All over the place. Gav and Matt are out fencing the new paddock. The roos knocked down a boundary fence last week. We lost a few sheep through the hole before we realised, so Danny took Robbie out to track them down this morning."

Aimee nodded. Danny was a phenomenal tracker and knowing he was passing that knowledge on to Robbie made her smile. "I bet Robbie's loving that?"

Sally chuckled. "He was up and had the horses saddled by daybreak. Practically dragged his dad out of bed."

"How did Miss Gerhardt appreciate her student being snatched away?"

Sally shrugged. "She's not here. Robbie finished his exams last week and she asked for leave."

Aimee raised her eyebrows. "Really? She left the station?"

"Apparently her sister is visiting and they're meeting on the Gold Coast."

"Sister? I never knew she had family."

"You didn't know her first name, so I'm hardly surprised."

"She will always be Miss Gerhardt to me." Aimee looked around the immediate vicinity. "So where's Joey and the new blushing bride?"

"He went to Tracey's wedding."

The cooling dark liquid Aimee had been swallowing came spraying from her mouth. Wiping her lips dry, she said, "He went to her wedding?"

Sally nodded. "Yeah. He wasn't planning to, but Amber convinced him."

"Amber?" Aimee shook her head. "So how long did their romantic dream last for? One week? Two?"

"Joey proposed to her."

"They're *engaged!*" Aimee looked wide-eyed at her sister, waiting for the punch line. None was forthcoming. "You're serious?"

"Very."

"Why?"

"Why what?"

"Why is he marrying her?" Aimee gasped. "He knocked her up, didn't he?"

Sally refused to meet her eyes, which answered the question loud and clear.

Aimee didn't know where to go with that news, so she slumped back into the chair and cradled her mug. "Wow," she said on a breath. "Wait. Why didn't anybody tell me?"

Sally bit her lip. "Joey asked me not to say anything. In fact, I haven't. So don't you dare let on that you know until you see him."

"But why? This is big news."

"Honestly? I think he's embarrassed."

"Because he's marrying a desperado?"

Sally chuckled before she could contain herself. "No, and stop that."

"Well, why then?"

Sally shrugged. "You're going to have to ask him that."

So she did. Two days later.

***

Her brother and his fiancée arrived just before lunch. Aimee noticed the plume of dirt announcing his return on her way back from checking the bores and troughs in the stocked paddocks. Smiling to herself, she clicked her tongue and urged her mount to hurry it along.

"Joseph," Aimee said, walking into her brother's office.

"Aimee. Hi."

"So…I see Amber is still here," she said, having heard the woman heaving in the bathroom on the way through the house. "Is she car sick?"

"Uh…" He shrugged.

"So…" Aimee said, sitting on the edge of his desk. "She's the one huh?"

"Yeah, I guess so."

Nodding, Aimee fingered some of the paperwork on the desk. "And Tracey?"

"Is now Mrs Chambers."

"I see."

Joey continued opening the mail piled on the desk.

Aimee heard him grunt and looking over at the envelope he was holding, she saw the familiar crest of Kevin's horse stud. *Oh, crap.*

"Well, I've got stuff to do. Catcha." She slipped off the desk and made for the door.

"Don't you dare!"

Aimee cringed and turned around.

Joey held up the letter. "You bought a horse!"

"Hmm?"

He slapped the invoice to the desk. "Why are we now the proud owners of a filly?"

About to explain why she bought the horse for Justine and admit to her brother that she wanted the woman in her future, she only managed to get out, "She's an investment. I—"

"Into what! Have you completely lost the plot! First, you send thousands of dollars down the drain when the stud covered Kite, and now you're spending more than that on a bloody pedigree filly! What the hell, Aimee!"

"Firstly, it's not my fault Handsome Boy got out and mounted Kite. Secondly, you're still getting a foal out of him, and thirdly, another pedigree stallion is coming to cover the other mares. Free of charge, I might add. So shove the attitude, Joe."

"Shove the…" Joey growled. "I've had it up to here with you," he said, indicating a level with his hand. "Sending you off the property was supposed to help you grow up, not invite you to spend money we don't have on horses we don't need. And another thing!" he said, picking up a file buried under other documents on the desk. "What's with the fuel bill? Armidale is a small town, so explain to me why you're spending hundreds of dollars on diesel."

"If you'd listen, I'd tell you, however, you're too busy flipping out on a power trip."

"A power trip? Jesus. I'm not putting up with this shit anymore, Aimee. We can't afford this. You're taking that filly back right now."

"I don't think so."

"You don't have a choice."

"Actually, I do." With a deep breath, she said, "Take the money for the horse and fuel from my trust account. That's what I had planned to do anyway, if you'd thought to ask like a regular person."

"What?" Joey blinked in surprise. The money Aimee set aside with regular payments over her lifetime was her nest egg. Her future. She had guarded her growing funds bitterly, refusing to touch them until they were large enough to fund a new breeding plan she had been planning for years.

"You heard me."

Joey shook his head. "No."

"It's my choice, Joe."

Joey continued to shake his head. "No. I'm not about to let you make yet another irresponsible decision. That's enough. It ends now."

"Irresponsible decision? At least I can pay for my apparent mistakes, but what excuse do you have?"

"Excuse me?"

Aimee scowled and said low and deep, "Knocking up a contestant. Nice example you're setting there, Joe. You're a real role model. Tell me, did you propose before or after she spread her legs for you?"

"Enough!" Joey's voice roared through the room and echoed down the hall. He charged across the room and looked ready to slap her. Aimee held her ground…just. "That's my future wife you're talking about, so show some God damn respect!"

Hot tears began to well in Aimee's eyes. "Start earning it then."

Joey growled and before he had a chance to react, Sally pushed them apart. "What the hell has gotten into you two?"

"Your sister has been living it up in the city, that's what! Spending my hard-earned money on stock we don't need."

Aimee took a step forward only to be pushed back by Sally. "*Your* hard earned money? Watch your ego there, Joseph, or soon you won't be about to fit out the door."

"I don't recall you doing a thing in the last quarter but spend it up, so yes, *my* hard earned money."

"At least I did my job when I was here. What did you do for half the year but stuff around and let the place fall apart?"

"So I let a few things slide, big deal. At least I'm not sending us broke. You can't spend that sort of money without asking, Aimee?"

"This from the man that prostituted himself to a TV show without asking any of us if we minded. I spent *my* money, Joe. Not yours. Not Sally's. *Mine.*" Aimee took a deep breath. "As for that ridiculous show…now you're stuck with one of them because you couldn't keep it in your pants. Great job, Joe. Want a pat on the back for successfully studding yourself?"

"Aimee," Sally said, shaking her head.

"You know what? I liked it better when you weren't here. There was no one here to insult my *fiancé*, disrespect my position as manager of the station, and bitch and moan about everything and sundry."

"Disrespect you?" Aimee said on a scoff. "Of course I don't bloody respect you. You've done nothing to earn it for months. Dad would have *never* let things get out of hand like you did."

"Yeah, well he's not here, is he? It's up to me to run this place."

"Into the ground?"

Joey's face turned thunderous and Sally was hard pressed to keep him back. "Fuck you, Aimee."

Aimee curled her lip and leant forward.

Sally shoved herself between the two warring parties and made a cut-it-out gesture with her hands. "Stop it, the pair of you."

Aimee refused to be silenced. Stepping away a little thanks to the pressure of Sally's hand in her sternum, she said quietly. "I've had it with you, Joey. You're not Dad, you'll never be half the man he was, so quit trying to act like him."

"I'm the only father you've ever known."

"No, Joe, you're not. I remember Dad. He respected people. He took time to listen. You're nothing but a wannabe with a superiority complex. Get over yourself already." Aimee stalked off down the hallway, forced to listen to Joey's parting shot.

"You know what, I'm glad you're not my kid. You're a selfish, petulant bitch!"

"Joseph!" Sally reprimanded him before Aimee ran outside and across the yard, tears streaming down her face.

***

Packing a bed roll and a supply of food, Aimee headed for the ranges on the western flank of the property and put as much distance between herself and Joey as she could. Sandstone and shale gravel clicked under the hooves of Skycatcher as the rolling pastureland changed into thick, tree-covered hills. She urged her mount to climb up the slope through the trees to the base of a sandstone rock wall hidden within the canopy. Here, she dismounted and let Skycatcher graze on the grassy clumps around her campsite.

They'd fought before, but never had their words been so ugly and harsh. Every syllable they'd uttered was spoken with the sole purpose to wound and bite. Swiping at the tears still rolling down her face, she poked at the fire she'd made at her campsite.

How did they get to this? They used to work as a synchronous family unit, each person knowing their role and fulfilling it, but ever since Joey applied for that damn TV show, everything had fallen to hell. Joey's choice to instigate his involvement in that show had seriously dented her respect for him. Once infallible and independent, now he appeared like nothing but a weak-spined fool on some ludicrous search for love.

"Stupid show," Aimee muttered, tossing a stick on the fire. She sighed as she thought of Justine. That show brought her into her life, and for that, she had Joey to thank. As bitter as that thought was, she knew it was undeniable. *It was a shame that when her love life finally found its feet, her relationship with her brother suffered.*

"Stubborn idiot," Aimee said, scratching at the dirt with her boots. *Who was he to say what she could spend her money on, and how dare he accuse of her being frivolous with it.* He barely asked why she purchased the horse before launching into a lecture. Something she had invested in as a token of what her future could hold had turned from hopeful to miserable in the space of five minutes. Angry and bitter, Aimee hurled a rock across the dark landscape and vowed to keep out of Joey's way. *The wanker could go jump off a cliff for all she cared.*

***

As the days went by in a muted war between Joey and Aimee, and despite Sally's efforts to mend fences, Aimee had felt like an alien in her own home. Restless and uncomfortable, she had kept herself as busy as she could once she returned from her seclusion in the hills, but every night, she'd lie back in bed and feel that ache again. It was similar to the hollow feeling in Armidale. Putting it down to being homesick while in the grey urban centre, that horrid empty feeling stayed with her like a leech sucking away her motivation. Immersing herself in the daily routine of station life, she couldn't seem to find her centre.

Sighing, she checked the wall clock. Nine p.m. Aimee smiled. Another sixteen hours and she would see Justine again.

Thoughts of seeing Justine tomorrow gave Aimee a sense of peace that she'd been lacking. With a smile, she picked up the letter Justine sent last week and reread it.

Aimee,
I miss you terribly. I know it's only been a few days, but knowing you're not coming to see us this weekend makes me ache with longing.

Aimee chuckled and rolled her eyes at the dramatic wording.

Aaron and I plan to head to his grandparent's place next Friday straight after school finishes. We'll pick up Dreamer and head to Yarrabee early Saturday morning. I can't wait. As you can imagine, Aaron is very excited and is begging me to skip the last week of school. I was tempted, but unfortunately, I'm working and my holidays won't start until school finishes.

I hope the next nine days goes quickly.
I love you.
Justine
PS: I've enclosed the complete season of Romancing the Farmer. Don't tell anyone you have it! Enjoy watching! I'll be quizzing you, so take notes. XX

With a rub at her chest, Aimee settled back against her couch and bit her lip as she stared at the silver disc with Justine's scribble on it. Aimee grunted in frustration. "Let's get this over with," she muttered, loading the DVD player. The theme song for *Romancing the Farmer* started and Aimee shook her head. *This was going to be tragic.*

Watching the process her brother had gone through to choose Amber, Tiffany and Brittney had been fascinating the second time around. It turns out that they had been the best of the bunch by a significant margin. Apparently, Joey was just as good as picking out potential females as he was at spotting pedigree horses and sheep. Joey's interview with the host came on screen.

"I live on a central New South Wales sheep property. Our closest town has about two hundred people, so as you could imagine, potential partners are hard to come by. I'm hoping to find someone willing to give it a go out on the station, and maybe fall for me in the process. We live on a remote property and make our own family from the people that work there. It's not an easy life, and everyone is expected to contribute. Any potential partner I have would need to be able to do that. It sounds like a lot of work, but it's rewarding and our little makeshift community is very close and just…well, great."

Joey shrugged and smiled.

Joey was introduced to all the women and the other farmers. Aimee blinked when she recognised one young man, a childhood friend from Victoria. Joey spent more time talking to him than picking women.

Fast forwarding through the interviews for the other men, she came to little snippets from the three girls Joey chose.

Flicking her hair from her eyes, Brittney said, "I'm ready to share my life with somebody. I want to find the one."

Tiffany's smile lit up the screen as she responded to the interviewer's question about competing for her farmer's affections. "I'm not used to coming second. I'm here to find love and anyone that gets in the way of that better watch out."

Tiffany then giggled until the screen cut to Amber.

"I've reached a point in my life where change is a necessity. Location doesn't matter, but what my heart feels does. If I feel a connection with the farmer, then I'll do what I can to nurture that."

Aimee found herself raising her eyebrows. *That had actually been a sensible answer.* "One point for you, Amber," she said quietly.

Flicking again through the selection process, she stopped when the familiar backdrop of the property came into view. *Wow, Justine really made it look amazing,* Aimee thought as she found herself immersed in the segment on Yarrabee Station. *Somewhere out there is my favourite hat,* she thought idly as the segment ended. Next, the three contestants took in the sights and Aimee chuckled, remembering how annoyed she was on day one.

Laughing as she watched the three girls trip over themselves in the shearing shed, break a nail or two on the fences, get covered in oil in the shed and mingle with the workers in the evenings, Aimee found herself highly entertained.

Then came date number one. Brittany.

"Oh, this is just so beautiful! I can't believe you live like right here on this place. You know?"

Joey smiled.

"So, like, how big is it? I mean, the house is like huge and like you've got a pool and all these cottages and stuff. It must be like a few acres or something. Right?"

Aimee rolled her eyes and groaned. *Listening to this woman pre-recorded was just as bad as listening to her live. Every second word was 'like'.* "Get a dictionary."

Joey answered the woman as he slapped a bug on his arm. "It's just over thirty thousand hectares."

"Oh." Brittany nodded, swatting at her own insects. "So…that's what? Like a hundred acres?"

"Over seventy-four thousand, actually."

"Oh, my God! That's like an entire country!" Brittany tipped her painted face back and laughed like a wounded hyena.

Aimee cringed at the screen.

"And so what do you do all day?" she asked once she composed herself, obviously not paying attention to all the work she'd done since she arrived.

"Well, we do like we did today. Herd animals, shear them, we also have a crop of feed we tend to and sell to other properties."

"What do you do on weekends?" she asked.

Aimee smiled remembering having this conversation with the other women.

"Well, we don't really get weekends. We work most days, but on Sunday, we just do the basics and take it easy."

"You work like *all* the time? Oh, my God. That *sucks*." Brittany began waving her arms around energetically at the persistent bugs.

Joey shrugged and looked ready to drown himself in the stagnant puddle in the creek.

"God!" Brittany screeched. "What's with all the bloody bugs!"

Aimee laughed and scanned ahead to the next date.

Date number two. Tiffany. The old shearing shed.

Aimee smiled as a beautiful afternoon lit up the screen over the old shearing shed and remembered the kiss she had shared with Justine against the wall.

Joey and Tiffany sat on the old ramp leading to the picnic area with a glass of wine and snacks Sally had made them.

"Are you enjoying it out here?" Joey asked Tiffany.

"Yeah. It's quiet, you know. The city is so busy and loud and I didn't notice that until coming here. You can practically hear butterflies fly."

Joey nodded. "Yeah, the quiet is one of the best things about the place."

"It's pretty," Tiffany said, looking at the approaching sunset.

"How do you think you'd go living out here all the time?" Joey asked a scripted question.

"It'd be different, but imagine the tan I'd get. No more salons for me."

Joey smiled at her, obviously wondering, like Aimee, if she was being serious or not.

"But really," Tiffany continued. "I'd do anything for the man I loved. That's the whole point, isn't it? Sacrifice your life for true love and all that?"

"I'd hope the person I loved would want to be out here with me and love the lifestyle as well. We live and breathe this property. It's our life and our livelihood. It's not for everyone."

Tiffany smiled. "I know what you mean."

"Yeah?"

"It's like modelling."

"It is?" Aimee said as Joey's voice echoed the same words from the TV screen.

"Yeah. Totally. Modelling is hard work. You never get to eat and you have to work out carefully so you don't get all muscly and boyish. You need to know how to walk in four-inch heels and look good doing it. A lot of women think they can manage it, but they just can't, you know? They're either too fat, too short, or too blotchy. It's a hard business, but I was great at it."

"Do you still model?"

"No. I got too old, so now I'm looking to settle down with a man that can provide me with everything I need."

Aimee frowned. She was sure Tiffany had been the youngest of the bunch, and was only in her early twenties.

"Like what?"

Tiffany's eyes widened as though she got caught looking for a free ride. "Oh, you know, love and stuff."

Joey smiled politely.

"Ugh…money grabbing wench," Aimee said, ending the nightmare and moving on to Amber's date.

"Do you want a family?"

"Yes. I do. I just need to find the right woman, you know? Someone who can handle the remote lifestyle. Be able to look after themselves and pitch in."

"Does it get lonely out here?" Amber asked.

"No. At least, not for me. My family is here. My sisters, their families. Life out here is what you make of it, you know? Yes, it's hard work, and yes it's isolated, but it's my passion. I couldn't imagine doing anything else."

Amber smiled at him. "I want to find that kind of passion. If I'm honest, I'm jealous you've already found it."

"I was born into it. I didn't have a choice."

"Would you chose anything else if you could?"

Joey thought for a while and soon shook his head.

"Exactly. A lot of people want what you have. What your whole family has. All of you look so content."

"It's in our blood."

Amber smiled at him again.

"What about you? What are you passionate about?"

Amber sucked in a long breath. "I don't know. I changed careers a few years ago. I went from accounting to nursing and I'm really enjoying it. Caring for other people makes me happy, so I think that's where my passion lies. In caring."

Aimee couldn't help but smile at Amber's response. At least Joey had chosen the woman with the most intellect. The fact that she was pregnant was still processing. *A little Joey running around the place would indeed be surreal.*

Aimee flicked to the final decision, already knowing Joey's choice.

"It's hard to choose because someone's going to go home disappointed. I didn't want to come into this to hurt people." Joey took a breath and looked off to the horizon. "I don't regret sending Brittney home, because I don't think she really enjoyed the life out here, and I need someone that can get their hands dirty. Someone willing to put most comforts aside and put in long days. Out of Tiffany and Amber, I have a pretty good idea who I want to have stay and maybe build a life with."

"You've fallen in love?"

Joey averted his eyes from the off-camera interviewer. Aimee knew Justine would have been the one asking the question, however, the voice had been dubbed to that of the official hostess.

"I think I have. I didn't expect to if I'm honest. I mean, like my kid sister, I didn't expect a show like this could bring two people together…not really. On the outside, it seems scripted and set up for heartbreak, but…" Joey stopped and smiled. "But, I think I found her…the love of my life."

Aimee pressed pause and stared at the screen looking for the falsehood. Sally finally confessed that Amber was nearing her second trimester, meaning that Joey had to have slept with her after the circus had finished. Assuming it was a one-night thing because he couldn't keep it in his pants, the look in his eyes told Aimee a different story. It was a look she recognised.

Aimee dropped the remote.

"Well, damn."

CHAPTER SIXTEEN

"When are they coming!" Robbie shouted across the yard at her as she left the stables.

"Who?" Aimee asked.

"Aaron!"

"Aaron? Who's Aaron?"

Robbie, who had run across the yard to reach Aimee, punched her in the arm. "Stop it."

"Ow!" Aimee rubbed her arm and flinched in sync with Robbie when Sally screamed at them from across the yard.

"Robert James Higson! If I catch you punching a lady ever again, I'm going to take the whip to you for a solid month!"

"But Mum," Robbie whined. "Aimee was teasing, and besides, she's not a lady."

Aimee gasped with offence. "You little brat!" Robbie took off laughing, giving Aimee something to chase. "Get back here you feral. I'm going to teach you about manners!"

Dodging and feigning, Robbie outwitted his aunt until taking a sharp left towards the machinery shed.

"Gotcha," Aimee muttered, pre-empting her nephew, and running around the outside of the shed as he ran through it. "Cheeky little sod!" she said when she caught him on the fly, hooking her arm around his neck and knocking off his hat to ruffle his hair. Spotting the dirty hay and horse manure she had just finished mucking out of the stables, Aimee grinned ruefully. "You, my darling nephew, are about to pay for hitting me, then inferring I'm not a lady."

Robbie saw where she was dragging him and did his best to anchor his feet into the ground. "No! Don't!"

Thankful for the strength working on the farm gave her, Aimee wrestled her constantly growing nephew to the waiting pile.

"Aimee! Don't! I'm sorry! *Mum!*"

Sally called across the yard. "Don't come crawling to me. You got into this all on your own. And Robbie? Don't you dare come near me until you shower twice and wash those clothes."

Aimee chuckled and shoved Robbie into the pile. What she didn't bargain on was his scrawny, but ruthless arm latching onto her and pulling her in after him.

With a screech, the pair of them belly flopped into the dirty hay and manure.

"Gross," Robbie moaned as he hurried out of the pile.

"Why'd you pull me in you little turd," Aimee muttered and threw a handful of manure at him.

"Hey!"

Aimee poked out her tongue and threw another lump of something at him.

"Stop it!" Robbie yelled before grabbing his own ammunition to toss at his aunt. Caught in a battle of hay flinging, neither heard nor saw the car pull up in the yard. It wasn't until the dust blew over them from the arrival, that they looked up.

"Shit," Aimee muttered.

"You swore. I'm telling."

Aimee narrowed her eyes at her dobbing nephew and smooshed a lump of mud into his hair. "Don't you dare. You tell, and I might mention to Mum about that magazine Gav showed you.

Robbie's eyes widened and he shook his head.

Aimee grinned at him and threw her arm around his shoulders. She quickly pulled back grimacing. "You stink."

"Yeah, and you smell like roses."

They looked at themselves and winced. "Gross," Aimee whispered.

"Will you two quit playing with the horse poo and get over here already!" Sally yelled at them from the front verandah.

Walking over with bits of hay and manure dropping from their clothes, Robbie and Aimee stopped when Sally held up a hand with a disgusted look on her face. "You two are revolting."

Aimee ignored her and looked at Justine. Smiling, she moved in for a hug but Justine yelped and jumped away.

"I don't think so. I may love you, but trust me, it only goes so far."

"If you love me, then you'd take me, manure and all."

Justine shook her head and smiled before leaning up for a chaste peck on the lips. "There. Now go sanitise yourself."

"Okay." Aimee grinned and turned to find Robbie and Aaron looking revolted, and Sally bouncing on the spot with her hands cradled to her chest.

"Oh, my God. That was just the sweetest thing I've ever seen."

Aimee scowled at her sister and went to walk past her into the house.

"Where do you think you're going?"

"For a shower."

"In my clean bathroom? I don't think so. See that hose over there...use it."

Aimee looked over to the patch of lawn they kept green all year around with bore runoff from the windmill nearby. Aimee shrugged and walked over, stripping her top off as she went.

"Ew!" Robbie complained as he was ordered to follow her. "Keep your clothes on!"

"I'm wearing a crop top for crying out loud. I wear less when I swim in the creek."

"So...that's bathers, not underwear."

"Too bad." Aimee kicked off her boots and tugged her jeans off, leaving herself in a crop top and boxer shorts.

"So gross."

"And you're still a turd," Aimee said spraying him with the hose as he tried to take his own shirt off.

"Stop it! You're wetting me."

Laughing, Aimee drenched the cheeky teen and once again found herself having to fend him off. The pair ended up covered in grass and mud.

***

On the verandah, Sally, Justine and Aaron all looked on. "She's a bloody child," Sally muttered.

"Can I go join in?" Aaron asked excitedly.

"You may as well," Justine said. "I think that party over there is for children."

Sally chuckled as Aaron sprinted across the yard and tackled Robbie to the sodden earth. Aimee quickly rinsed herself off and left the boys to their fun. Sending a wave in Justine's direction, she hurried to her loft to change.

"So…love?"

Justine, who was left smiling as she watched her barely-dressed girlfriend saunter across the dirt, turned to look at Sally. She nodded. "For me, yes."

"And Aimee?"

Justine shook her head with a silent chuckle. "Has trouble saying it."

"Saying what?"

"That she loves me."

Sally groaned. "Sounds like she got the same emotional deficiency Joey has. Two perfectly capable and confident people, but get them to talk about feelings, and pfft!" Sally waved her arms as if creating a small explosion. "Their brains turn to mush."

"I hear congratulations are in order for Joey and Amber." At Sally's odd look silently saying, 'how did you *not* know they were engaged?' Justine explained. "Aimee told me about the baby."

"Ah. Yes." Sally beamed. She was looking forward to becoming an aunt…finally. Shifting her gaze to the boys now covered in mud, she wondered if Aaron was about to become a nephew sometime soon.

"Mum," Robbie said as he started to slop his way over with Aaron. "Can we have a swim?"

"Not until you shower. I'm not risking getting horse manure in the pool. If it's all right with Justine, you boys can go shower down at the shearers quarters then go for a swim."

Justine smiled and nodded as two pairs of pleading eyes looked her way. "I'll put your swimmers by the pool."

"Thanks, Mum!" Aaron said loudly before running off with Robbie.

Smiling indulgently at the boys, Sally turned to Justine and said, "Right! Let's get your bags and unload your horse."

***

Aimee returned to the yards in time to find Sally and Justine hefting luggage from the back of the four-wheel drive, and to hear her sister say, "Where do you want to sleep?"

Aimee blushed as she walked up to them. "Umm…Justine, can I have a quick word."

The woman gave her a quizzical look, but let Aimee draw her away from Sally, who chuckled to herself. "I was wondering, if it was okay with you, if maybe, uh, you'd like to stay with me in the loft?"

Justine nodded as though this news was obvious. "Of course."

"Umm…and maybe Aaron could bunk with Robbie in the house?"

Justine smiled. "He'd like that."

Nodding, Aimee said, "Yeah, I figured he'd want to hang with Robbie, you know because they're really good mates."

"Mmm." Justine's eyes twinkled up at Aimee, seeing through the very thinly veiled plan to get the woman alone in her bed.

"So, uh, yeah. I'll put Dreamer in the stables."

"Okay. Thanks."

Both Justine and Sally were grinning at Aimee as she unhitched the horse from the shady side of the float. *Man, that shouldn't have felt as embarrassing as it was. There was nothing wrong with wanting alone time with her girlfriend, was there? They'd been sleeping together for months.*

"Hey boy," she cooed at the wary-looking stallion. Coaxing him gently across the yards, Aimee stalled him in the fan-cooled stables and found him some sweet hay to eat. "Kite here will look after you," she said to him. "Won't you girl?" Giving Kite a cube of sugar, she stroked her mare's muzzle and moved on to the next stall and gave the same treatment to Nameless.

The young filly, not as nervous as she was when she arrived, was more than ready to be handled and taught some basic groundwork by her new master. Smiling when that very person walked into the stables with her bag, Aimee crossed over to Justine and wrapped her in a much-needed hug.

"I've missed you," Justine whispered into her neck.

"Me too," Aimee said, lifting Justine off the ground and holding her tight. "I want to show you how much, but first, I have introductions to make."

"Introductions?"

Aimee smiled and gave Justine a chaste kiss. Leading her by the hand to the yearling's stall, she let Justine look the young horse over.

"Who's this?" she asked, pleased when Nameless nuzzled her hand, sniffing for more sugar and snorting when she was disappointed.

"That's up to you. She's fourteen months old and has been waiting for her new owner to come to train her."

Justine was smiling at the horse allowing her to stroke her nose. "She's beautiful."

Aimee's heart swelled. "She's yours," she said quietly.

Justine stopped moving and her eyes snapped to Aimee's. "Pardon?"

"Umm…I thought that maybe you might need your own horse for when you're on the station."

"You bought me a horse?"

Aimee licked her lips unsure if this was such a good idea after all. *Grand gestures were nerve-wracking.* "Yes."

Justine's gaze turned back to the young horse.

"Aaron helped me chose her."

"What? When?"

"Remember the secret stuff?"

"*That's* what you two did?"

Aimee nodded. "So…do you like her?"

Justine took a deep breath and studied the horse. "She's a wary one."

Aimee nodded at the assessment.

"She'll require gentle training and a lot of handling."

"She will."

"She'll need a consistent guiding hand."

"I know."

Justine turned her attention back to Aimee with her eyes twinkling. "She's a big commitment."

Aimee's mouth curved into a smile, no longer sure if Justine was talking about the yearling or herself.

Justine purposely looked Aimee up and down taking away all doubt the focus of the subject. "I'll need to spend a lot of time with her."

Aimee nodded and swallowed down a lump the size of a brick. "Will you stay with her? Maybe…" Aimee felt her ears burn and her head start to spin. "Maybe, umm, you know, like, maybe permanently?" she managed to stutter. She felt like an idiot.

Justine looked amused by her awkward delivery, but refrained from laughing in her face. "Yes, I think I might."

Aimee shuddered when she pulled Justine against her for a kiss. She was certain that she'd just had the most important discussion of her life. The way Justine responded with a deep moan and arms that latched around her, she suspected she felt the same.

"I think...we should...get your bag upstairs," Aimee said between kisses.

Justine tugged her toward the stairs, not caring whether the bag came or not.

***

Whistling and feeling like she was floating on air, Aimee entered the homestead on her break-of-dawn quest to find milk to restock her small fridge. Justine liked lots of milk in her coffee and considering she liked coffee when she woke, Aimee wanted to be prepared. She pulled up short when she found Joey sitting at the breakfast bar eating toast. "Oh."

"Good morning to you, too," he said, sipping at a steaming cup of coffee.

"Yeah. Morning," Aimee muttered and went to the fridge, wanting this exchange to end as soon as possible. It had been a frosty two weeks since their argument and despite seeing truth in his words after watching *Romancing the Farmer*, Aimee had avoided her brother like the plague. Pouring some milk into a smaller bottle, Aimee looked up through her lashes at Joey. She frowned. "Why are you trussed up like a turkey?"

Wearing his version of a suit: tan slacks, crisp white shirt and his best boots, he looked ready for a fancy dinner.

"I'm off to Melbourne."

"Why?"

"It's where Amber lives."

Aimee nodded and returned the larger bottle of milk to the fridge, capping the decanted smaller glass one. "Right. Amber. So...is she moving up here?"

Joey narrowed his eyes suspiciously while he contemplated the question. "Yes. I'm helping her move in."

"Right." Aimee nodded again and gave him a closed-mouth half-smile. "So...a kid huh?"

"Yeah."

"Yours?"

"Aimee!"

"What? I'm just checking!"

Joey huffed, climbed off the stool, and shoved his breakfast plates in the sink. Whirling on his sister, he propped his hands on his hips. "Yes, the baby is mine. Yes, we're getting married. Yes, I love her. This may seem stupid to you, but I'm ready to make a life with Amber and our child."

"I never said it was stupid."

"You implied it."

"No, I didn't!"

"You're questioning her morals."

"No, I'm looking out for my brother. It's what we do. Obviously, you've forgotten that little fact because you've done nothing but bark at me for months. Guess what, Joe? I get to make stupid decisions, too. It's my life, so butt the hell out."

"Your decisions are costing me money."

"No, they cost *me*. That filly is an investment—my investment—but you're too busy playing Scrooge to see that."

Joey pursed his lips. "Fine, but what about Justine? How's that going to work out? There's a little boy just down that hall that's going to get hurt."

"No, he isn't, because I won't allow it."

"Come off it, Aimee. Since when are you so committed? I can't see you settling down…ever."

Squeezing the top of the bottle and thankful it hadn't smashed beneath her grip, Aimee shook her head at her brother. "One could say the same about you." Turning away from him, she stormed away.

"You're a bloody idiot!" Sally snapped at him from the hall entrance.

"She's playing with fire."

"God, you two are so alike it makes my teeth ache." Sally shoved past Joey and began to boil the jug. "Justine is in *love* with her, Joe."

He scoffed. "More fool her."

"Jesus, Joseph, will you stop that? Can't you see Aimee is in love, too?"

"Aimee? Right…"

Sally looked to the heavens and shook her head. "She's been in a relationship for four months. That should tell you something for starters. She spent every weekend she could with Justine and her boy, and is trying to set a life up for them here."

Joey frowned. "She went to Sydney every weekend?"

"Mostly, yes. Aaron show jumps, so they've travelled all over the state."

Joey blinked. That made all the fuel transactions make a lot more sense. "What else?" he asked.

"That filly needs to be handled, and Aimee hasn't gone anywhere near the training yards with it for two entire weeks. What does that tell you?"

"That she's been busy?"

"That's it's not *her* horse."

"But she…" Joey's eyes widened. "She bought it for Justine?"

"That's where I'm putting my money." Sally poured herself a cup of tea. "Aimee's been talking about extending the loft. She wants to put in a bathroom and a second room."

"Really?"

"There's plenty of room for it."

"I know, but…why?"

Sally put a hand on her brother's shoulder. "She's found her other half, Joe. I think she wants to ask them to live here."

"But…what if it doesn't work out?"

Sally smiled. "Then let them sort it out."

"But—"

"No, buts, Joe. Leave her be. I really think she's happy. Can't you let her enjoy that?"

Joe scrubbed at his newly shaven chin and sighed. "Yeah…I guess you're right."

"Damn straight I'm right. Now, off you go, Romeo. You have a fiancée to pick up and in-laws to meet."

Joey's face crumbled to a grimace. "Yeah. Great. Awesome."

Chuckling, Sally waved him away. "See you in a week. Play nice!"

"Yeah, yeah."

***

"What's wrong?" Justine asked when Aimee strode into the loft and slammed the door.

Briefly startled, Aimee eventually answered, "Joey! He's an arsehole."

"Why? What happened?"

"Nothing." Aimee slammed the milk bottle to the bench and tried to escape Justine's proximity before she became too exposed. Too late, Justine snagged her arm and spun her around.

"Oh, honey," she said, using her thumb to brush away tears. "What happened?"

Taking a long breath to compose herself, Aimee said, "He doesn't think this is serious."

"What? *Us?*"

Aimee nodded.

"Are we?"

Aimee froze. "Umm…" Aimee looked away and shrugged. *How the hell was she supposed to know what was serious or not?*

"You don't know?"

"Well…I mean, I think I know, but…you know…" Aimee could feel the heat of a blush moving up her neck. *Why were feelings so hard to turn into words?*

Justine smiled and leant up to kiss Aimee on the cheek. "Yes, we're serious. Stop panicking."

Aimee's face lit up into a smile and she let out a breath of relieved air.

"You know I love you, right?"

Aimee nodded.

"You're the first woman I've ever loved, did you know that? The first *person* I've ever been in love with, actually."

Aimee shook her head.

"And you're going to be the last. Do you understand me?"

Aimee went back to nodding and was feeling a little dizzy from the seriousness of the conversation

Justine cupped her cheeks. "I'm new to all of this as well. I've never been in an adult relationship before. I don't know the rules, but I know what I feel. What I feel is undeniable. Okay?"

Aimee gave her a small smile and said, "Okay."

"Now. I need coffee." Justine snagged the milk from the bench and made her way over to the kettle. "Want some?"

Aimee's eyes scanned her girlfriend and recognised that she was in nothing but a t-shirt. The small smile playing on her face from the heart-to-heart conversation turned decidedly evil. "Oh, yes. I want some."

After making Justine squeal when she made her intentions clear, the women returned to the bed and had missed the coolest part of the morning by the time they exited the loft. Aimee walked into the rapidly heating day with a spring in her step and a sore but loved body. As the day progressed and dust stuck fast to the sweat on her brow, her mood remained upbeat.

Everyone noticed.

"Aims, mate, you're bleeding," Gav said after she returned from a maintenance run on a bore.

She inspected the skin missing on the back of some of her fingers. "Yeah, the nut on the pump got stuck again. Bashed my hand on the casing." She shrugged and smiled before stowing away the tools she had taken with her.

"Okay," Gav said slowly, expecting a burst of profanity about the injury. "Right. Danny an' me are headin' out to the north-west corner. The Ritters next door reckon some bloody yobbo's been shootin' roos up there. Gunna go take a squiz. Make sure they haven't wrecked the fences like last bloody time. Stupid wankers."

"I hope for their sake they haven't," Aimee said, exiting the cage where she stored the oil canister she had used.

"You comin'?"

Aimee took a deep breath and considered it. In the north-west corner of the station was a rocky outcrop that glowed in the sunset light. It was a good spot to enjoy a hard-earned beer. She checked her watch. It was nearing three in the afternoon. "Got a coldie on board?"

Gav scoffed at the question.

Aimee grinned. "You're on. Let me grab Justine and Aaron. Back in five." Aimee ran from the machinery shed across the dirt quadrangle now pounded into fine dust from the lack of rain. Despite the dry heat, the fields still flourished with thick grass from their rotating grazing management, the plentiful summer rains last season, and the late winter showers before the TV show came to take over their lives. What a rollercoaster it had been since then.

Bursting through the kitchen door, Aimee was met with a scream.

"Jesus Christ!" Sally yelled dropping the plate she was carrying. It hit the floor with a loud shatter. "Damn it, Aimee! What the hell are you doing?"

Aimee cringed and bent down to help pick up the scattered ceramic. "Sorry. I was trying to find Jac."

Sally stopped in her attempt to clean the mess and frowned.

"*Justine*. Where is Justine?"

"Oh. Out on the patio watching the kids in the pool."

"Great. Thanks. Sorry about the mess." Rushing off before she was reprimanded further, she gathered Justine and Aaron, found herself joined by Robbie as well, and left behind a cranky Rolly because her mother wouldn't let her come along.

"Where are we going exactly?" Justine asked as they all clambered into the tray of the ute. "And I'm pretty sure this is illegal," she said as the car began to move and she made a grab at the side. "Aaron, hold on."

"We're on private property, this is fine. Gav won't be an idiot, and we're heading up to the north-west for a cold drink."

Justine frowned and Aimee grinned at her. "You'll see."

The boys made a game out of the ride in the back of the ute, and Justine slowly relaxed and enjoyed the view. Aimee watched the same scenery pass by with a more studious expression. The feed on the ground was better than could be expected, and the sheep looked fat and lazy as they hid in the shade while the sun still rode high in the sky. The vegetation on the road was more concerning. The grass was long and thick along the fence boundaries, and it was a trend she was finding across the entire station since she returned. Close to the homestead, the vehicles had suppressed the grass and made the area a dust bowl. Further out, the road became two-wheel tracks and she could smell the burn of grass beneath the car engine as they warmed it on their path.

Aimee banged on the roof of the cab and leant around to the passenger side. "Danny, we gotta grade this," she called out over the noise of the car.

"Yep," was all he said in response.

Furrowing her brows, Aimee felt Justine tug her arm.

"Grade it?" Justine said.

"Clear it. Not only does it make checking fences easier, but it acts as a fire break." With a glance at the boys and seeing them preoccupied in discussion and pointing to the passing countryside, Aimee said, "Joey's been slack this year. All this should have been done a few months back, but with the TV show and his trip to the city, it obviously wasn't high on his list." Lowering her voice and moving closer, she added, "*He* should have noticed," she said, gesturing to her brother-in-law. Whispering in Justine's ear, she said, "I think something is going on between him and Sal."

"Like what?"

Aimee shrugged. The car slowed and Aimee jumped off the back to open and shut the gate. A few minutes later they were riding the boundary between their property and the one to the west. "See the difference," Aimee said, pointing out the bare strip on the neighbour's side of the fence.

A burst of profanity from the front cab made Aaron turn bright red and Justine raise her eyebrows. "Those bastards," Gav yelled as he stopped the ute. "Look at that."

A section of fence had been cut by trespassers. Swearing again, Gav called the neighbouring station over the UHF radio with the news and got on with the task of fixing the hole.

Having their refreshments when the task was done, they drove home in the dark as the boys on the back amused themselves with the spotlight.

With her arm around Justine, Aimee sipped at her beer and stole the occasional kiss.

"Woah! Aims! Look," Robbie said.

"At?"

He pointed behind them. Turning her head, she saw the flash of lightning in the distance. *I hope it brings some rain,* Aimee thought, watching the light show for a few moments. Her eyes flicked to the overgrown road they were driving on and she shook her head.

***

"Joseph Turner, explain yourself," Aimee said the moment her brother returned to the station a week later.

He rolled his eyes and walked away from her.

"Hi, Aimee," Amber said, climbing out of the other side of the car.

Aimee spared her a quick "Hi" and a nod before charging after her brother. "What the hell have you been doing since I left?" she yelled, opening the door to the office that he slammed in her face. "You said you took care of everything."

"Not now, Aimee."

"Yes, now. Why is half the stock still up in the middle paddock?"

"There's good feed up there."

"Maybe for a few more days. We agreed on rotating the stock. It's sustainable and it works, but apparently in your wisdom, they've been in that paddock for a month, and in the previous one for five weeks. If you moved them every two weeks, the feed will recover faster. You know that."

"So move them," he said, giving her a dismissive wave and sitting at the desk.

"Jesus, Joe. Do you even care?"

"Of course, I bloody care."

Aimee scoffed. "Yeah, I can tell."

Joey gritted his teeth. "Look, it's been a rough year. Shit happens."

"Yeah, it does, but it happens all the time and you've never let the management slip this bad. None of the fire breaks have been seen too. I spoke to Gav, and he's still waiting on that disc planter. The bloody sorghum seed is still sitting in the shed going off. According to Danny, the gen set is due for some serious maintenance, but you've put it off. Need I remind you that if that breaks down, we've got no power."

"I know, Aimee. I've been talking to someone about getting it replaced. What's the point of fixing the old one if we install a new one?"

"So tell Danny that. All he's aware of is that you've been sitting on your arse for months."

"Bull*shit*. And Danny has no room to complain. He's been unreliable since last summer. He's bloody lucky he's Sal's husband, or I would have fired him by now."

"Fire Danny?" Aimee scoffed. "Shame you can't fire yourself."

The UHF crackled to life on the desk and Joey turned it off with an angry flick of his finger. "I don't have to explain myself to you."

"That's the thing, you *do*. This property is *ours*, Joe. Not *yours*. Once upon a time, you used to be on top of things, and when Grandad retired, you stepped up. I used to look up to you, but lately…" Aimee shook her head and started to walk towards the door. About to pass through it, she paused and said quietly, "When are you going to stop thinking with your dick?"

"My—" Aimee shut the door before Joey was able to throw something at her. "You can't bloody talk!" She heard him yell as she strode away. "I didn't spend thousands on a horse!"

"Everything okay?" Sally asked as Aimee reached the kitchen.

"Marvellous. You?" Aimee said, slumping into one of the stools at the kitchen bench.

Danny entered the kitchen, hesitated when he spotted Sally and Aimee, and quickly moved away.

"Yeah…just bloody marvellous," Sally muttered, going to the fridge and pulling out two beers. "Cheers," she said, knocking her can against Aimee's.

"Cheers. Here's to wankers who can't keep it in their pants."

Sally nodded and downed half of her can. "Yep."

CHAPTER SEVENTEEN

The air was turbulent and crackled through the night sky in a blaze of static discharge. The summer storm came bearing nothing but dry air and electricity. Its powerful electric tendrils blasting their charge to the caked crust of the ground below. The intense heat bursting the dry vegetation in its path, and as the cluster of dry thunderstorms branded their path across the sky, so did they burn the land in their wake. On the north-west boundary of Yarrabee Station, the gusts created by the steep pressure lines of the storm front fanned and fuelled the grass and trees that had been turned to embers by the storm. The wildfire built as hungry flame chewed through the dry debris on the landscape. Four seasons of spectacular rains and growth proceeded the dry, hot summer, and now, the ground was littered in a smorgasbord for flame to find.

And find it, it did. In the dead of night, hot northerly winds encouraged and nursed the small fires scattered around the station until they raged, angry and hot on a mission to devour all it could find.

The homestead, nestled beside the creek running along the south, was quiet as most persons forgot their arguments and worries as they slumbered. In the paddocks beside those being torn apart by fire, the animals sniffed and panicked. Wild-eyed, they charged south through the valley towards the creek. Like a demon, the fire followed their tracks, fire and beast taking the quickest and easiest path south.

***

Sighing in her sleep, Aimee gave up on the pretence of rest and slid out from the woman hugging her like a koala. Giving Justine a soft smile and a kiss on the temple, she whispered her love to the woman before quietly shuffling to the kitchenette. Mitsy greeted her with a wiggle and a whine.

Water on the boil moments later, Aimee soon nursed a cup of chamomile tea as she started the final episode of *Romancing the Farmer*. Careful to keep the volume to a minimum, she turned on the subtitles and contented herself with reading the goings-on of all the desperate farmers. Flicking to Joey's segments, she sipped on her tea and watched as the sound of distant thunder echoed through the night.

"I knew almost instantly who I was attracted to the most," he told Tiffany and Amber as they hung off every word. Studying Amber, Aimee could see the way her eyes shined as she looked at her brother. *Was she pregnant yet?*

"She makes me feel less lonely…like there's someone out there in the world that might be prepared to take me as I am. Living on the station is a lonely life without people around you that you love and respect. I'm lucky enough to have family and friends to make life on the station the best place in the world for me to be…but…despite having those people, I have no one to stand beside me until my dying day. No one to share my life with; no one in my bed; no one to raise a family with…" Joey trailed off. "I guess I just want to find what my parents had."

The show cut back to the faces of the female contenders. They looked moved by Joey's words, and Amber was visibly crying.

Mitsy put her head in Aimee's lap and whined again.

"Shh, girl."

"And the person I feel—no—that I *know* can be the one I need through my ageing years is…Amber."

Amber sobbed and ran to Joey, wrapping her arms around him tightly. The hostess of the show looked completely swept away by it all, and when the camera cut back to Tiffany, she was pouting.

Skipping through to the final interview with the new couple, Aimee took a deep breath and smelled something she wasn't expecting. The fast forward motion forgotten, the DVD skipped right through the credits as she frowned, alert and concerned.

Smoke.

The storms in the north had been ignored thanks to the multitude of distractions. Now, however, they concerned her. Sneaking past a slumbering Justine, she looked out of the north-facing windows of the loft and her heart sank right to her toes. There, over the horizon, was the tell-tale orange glow of fire.

"No," she said on an outward breath.

Mitsy barked.

"Wassup?" Justine slurred in her sleep.

"No, no, no," she continued to chant as she tugged on a pair of jeans and threw a flannelette shirt on over her singlet top.

Groggily, Justine sat up as Aimee picked her shoes up off the floor and pulled them on without bothering with socks.

Aimee finished her task and looked at Justine as a northerly gust rattled the windows for a moment. If the fire was fed by those winds, then it was headed their way. Aimee walked around the bed and took Justine's hands. "I want you to get dressed."

Justine looked at the clock. "It's three in the morning."

"And there's a fire in the north. I need to get Joey and try and stop it before it gets too far."

"A fire?"

Nodding, Aimee said, "I need you dressed and I think you should go down to the house with Sally and the kids."

Justine burst into action and did as she was advised.

"I have to get Joey." Aimee kissed her on the lips and ran from the loft.

***

"Joe!" Aimee said in a whispered shout as she knocked on his door. "Joe."

"What?" the man said as he pulled the door ajar.

"Fire in the north."

Joey straightened for a moment as that news sank in. With a curt nod, he shut the door and Aimee moved on to Sally's room.

"Sally?" she said with a soft knock. It took a minute of knocking to wake someone inside.

"Aimee?"

"I need Danny. Fire in the north."

"What?" Sally looked at her in shock. "But the stock is grazing up there."

"I know. That's why I need Danny. Can you wake him?"

For some reason, Sally looked heartbroken. Aimee reached out to her instinctively.

"He's down the hall. We…uh…don't sleep together anymore."

The implications behind those sadly murmured words hit Aimee straight in the chest. "Oh, Sal," she said, squeezing her sister's shoulder.

Sally shrugged. "We're trying to work it out." Pointing, she indicated the room at the end of the long hall. "He's in the green room."

The phone began to ring in the study. Sally and Aimee shared a stone-faced look. "I'll get the phone. You get Danny."

Nodding, Aimee moved to the room with an apt name. Green paint, green curtains, green carpet. It was horrid. Knocking loudly knowing how deeply her brother-in-law slept. "Danny! Wake up!"

Danny opened the door with a rush and said, "What? Where's the bloody fire?"

"North paddocks."

He blinked at her for a moment, his eyes dark as though sleep rarely came to him. "Are you serious?"

Aimee nodded. "I wish I wasn't."

"Christ." Danny left the door open as he tugged jeans on over his boxer shorts and threw on a shirt. "Is Joey up?"

"Yeah," Joey said as he joined the group at the door. "Danny, get the guys and get the dozers on the move. Aimee and I will take the water trucks. Let's hope it hasn't reached the grazing paddocks."

"The rural fire brigade has just mobilised everyone," Sally said, rushing to the group. "They've been dealing with the fires since midnight, but in the last hour, they all got out of control. The UHF was off."

Aimee and Joey shared a grimace.

"How bad is it?" Danny asked as they all moved outside in a jog.

They paused as the horizon glowed at them ominously.

"Bad," Aimee said, voicing their thoughts. With an unspoken command, they all ran to their tasks.

Justine, dressed and looked adorably rumpled from sleep, caught Aimee as she ran across the yards to the machinery shed. "I want to come with you," she said.

The breath escaped Aimee's lungs in a rush of fear. "No. Not happening."

"But I can help."

"Jac, I can't have you near the fire." Aimee's eyes found the horizon. "If it's as bad as I think it is, I don't even want you here. Get Aaron, get your things and go into town."

"I'm not leaving."

Aimee huffed out a rush of air. "You must."

"No. Not unless you leave with us. If I can't come and help, then I'm waiting right here." Justine emphasised her words with a sharp point at the ground at her feet.

"Promise me you'll be ready to flee if you have to. Sally will know if it's too dangerous to stay. Don't fight her. Promise me."

"Then be here if we have to leave, because I'm not going anywhere without you. I promise you that."

"Jac—"

"I love you, you stubborn farm girl. I'm not going to leave you to burn."

"Aimee!" Joey yelled at her from the sheds.

Aimee gave Justine an exasperated shake of her head. "I'll come back," she promised before kissing her soundly and running to the sheds.

***

Gav and Danny were starting up two bulldozers as Joey and Aimee took the water truck north. Followed by two other vehicles driven by station hands and full of equipment they'd need, they reached the crest of the low hills that afforded them a view of the land to the north.

"God," Aimee said in a low whisper.

Joey gritted his teeth. "Start praying, Aimee."

The fire extended in a broad band through the dried grass and low shrubby acacia bushes. Channelling into a 'V', it ate up easy ground and was burning towards the thick vegetation of the valley cutting a path through the hills.

Joey picked up the radio handset. "Danny, mate?"

"*Yeah, Joe?*"

"It's big, mate. The north paddock is on fire and it's heading for Huntsman Gap. We need to stop it there."

Aimee nodded, silently agreeing. The fire had a clear shot through the rest of the paddocks to the river from that point. Crawling up the hills, however, it would soon run out of fuel as rock and bare soil adorned each of these particular crests. The backs of fleeing sheep could be seen from their slightly elevated vantage point, and Aimee wished she had Kite with her. The flock was headed for a barbed-wire fence that they would no doubt mow down in their panic. Injured sheep was something she didn't want to see happen. She eyed the panting dog on the seat beside her. Her shadow, Mitsy, could save the day.

"I'm taking a ute," Aimee announced, jumping from the cab of the water truck and running to the two cars waiting behind them.

"Wait," Joey said, following her. "What are you thinking?" he asked, genuinely wanting to understand his sister's plan.

"I'm taking Mitsy and getting the flock out of there."

Joey nodded. "Take them west."

Aimee blinked. "East."

"The wind is supposed to swing around from the west later. You'll be leaving them in the path of the fire if you go east."

"West takes us to the Bowl."

"And away from the fire."

The Bowl, so named because it was surrounded on three sides by the rocky peaks of low hills, was a large plain of tilled soil currently fallow with thick grass and waiting to be sown with sorghum. The tough rows of sorghum yet to be planted was a crop that was meant to feed the sheep through winter in case of drought, or to sell on to other farmers. Aimee let the fact it was yet to be planted slide.

"You're sure?" Aimee asked Joey.

"Yes."

Instinct told her otherwise, but this wasn't the moment to start an argument. "Okay then." Aimee whistled for her four-legged companion and bumped her way down into the valley towards the sheep. Already they had begun to gather against the sharp wire, and the strain on the fence was growing. Sheep baaed in pain as the weight of the mob pushed those closest into the wire. "Mitsy, go," Aimee said, releasing her dog as she slowed. With a series of whistles, the panicked sheep were reluctant to follow the orders of a dog and its master. Smoke billowed thick in the wind, and Aimee could taste the ash in the air.

She could see the flame as it flickered and licked at trees and air. *It was close. Too close.*

Continuing to shout and whistle at her border collie, Mitsy began to nip at the hindquarters of the stubborn woollen animals and for once, Aimee didn't bother to correct her methods. Panicked animals were hard to encourage, and with well-placed bites, the sheep began to shift along the fence to the west. Driving ahead as Mitsy spurred them onwards, she opened the gate and used the car as a barricade. Sheep, running and scared, came at her. Relying on their self-preservation, she nevertheless braced herself in case they trampled her. The forerunners turned sharply through the gate at the last minute, and behind them, the flock followed with the occasional sheep hitting her legs. The last of the flock leapt and bleated while Mitsy nipped at its leg. Jumping and hitting Aimee square in the chest, she was driven backwards against the car, and her breath expelled in a rush.

Winded, and uncertain her recently healed ribs fared well under the weight of the sheep, she climbed back into the car and drove after Mitsy, for once not bothering to close the gate behind her. Slowly, they guided the sheep west and out of the path of the fire. She looked up at the ridge seeing the other four-wheel drive parked beside the water truck as it overlooked the valley. She hoped Joey could contain the flames before they escaped the narrow gap.

***

Seeing Aimee get knocked down in the dull light of the fire glow had made Joey wince. His sister, ever resilient, got off the ground and continued after the flock now rushing away from the fire. Silently wishing her luck, he turned to Johnno and Mike. "Get the hose on," Joey told Johnno. "Mike, shovel." Grabbing the UHF radio again, he spoke into the handset. "Danny, how far off are you?"

"*Twenty minutes.*"

"Roger." Joey put down the radio and sighed. *Twenty minutes was going to be too long.* A gust of hot air rushed over him to prove the point. The fresh oxygen fanned the flames below and they flickered brighter. "Mike, follow me."

Grabbing a shovel and a steel rake, the two men scrambled down the sparsely vegetated rocky slope and rushed to the fence line where Aimee had been. Berating himself for not getting the fire lines bulldozed along each fence line months ago, he studied the layout of the land in front of him.

The valley, which was more of an undulation in the hills, was thirty metres wide at this end. Behind him, a vast plain of thick trees and grass leading up to the dense trees blanketing the dry creeks around the homestead.

"Okay, start clearing along the fence line, and up to the rocks." Joey pointed to the outcrop of rocks on each side of the valley.

Mike nodded and got to it. It was hard, but desperate work, and it was taking longer than it should have. They needed the dozers, and they needed them now. Progress to the fire path was slow, and twenty minutes had provided enough time for the fire to practically be on top of them with no bulldozers in sight. Johnno had given up on dousing the fire from above and was now in the middle of the cleared ground spraying the flames only five metres away.

Mike and Joey threw dirt on each newly kindled tuft of dry grass, but their efforts proved hopeless. The fire raged and burned to the sides, eating up the fuel it found at the entrance to the valley.

"We need to move back," Joey shouted over the roar of flame that started to trickle to the sides, knowing if they didn't move now, they'd be stuck.

Joey climbed onto the water truck that Johnno drove out of the paddock through the gate Aimee had left open for them.

"Mike, get the ute," he said. "Danny, where are you?" Joey barked into the radio.

"*Five minutes away.*"

"The fire broke through Huntsman Gap."

Silence.

Joey's mind raced. They couldn't contain this here. That opportunity had come and gone, and as the water truck continued to slowly move away from the fire front, he wracked his mind for ideas. "Ironwood Stock Route," he said.

Johnno looked over at him. "You sure?"

Joey nodded. "It's long enough and wide enough." Into the mike, he said, "Danny, turn back. Get into the stock route and clear it as you drive."

"*Roger that.*"

"Get to the nearest bore, Johnno, we need water."

***

213

As Joey and the station hands tried to put a gap of bare soil in the path of the fire, Aimee slowly made her way across kilometres of dry fields. The darkness of the night was absolute out of the path of the glowing fire. The moonless sky did little to assist her plight, and she knew with certainty that they'd lost some of the flock on the way. The spotlights on the four-wheel drive helped to a point, and Mitsy was doing her damnedest to get the unruly sheep under control.

Constantly looking behind her, her heart dropped when the glow refused to dim. "Come on, Joey," she muttered.

"*Danny, where are you?*" came through the radio.

"*Five minutes away.*"

"*The fire broke through Huntsman Gap.*"

"No," Aimee said on a breath. Thinking fast, she picked up the mike to suggest the stock route and heard her brother's voice again.

"*Danny, turn back. Get into the stock route and clear it as you drive.*"

"*Roger that.*"

Aimee nodded. If they moved fast and the wind stayed fickle and gusty, they stood a chance, but would lose a lot of good grazing ground. It was a small price to pay to keep the flames away from the flock and homestead.

Concentrating once again on the sheep she was moving, she whistled to Mitsy to gather up a straying group and slowly, they trekked west. The crackle of the radio keeping her company.

"*Gav and I are moving northeast from the bottom of Lone Gum Paddock. Where are you, Joe?*"

"*The other end at the bore. Johnno and I are going to douse the fringes.*"

"*Danny, it's halfway across Lone Gum. I think we have two hours, tops.*"

"*Two?*"

Aimee shook her head. *It was moving quickly. Too quickly.*

"*Mike, come back.*"

"*Copy you, Joe.*"

"*What's your position?*"

"*Two clicks west of the gate.*" No further information came through the radio. If her reckoning was right, Mike was two kilometres in her direction, meaning the fire had a mind of its own. It was travelling in all directions despite the northerly gusts. Granted, it was moving south faster than it was moving in the other directions. Looking at her odometer, she reckoned she'd travelled five kilometres in the hour since she left the fire front. A check in her rear vision mirror showed the glow only a few kilometres behind her.

With a deep breath and a silent prayer, she continued on her task and kept an ear on the radio chatter.

"*Joe,*" Sally's voice said a little while later. "*Joe, you copy?*"

"*Go ahead, Sal.*"

"*I called George, see if he has some guys available. He's got fires in his stockyards, but is sending over two blokes.*"

"*Roger that. Send them to the stock route to find Danny.*"

"*The rural fire service has guys out around Roper Creek. The storm set off more than fifty bushfires. They're waiting on reinforcements from Condobolin, Parkes and a truck from West Wylong. All the rural firies have been called in. Most are at a fire near Roper Creek.*"

"*Roger that, Sal.*"

"*Come in, Joe,*" Sally said as the sky in the east began to lighten.

Aimee swallowed hard when the lighter sky revealed something she didn't want to see.

"*Yeah, Sal?*" Joey replied five minutes later.

"*There's a storm building out over the plains. A big one.*"

"*How big?*"

"*The bureau has a severe weather warning out for it.*"

"*Shit. Mike. Come in.*"

"*I'm already moving,*" Mike said.

Aimee grimaced. She could see the darkened clouds in front of her contrasting against the backdrop of the lightening sky. Stopping her car, she climbed out and waited. The air was still, but her fears were recognised an instant later. A trickle of wind blew directly behind her, making a path towards the storm. The rapid uprising of air and decrease in pressure generated a gradient that the air rushed to fill. As the winds slowly picked up to balance out the storm in front of her, so did they bring the smell of smoke.

"*Aimee, you copy?*"

She dove into the car to grab the mike. "I heard, Joe."

"*Move.*"

She nodded to the radio. She had no intention of staying here to let the winds racing towards the storm bring with them fire and ash determined to burn her.

"On it. Heading south."

***

"What does that mean?" Justine asked Sally as the woman went pale.

"It means the wind is going to change."

"Meaning?"

"Aimee was sent the wrong way."

"She's in the path of the fire?"

"Maybe. It's hard to tell which way the wind will shift, but it's possible it'll turn west. She'll be fine. She's got warning and is already moving."

"Show me where she is," Justine asked, looking at the map of the station and surrounding properties that was spread out on the desk. Sally had marked the area of fire with pegs and the map was littered with them.

"Around here," Sally said, pointing to the west of the fire.

"That looks so close."

Sally nodded. The scale didn't help. "Danny and Gav are here," she said, moving two coloured rocks she had found in Caroline's room. "Joe and Johnno are here, and Mike is joining them from here." They both stared at the map and the little pieces for a few heartbeats.

"What can we do?" Justine asked again.

"We get them something to eat and drink," Sally said, leaving the study and heading for the kitchen. With the sun rising, and the guys having been out there for a couple of hours already, it was time to replenish them.

"Morning," Amber said, walking into the kitchen as Sally and Justine finished packing thermoses of coffee and containers of sandwiches. "You're all up early. What's going on?" she asked.

"Fire. Everyone is out fighting it."

Amber's eyes widened. "Are they okay?"

"They're fine."

"*Sal, come in,*" the radio crackled with the sound of Joey' voice coming down the hall. Sally, followed by Justine and Amber, walked into the study.

Crossing the room to the desk, Sally said, "Go ahead, Joe."

"*Winds turning easterly. Confirm wind predictions for the remainder of the day.*"

"Will do. Give me five."

"*Roger that.*"

"What does that mean?" Amber asked.

Sally held up a finger and looked at the fax sent through five minutes ago. The rural fire service was keeping all the properties up-to-date with the weather details. "Joe, wind predictions are northerly at thirty to thirty-five kilometres an hour, gusting up to fifty."

"*Roger that. Danny, you copy?*"

"*Yeah, Joe.*"

"*Finish the stock route. Send Gav back to clear the route to the west.*"

"*Copy that.*"

Amber looked at Sally for an explanation. "They're trying to put in a firebreak to hold the fire up. There's a storm to the west that's generating easterly winds and widening the fire front. Gav is going to create a firebreak to the west of the one they're making to the east."

Amber blinked at her. "Can we expect injuries?" she asked after a few minutes of map studying.

"Blisters, usually," Sally answered, thinking back to the handful of times they had fought bushfires over the years. She remembered from her parent's retelling *The fires in seventy-six were the worst.* The entire property had been rendered into ash and charcoal. Everything since had been classified on a scale of puny and hardly worth putting out. Nearly forty decade's worth of fuel littered the gullies and hills, and Sally knew the firebreaks on the pastureland had only just begun to be re-dozed. None to the north had been reached yet according to the map on the wall showing recent fire prevention actions.

Sally looked at Amber. The show and his impending fatherhood had distracted Joey. Still, Danny should have taken up any slack as manager. Of course, his imploding marriage had done what it did to Sally. Rendered her depressed and barely able to function with the basics. More than one person had asked her if Danny was all right over the past few months as his work ethic faded off. She had smiled and assured them he was just getting old. *If only people around her knew how hard she was fighting to keep it together. How desperate she was to maintain a façade for the kids and workers alike.* Only behind closed doors had she let herself fall.

"Sally? Are you okay?" Justine asked.

"Huh?"

Justine reached up and wiped a tear from her cheek. *When had she started crying?* "Sorry. Tired."

Justine frowned at her, but didn't pursue the conversation.

"How about we get these guys some food?"

Nodding, Justine said, "How?"

"Bike. It's fastest."

"Okay, I'll go."

"What? No? I will. I know where everything is."

"You also know how to operate all of this," Justine said, sweeping her hand at the room full of radios, maps and whirring faxes.

"Why don't you both go? I'll man this fort and mind the kids," Amber said, rubbing a hand unconsciously over her still-flat stomach.

Sally stared at her for a moment. Sending Justine out to Aimee would save her a fair amount of time, besides, the bike would be useful to help Aimee herd the sheep southward. Nodding, Sally turned to Justine and hoped Aimee wouldn't permanently maim her for sending Justine out there on her own. "You'll find Aimee here." Sally traced a path with her finger along the most prevalent road heading north-west. "Stay on that until you reach a windmill. You'll find a track going off towards the western hills with the lone tree on it. A couple of k's up, and you can start looking around for Aimee. Give her a hand with the sheep and take one of these," she said, pulling a handheld radio from a charger. "I'll refill the boys and come back. Amber, ask Robbie and Aaron to mind Rolly."

"Aye, aye," Amber said, saluting.

Giving her a wry smile, Sally led Justine to the shed.

CHAPTER EIGHTEEN

"Come on, come on," Aimee said to the sheep as they continued to panic with the renewed smell of smoke from a north-easterly gust. The storm to the west had grown and looked to tower over her in the early morning light. It flickered and slashed light through the air as currents swirled and charged the particles within the clouds. Greedily sucking in oxygen, the winds had increased from the direction of the fire front and had rained ash and smoke around the slow-moving herd. The glow on the horizon had gone, replaced by air thick and grey. Aimee's stomach felt loaded with rocks at the dread that created.

"Mitsy!" Aimee whistled loudly and urged the panting dog to tuck in the wandering sheep at the left flank. The flock, nearly six-hundred beasts thick and containing three-month-old lambs, was stubborn and panicked. Climbing down from her vehicle, she ran to the right wing of the flock to drive them forward with shouts and claps. It was futile. The smoky air, the nipping dog, and the blast of the car horn had dazed them all. Wandering around aimlessly, a few took off behind her, another group went west and some bolted forward. "Shit," she muttered to herself. With the strong northerly winds expected soon, she knew she needed help.

No sooner had the thought crossed her mind than a quad bike crossed the paddock to reach her.

"Sally. Thank God," she whispered, waving the person over. When Justine's figure appeared as she approached through the smoke, Aimee's heart stopped beating. "No," she said under her breath and glanced at the fire front behind her. "What the hell are you doing out here!" Aimee screamed when Justine stopped beside her with a smile. The smile slipped off her face instantly. "Turn around. Get your stuff and leave!"

"I will not," Justine said, climbing off the bike.

Aimee grabbed her shoulders, spun her around and pushed her towards the bike. "Yes, you bloody well are. Get out of here."

"No!" Justine shrugged her away. "I'm here to help."

"I have everything under control. I don't need your help," Aimee said, unable to stop glancing at the fire front. The black smoke marking its presence was starting to flicker along the horizon line. Flame. Aimee swore under her breath. *If she didn't move fast the flock would be caught by the fire when the winds changed again.* Aimee huffed. "Fine. You take the car, push the mob from the centre and Mitsy and I will drive the edges. We're going that way." Aimee pointed to a tree line in the distance. "If we get across that creek, it should give us enough of a firebreak to push the flock south-east to the bottom paddocks."

Justine nodded. "Here," she said, handing Aimee the helmet she had been wearing.

Aimee shook her head. "I need to be able to shout and whistle."

Justine handed her a water bottle and a sandwich instead.

"Thanks. Let's go."

The storm on the horizon flashed and grew, widening the fire front behind them as winds rushed to the epicentre of the thunderclouds. As long as that storm continued to build, their hopes remained high, and finally, the smoke thinned as they broke free of the front. Breathing a sigh of relief, Aimee mustered the sheep another hundred metres before calling Mitsy over for a break.

"Hey, girl," Aimee said, rubbing Mitsy's head fondly and tipping some water into the dog's greedy mouth. "Good girl."

Justine climbed from the vehicle and jogged over to them. "Are we getting there?"

Taking a sip of water, Aimee wiped her mouth with the back of her hand and said, "Slowly. Any news over the radio?"

"Amber relayed—"

"*Amber?*"

Justine nodded. "She's back at the homestead."

"Where's Sally?"

"Running food to the rest of the guys."

"Leaving Amber to mind the radio and the kids? Is she *insane!*" Aimee climbed down from the bike and gestured to Justine to get on. "You're going back to the house."

"What? No, I'm not."

"Amber shouldn't be left alone back there."

"She's perfectly capable."

"She's a city slicker! She has no idea what she's doing!"

"No, Aimee. She's an independent, competent woman who is about to become your sister-in-law. She's got just as many degrees as you, so put away the preconceptions and insults already."

Aimee averted her eyes and nibbled on her lip. "Fine, but if you hadn't noticed, this place is on fire. I've never seen anything like it before and I want someone I trust manning the radios. I don't care how competent Amber is, she's never had to deal with something like this before."

"You just said you haven't either."

Aimee scowled. "Maybe not, but I know how to—" Aimee stopped and cocked her head as a crackle came from the car. Running over to it, she heard the end of the transmission.

"*—do you copy?*"

Aimee picked up the receiver and waited.

"*Aimee, do you copy?*"

"I copy. Go ahead."

"*The front has beaten the west firebreak and made it into Bowl Paddock.*"

Aimee's eyes widened. The fire front had spread significantly. When the winds shifted northerly, the fire was going to cut a swath down the guts of the entire property. They'd be lucky to stop a quarter of it from going up in flames. "Copy that," she said into the mike to Joey.

"*Where are you?*"

"Half a click from Steven's Creek."

"*Okay. Get the animals across and head to Middle Bore. I want to push the flock there as far east as possible.*"

Aimee pinched the bridge of her nose. Having lambed in the past few months, the majority of their stock was in the middle paddocks getting fat. A thousand sheep lay in the path of the fires if the firebreak at the stock route failed. Considering Joey was asking her to move the stock meant he wasn't confident. "Roger that," she said, looking to the north and seeing smoke thickening from one side of the horizon to the other.

"Everything okay?"

Jumping at the sound of Justine's voice, Aimee tore her eyes from the carnage in the north. If Joey didn't think the firebreak was going to work, then the homestead lay unprotected if the fire made it through the middle paddocks. "No. You need to go back to the homestead. Get the kids and head to town." Justine was about to shake her head when Aimee grabbed her shoulders. "I need to know you're safe. That the kids are safe. Please. The fire is heading straight for them."

Justine looked over her shoulder and a northerly gust hit her face, bringing with it the smell of smoke. The winds increased into a full-blown breeze making Aimee turn back and frown. Glancing to the storm to the west, she noticed the clouds that had once been strong and thick, had begun to break up. The storm was easing and with it, so were the winds dragging the fire to the west. Now, the fire was coming for them.

"Get in the car and go," Aimee snapped, running back to the bike and whistling to Mitsy.

"You're coming with me!"

"I can't. I need to get this lot across the creek and go and help Joey."

"I'm going to help you."

Running out of time to argue, Aimee quickly kissed Justine on the forehead and started her motorbike. Pushing the flock south once again, she clenched her teeth as Justine resumed her role in the centre to help drive the beasts across the creek.

With Justine's assistance, the flock was easier to control; however, the pace was still too slow for Aimee's liking. Her voice, hoarse from shouting and whistling at Mitsy, was beginning to be impeded by the thickening smoke.

This is hopeless.

***

Eight hours and forty-five minutes, Aimee noted when she checked her watch. That's how long they'd been outrunning the fire. Exhausted, covered in ash, and barely able to talk, she panted as she sucked down as much water as her stomach could hold. Beside her, Justine slumped down against the car with her head in her hands. She looked as dejected as Aimee felt.

All impressions of control over the hungry flames had vanished the instant the fire jumped the firebreak in the stock route an hour ago. Barely noon, and the fight was already over. Life was in the balance and so was the century-old livelihood of the property. *Gone in one lightning strike*, Aimee thought to herself. *Poof. Up in smoke.*

Screwing the lid back on her bottle, Aimee walked to the refuelled quad bike and stashed her water bottle in the holder. Staring at the smoke-filled air, she took a deep breath, tasting the ash and smell of burning gums on her tongue. They had driven the flock in their care south-west and out of immediate danger, however, they had thousands of head of sheep in the path of the flames. The dozers had been abandoned to be replaced by stock trucks to cart away sheep when the possibility of halting the fire had become impossible. Small, and only able to ferry eighty head at a time with panicked woollen animals, the mass exodus of the flock had only just begun. They needed help. They needed to keep working the dozers. With a sharp nod to herself, she turned to face her girlfriend. Justine wasn't going to like what she was about to do.

"Okay. Here's what's going to happen now. You're going to take the car, get Aaron and the kids as far away from here as possible."

Justine lifted her head up and squinted into the smoky light. "No."

"I'm leaving you no choice," she said as she climbed onto the bike, securing the helmet. "You need to get back to the homestead and make sure everyone evacuates."

"But—"

"It's not up for discussion!" she shouted. Starting the bike, she pursed her lips, hating the wounded look on Justine's face. "Go! Take Mitsy with you." In a swirl of kicked-up dirt, Aimee floored the bike and spun the wheels, racing at pace to the epicentre of the disaster. She hoped with all her might that Justine would take her cue and return to the south-east, away from the devastation.

***

The sun disappeared behind thick, black smoke, basking any remaining visibility in a curious yellow-orange haze. *I'm on Mars*, Aimee thought to herself as she tore across the unburned paddocks. Ash rained down in little flakes and filled her mouth with the taste of devastation. Coughing to clear her airways, and brushing the particles from her eyes, Aimee made it to the middle of the chaos.

Sheep were being herded, with little care for being gentle, onto the waiting flatbed trucks. Running over, Aimee watched her brother pick up a lamb and all but throw it into the truck. The mother bleated pathetically at its ungraceful journey and soon found herself shoved over the short rails to join it. Opening her arms and shouting, Aimee helped the boys load as many sheep as the truck could carry. It began its journey away from danger before Joey realised she was there.

"Aimee? Where are the—"

"Safe across the river. I sent Justine home to evacuate the kids."

"Amber?"

Aimee shrugged. "With Sally back at the house?"

Joey shook his head and pointed to an arriving truck. "Sally is here."

"Then I don't know. Probably manning the radio still."

"I want her to go with Justine."

"So call them up and say so. We have a fire to deal with right now." Aimee pointed to the thick smoke to the north. Flames, angry and hot, were visible only one hundred metres distant.

Joey grabbed her arm. "I want you to go back to the homestead. Get them out." Aimee started shaking her head and opened her mouth to speak when Joey squeezed her arm. "I need to know she's safe."

"Justine—"

"Do you really think she'll leave you behind?"

Aimee gritted her teeth. She willed Justine to leave but had a nasty feeling that the stubborn woman would likely stay until the death to assure she was safe. About to answer in the negative, she was interrupted when a strong gust of wind hit them, bringing with it a rainstorm of burning embers. Just as Sally pulled up in the truck with Danny, the dry grass around them burst into flames, scattering what was left of the flock.

"Go! Now!" Joey screamed at Danny as he floored the truck out of danger. Joey turned and ran for the four-wheel drive parked nearby, but stopped as little brush fires continued to light up from the embers on the wind. "Aimee, leave!"

Hissing and brushing off the embers that hit her arm, Aimee watched as her brother made it to the vehicle safely and started south. Hopping on the bike, Aimee looked around as if the world had slowed. Sheep ran in haphazard lines, the truck and four-wheel drive kicking up dust as the wheels spun with urgency, abandoned vehicles slowly becoming engulfed in smoke and flame, and nearby, the dozers were backlit by the oncoming rage of fire. Fleeing were her siblings, brother-in-law, and co-workers. Safe, for now, was her girlfriend, family, and dog. Alone she sat on the bike wanting nothing but to make sure they remained that way.

Aimee bit her lip and stared at the dozers, then her eyes widened. Running to one of the machines, she climbed in and started it up. Heading south as fast as she could manage, she made for the one thing that might save the homestead and all that were in it. She had to make it.

CHAPTER NINETEEN

Sally's heartbeat refused to slow as Danny gritted his teeth and outran the smoke and embers. They were less than five kilometres from the homestead, but it felt like it was too close. Far too close. The fire ridge had gained momentum faster than predicted, and they should have evacuated the kids before now.

"We're too late," she said in a burst of panic.

"No, darlin'. We're not," Danny said, letting go of the steering wheel and reaching across the wide cab for Sally's hand. She took it with desperation. "We're going to get the kids, and everything will be okay."

Oh, how she wished that was the truth. She'd do anything to make everything okay again. For the past few months of emotional confusion to be over. For Danny to be hers again. Only hers, and not be soiled by some random trollop in Wagga. Sally couldn't help the sob that came out of her mouth. She'd been so strong, so resilient, but today, with everything she held so dear balancing on the edge of destruction, she couldn't take it anymore.

"Sal? Babe?" Danny asked, squeezing her hand.

"How!" she yelled. "How is it going to be okay? Our property is nothing but ash, Danny! Our family is falling apart, and now we have nothing. *Nothing!*"

Danny's grip remained tight on her hand, and as silence filled the cab, they held one another like a lifeline. They knew that once they let go, everything would crash down around them. And it did.

"Where's Aimee?" Justine shouted across the yard as they pulled up.

Sally looked behind them, seeing Joey's vehicle entering the yard, and waited patiently to see Aimee arrive. In the slower vehicle, it was safe to assume she wasn't too far behind. Joey pulled up and jumped out. "Are the kids ready to go?" he asked Justine. "Where's Amber?"

"Inside."

"Joe!" Gav yelled from the machinery shed. "I've got the lads making a firebreak out the back."

"No. Forget it. The fire is jumping. It won't matter. Maybe if we had the dozers." Joey sighed and stepped towards the house.

"Joe," Sally said quietly. When he looked over at her, she continued. "Where's Aimee?"

"She was right behind me," Joey said, swinging around to look up the road. "Wasn't she?"

Sally's skin prickled. "You don't know?"

"She was on the bike as I left, I assumed—"

"Assumed!" Justine screamed as she yanked violently on Joey's arm. "Where is she!" Justine spat at him before glancing over at the truck. Sally and Joey latched on to her arm as she made to bolt over to it.

"No," Sally said, shaking her head.

"Let me go! I have to find her."

"It's too dangerous. Aimee will be okay."

"How do you know that? She's out there where the world is burning down." Turning on Joey, Justine lashed out viciously. "How could you! How could you just leave her out there?"

"I didn't—"

"You did!" Justine shrieked. "You abandoned her again! You turned your back on her once more, thinking about nothing but yourself. You bastard!" Justine screamed as she began to pummel the man's chests with her fists. "How could you?"

Danny and Sally leapt into action, pulling the flailing woman away from Joey, who shook his head lamely, looking lost and shocked.

"Joseph?" said Amber as she joined the group, warily eyeing the restrained woman struggling against Danny's chest.

"Let me go," Justine said quietly. Releasing their grip, Sally and Danny stepped back. "Call her," Justine said to Sally. "Get her on the radio."

"She was on the bike. She doesn't have one," Joey said.

"So she's alone. Cut off from her family. *Again*." Justine's eyes held reams of accusation as she stared resolutely at Joey. Joe was unable to hold her gaze for long before his eyes dropped away guiltily. Aaron ran to his mother and wrapped her in a hug, stealing her resolve.

As Justine broke down, Sally's hand covered her mouth as she hid the sob held there and felt Danny's arms come around her in a comfort she had long missed. Joey allowed himself to be held by Amber, crumpling into her outstretched arms. To the side stood

Justine with Mitsy by her side and Aaron on the other, staring up the road waiting for her partner to return. Sally could pinpoint the moment Justine snapped. Her eyes hardened and her fists clenched. A moment later, she was gathering her son in her arms, she whispered words of love. "You need to leave," Justine said, directing her son to the car Robbie was helping to pack. "Stay with Robbie and mind what Sally says. Okay?"

"Go get her, Mum," Aaron said.

"No!" Sally yelled out, but it was too late. Justine was sprinting to the four-wheel drive in a desperate attempt to boldly rescue Aimee. Victorious, Justine made the car and locked the doors before Danny and Joey, who chased her, were able to reach her.

"Open the door!" Joey shouted.

Justine rolled the window down enough to shout through before she drove off, "Look after Aaron."

"Dammit, Justine. Get out of the car!" Joey shouted as the vehicle began to move, Mitsy leaping into the back opportunistically. "No! Shit!" he yelled as the car vanished into dust.

"Oh, God. Danny," Sally said, joining her husband and wrapping a hand around his waist.

Slinging an arm around her shoulder he said, "We need to think of the kids. I can't lose them, too."

Sally looked up at her husband's glassy eyes. His words were choked, heralding the rift that had occurred between them as they grew apart from his indiscretion. "No," Sally whispered. "We can't."

CHAPTER TWENTY

The airstrip. An abandoned clearing two hundred metres wide that sat adjacent to a sparsely vegetated holding paddock. *It was perfect.*

Driving the dozer to the southern side of the airstrip, Aimee cleared a frustratingly slow strip of grass, before returning along the one-kilometre length of the strip to add another cleared path.

"Now for the risky bit," Aimee muttered to herself as she fished something out of the dozer cab. *Thank goodness for smokers*, she thought as she gripped the lighter and ran across to the grassy side of the strip. Bending down, she rolled the flint only to find a spark without flame. "Shit." Shaking the lighter, she could feel the diminutive weight of gas inside it and tried again. Successful, she lit up the grass and was forced to jump back as the dry tinder took the flame hungrily. Running along the length of the strip, she lit spot fires as fast as she could before sprinting back to the dozer to watch.

"Come on. Come on. Come on," she said in a chant. Slowly the small flames picked up and ran with the life they were given. Hot winds fuelled their paths and soon, tendrils of fire reached across the width of the airstrip, slowly building to a fiery crescendo. Reaching the strips of dirt carved out by the bulldozer, the flames halted and seemed to growl at the restriction of fuel. Vainly trying to leap the six-metre gap, the flame was too cold and too low to jump across. Over an agonising sixty minutes, while widening the gap as much as she could, Aimee cheered as the fire died away, leaving behind nothing but charcoal and ash. Leaving behind nothing that could burn.

She blew out a breath of air. Now to extend the firebreak, she thought as she looked to the north. In the ninety minutes since she left the fire front, it had steadily moved closer and closer. Better move quickly. Starting up the dozer, briefly concerned at the lack of fuel in its tank, she made for the western end of the airstrip. Realising she had been so focused on her plan, that she was yet to radio in, she glanced at the radio and noticed its display was dull. Frowning, she tapped the top of it and flicked a few switches. It crackled to life. *Shit, how long was that off?*

Picking up the mike, she was about to talk into it when it burst into life with Joey's voice.

"*Justine! Come in! Damn it, I know you can hear me. Where are you?*"

Blood froze in Aimee's veins.

"Joey, come back."

"*Aimee? Where the hell are you?*"

"Never mind that. What's going on? Where is Justine?"

"*I'm right here,*" came her voice through the radio.

"Oh, thank God," Aimee muttered to herself.

"*Justine is looking for you,*" Joey said.

"What!" she yelled into the mike. "Justine, where ever you are, head back now!" Aimee looked towards the north again and grimaced. It was a wall of thick, black smoke covering the entire horizon. Nothing stood a chance in front of that. Probably, not even this, Aimee thought, looking at her firebreak.

"*Where are you?*" Justine asked.

"I'm at the old airstrip. Where are you?"

There was a long pause before Justine said, "*I don't know.*"

Aimee stilled and stared out of the dozer windscreen. Somewhere out there was the woman she loved with a force-ten disaster closing in on her. Closer still was her family and their home. The home that held all the memories of her parents and the life she had carved out with her siblings. A home that was going to burn. Her eyes flicked to the encroaching wall of smoke, flame and crackling carnage.

"Joey, get everyone out. We've lost." There was no response. "Joey?"

"Copy that."

Aimee shut her eyes and pressed the mike against her forehead. She couldn't leave Justine somewhere in this disaster *and* save the homestead. She was no superhero. With a quick huff of air, she made her choice. Bringing the mike to her mouth again, she said, "Justine, head south, away from the flames. I'm coming to get you."

"Aimee, no—" Aimee cut off the sound of her brother's pleas with a flick of a switch and revved the dozer she was driving. Making a beeline for the homestead, she cursed the machine for its slow speed and ignored the heat building behind her.

***

Joey ran outside to the hurried evacuation of the property and personnel. One car was being loaded with vital records and computers, another with historic and personal memoirs, and the other was full of station staff.

"Head to Roper Creek. We'll meet you at the oval," Joey said to Mike in the driver's seat.

"Will do, mate. You got everything under control here? We can—"

"It's fine. Just get out of here while you can." Joey banged the side of the four-wheel drive. "Go."

Mike nodded once and accelerated, taking four people with him to safety.

Joey paused, gritting his teeth at the view to the north. Thick and black, the fire was only a couple of kilometres away now. Their only remaining choice was to flee. Nothing could contain the heat and raging chaos of what was coming. "Nothing but a god-damned miracle," Joey muttered. He sprinted to Sally's vehicle. "Got everyone?" he said, peering into the car to find three wide-eyed children. Robbie had his sister tucked against his side, and Aaron looked pale.

Sally nodded and took her brother by the crook of his arm, leading him away from the kids. "Did you reach Justine?"

Joey nodded slowly. "She's lost."

Sally shot a look at the back seat of her car and her hand covered her mouth.

Joey took his sister by the shoulders. "We found Aimee." Sally's eyes snapped back to him. "She's going after Justine."

"What? No!" Sally cut her eyes to the horizon. "It's so close. She's going to get herself killed!"

Joey squeezed her shoulders. "I need you to take the kids and Amber. Get out of here. Now." Joey looked to the east. "Before the roads are cut off."

Sally began shaking her head. "I'm not leaving you here. I'm not going to drive off without my family."

"Yes. You are. You know you have to get the kids out." Sally held his determined gaze for a long time, but Joey saw the give in them. "I'll find Aimee and bring her out. I promise." Sally's eyes found Danny as he vainly pumped water over the roof of the house. "I'll bring everyone out," Joey said softly. "Somehow."

Sally deflated. "You promise?"

"I promise."

Standing up straight, she pursed her lips and strode off to the waiting car. "In that case. We'll see you soon."

Joey nodded. His eyes met Amber's through the windscreen and held them as Sally accelerated sharply. Watching them leave through the gate, with one of the several horse floats in tow, took a significant weight from his shoulders. Now to achieve the impossible. He looked back at the smoke. *How the hell was he supposed to find Aimee?*

Joey blinked as something moved on the hill behind the homestead. Something big, yellow and slow. "Shit! Danny! The dozer!"

Danny whirled around, sending the hose offline and painting a wet mark across the grass beside the house. "What?"

Joey pointed. "Aimee's bringing the bloody dozer!" Running over to the shed, Joey snatched up a motorbike and raced to his sister.

***

Aimee almost cheered at the sight of her brother careening out of the yards and across the few hundred metres separating her from her goal. Joey stopped the vehicle beside her in a plume of dust and Aimee jumped down from the machine. "I need that," she said, pulling the bike from his grip.

"And I need that," he said, pointing to the dozer.

"She's at the old fort," Aimee yelled as she approached.

Joey stared at her for a heartbeat. Aimee knew what he was thinking. It was close to the fire front. Joey snagged her arm. "Aims…"

"Save it for when I get back."

"But—"

"Save it." She squeezed her hand over her brother's and gave him a smile. "I tried to make a firebreak at the old airstrip." Joey nodded. "See you soon, Joe."

Joey smiled. "Will do, Bug. Now go save the woman you love."

Aimee's face hardened with resolve. "Absolutely."

Three minutes. That's how long it took to get Skycatcher out of the horse float and climb on her back. The large, flighty horse was a reluctant rescue vehicle, but Aimee's years of experience wrangled the unruly beast to her will. North-west she galloped bareback to the place she had Justine describe to her on the slow dozer ride back to the homestead. She had at least five minutes until she crested the ridge that would afford her a view towards the Old Fort. Gum trees – low scraggly ones – Justine had said. Cracking dirt that she could peel off in a palm-sized plate from the ground. Rocks that looked whiter than most. An abandoned platform in the trees. Aimee had almost passed out with relief when Justine described her location. The Old Fort was a small depression surrounded by a rocky outcrop. A place of imagination and play from her youth that was hard to reach in a conventional vehicle from the south, but was only a sedate twenty-minute ride away on horseback from the homestead. The small valley leading into the depression took a car through a circuitous route from the north. It appeared Justine had unwittingly driven into it as she tried to return to the homestead.

Blood roared in Aimee's ears and her heart seemed to seize and pound simultaneously making her fists clench and her breathing jagged. Her teeth began to grind as her jaw tightened. Breaths now coming in short bursts through her nose. Panic had long passed for anger at her girlfriend's foolishness. "Idiot!" Aimee screamed. *You shouldn't be out here*. A breath. *I'm not worth dying for.*

She made the crest and fear nearly dropped her from the horse's back. The rise wasn't great, but it was enough to hide uncontrolled destruction from the homestead behind her. She could see the depression as the shadow of death loomed over it.

"No," she gasped out before clicking her tongue and urging Skycatcher to speeds that she hadn't reached in years. Ash rained down on her and the smoky wind whipped through her hair. Somewhere to her right, the edge of the airstrip was engulfed in flames. To a deity she had ignored for years, Aimee prayed with every atom in her soul that the firebreak would buy her time to collect Justine and return to the homestead. She added an extra prayer that her brother would get out before it was too late.

She lost sight of the southern outcrops of the Old Fort as she descended from the rise through little gullies and washouts that marked an old creek bed. Thick bushes and long grass hindered Skycatcher's progress, but Aimee pushed the horse through the discomfort. Branches that would soon provide fuel for the devil snagged and clawed at both woman and beast. With a hiss, the sting of a branch that tore at the flesh on her face was quickly pushed aside.

In a feat of horsemanship, Aimee and Skycatcher dodged and weaved the obstacles before them and burst through into woodland that provided them a clear shot to the outcrop. An outcrop now covered in flame.

"Hah! Hah!" Aimee yelled at Skycatcher urgently, kicking the horse hard in the sides. Skycatcher, who had responded to her urgency from the moment the woman climbed bareback onto her hide, lengthened her strides. The loud bite of her hooves hitting the rocky dirt was accompanied by the harsh snorts of air and foam exiting the horse's mouth.

Please don't be dead. Please don't be dead. Aimee chanted in her mind as flame ate more of the outcrop in its path south. *Please. Please. Please.*

Darkness blew over them as a gust of wind pushed thick, suffocating smoke over them. Spot fires burst around them and sharp whirlwinds of air blustered ash and ember through the air. Coughing, Aimee began to shout in long bellows. "Justine! Justine!" Weaving Skycatcher around the rocks and shrubs making up the bottom of the outcrop, she called again. "Justine!"

She heard a faint bark on the wind.

"Mitsy?"

"Aimee."

Aimee froze as the faint sound of her name met her ears. "Justine!"

Narrowing her eyes and concentrating hard on anything but the roar of flame coming over the outcrop, she whipped her head around as another faint call reached her. Aimee gasped. To her left, Justine was sprinting away from the outcrop with her hands held over her head as if to protect it from the heat of flames cresting over the rocks behind her. Next to her was Mitsy with her ears laid back flat, but refusing to leave Justine's side.

Screaming Justine's name again, Aimee kicked Skycatcher hard in the sides and urged her forward. It was fifty metres at most, but it was the longest distance Aimee had ever crossed. Spot fires burst around her as the air crackled with heat, drying and combusting anything flammable with a mere ember and a breath of wind. The roaring storm that was the flame front intensifying the closer she got to Justine. Reaching out a hand, she screamed at the woman, "Reach out to me!"

Justine did, and with barely a falter in Skycatcher's step, Aimee hooked Justine under the arm as the woman clutched at her. The momentum almost dragged them both from the horse, but using every ounce of strength she had, Aimee gripped Skycatcher's back with her knees and felt her shoulder pop as she reefed Justine behind her.

"Hold on to me," she cried unnecessarily as they galloped away from the encroaching flame. "Mitsy, come!" Outpacing the disaster, they soon broke free of the dense blanket of smoke and headed for the homestead.

The thick vegetation and uneven ground at the bottom of the next rise finally beat Skycatcher. Stumbling as they scraped their way through bushes and gullies, the horse fell forward, launching her riders into a bush. Aimee hit the tree base hard and felt the spike of a dry branch snap deep into her skin as her thigh impacted the wood. Somewhere on the other side of the spindly tree, she heard Justine hit the ground with a dull thud and a grunt of air.

"Justine?" she said through gritted teeth. Whatever had hit her leg burned pain through her entire side.

Coughing proceeded Justine's words. "I'm fine. Are you okay?"

Aimee nodded to herself and shutting her eyes tight. She refused to look at the damage she knew she'd suffered.

"Aimee?"

"I'm fine," she said, getting to all fours. Just. Growling at the pain in her leg, she made to stand only to find she had little to no movement in her right leg. Mitsy licked at her face.

Arms were quickly touching her, assessing the truth. "Oh, Aimee," Justine whispered when she discovered the butt of the branch sticking from the side of Aimee's thigh.

"Skycatcher?" Aimee said on a groan, feeling her stomach tip when she saw the wood in her leg.

"I don't know." Looking around, they saw no sign of the spooked horse. "Come on," Justine said, hooking an arm under Aimee's. "We can't stay here."

They looked in unison to the fire front boring down on them. *Could they even out-run that?* Aimee thought to herself. "No," she said, answering her own question. "You run back to the homestead," she said, trying to fend off Justine's assistance.

"What? No! Are you insane?"

"Justine, we have no choice. We can't beat this, but you can. Run, Justine!" Aimee gave the woman a shove and stumbled back, nearly landing in an unbalanced heap in the dirt.

"Damn it, Aimee. We don't have time for this."

"Exactly. Now get a move on! Run. Get a bike, come back for me, whatever, just get the hell out of here already!"

"No!" Justine's face contorted into something half-furious, half-devastated. "You don't get to make this decision on your own. You have no right to say who gets to live and who gets to die."

"I'm injured."

"So start hopping." Justine swooped against Aimee's side and began tugging her along. "Like it or not, I'm not leaving you here. Now, quit arguing with me!"

Mitsy barked her agreement.

Given little choice but to hop furiously or land face-first in the dirt, Aimee hopped.

"You're a bloody martyr, did you know that?" Justine snapped.

Aimee scoffed and hopped, scowling at the pain each movement created. It was intense, relentless and like a hot coal burning through her. "This from the…woman that…drove into a fire to…find me."

"You gave me no choice."

"Aaron should be your choice, not…not me."

"He was my choice, but he's safe. You weren't."

They reached the bottom of the crest Aimee had surveyed the carnage from earlier. Hopping up an incline was deadening her other leg, and soon she involuntarily hit the ground and winced at the pain shooting through her knees from the contact.

"Crawl," Justine said, leaving no room for argument. The woman sounded livid, but she remained by Aimee's side as she clambered up the slope on her knees, and maintained a consistent touch at her shoulder.

Progress was slow, and Justine's touch turned to fingers clutching at her shirt almost trying to pull her forward.

"Leave me," Aimee panted, guessing the fire was eating its way across the gullies they had just traversed.

"No."

"Why?"

"You aren't safe."

"I was until you got lost. I was…just over…there." Aimee pointed to the airstrip as they neared the crest. It was a scar on the landscape that the fire had to circumnavigate to continue its path. "It worked," Aimee said, smiling at the lack of fire between the strip and the homestead. She wished the same could be said for the fire behind them. Gasping as she saw it burn away the washout that had caused Skycatcher to stumble, Aimee felt dread send everything numb. "Justine, you need to go!" She pushed at the woman's legs.

Justine responded by pulling Aimee to her feet. "Run, Aimee."

"No!" Aimee pulled off the woman and fell. "You have to go. Please. Please." Tears began their hot trail down her cheek. "I can't have you waste your life trying to save mine. Just go."

Justine stepped forward and slapped Aimee across the cheek. "I love you, you idiotic woman. I will never leave you behind. Now get on your fucking feet and move!"

Howling with pain, and damning the woman at her side, Aimee took as much weight as she could on her leg when Justine once again pulled her to her feet. "Fuck you," Aimee growled as pain, adrenaline and absolute fear fed her body.

"Sure, but first, we need to live."

Aimee couldn't help it, but she burst into manic, completely inappropriate laughter. As the hysteria quickly abated thanks to injury, flame and the need for oxygen, she muttered, "God, I love you."

"I know," Justine whispered. "I know."

***

"Here it comes!" Joey yelled to Danny, as he waved his arms trying to attract the man's attention over the sound of the dozer. The smoke had thinned enough to reveal flame lapping at the hill he saw Aimee disappear over twenty minutes ago. Danny lifted an arm in response. "Come on, Aimee," Joey muttered to himself, searching the area to the northeast for signs of his sister.

For the last twenty minutes, they cleared as much as they could from around the house. Trees that had stood for hundreds of years had felt the bite of the chainsaw, and their remains were pushed far from person and property. The moonscape left behind made Joey's heart ache, but if this was going to save the house and the stock crammed into the yards nearby, then so be it.

Watching the dozer take another lap around to increase the cleared ring near the sheep, Joey turned to rush back to the house to find Skycatcher running into the yards from the west. He stared at the horse for a moment before he swore loudly. "Damn you, you stupid, bloody idiot!" Tearing over to the bike Aimee had abandoned by the stables, he thrust it to life with his foot and spit dust across the vicinity as he raced up to the crest of the hill where the flames were showing their ugly heads. There had been no time to put on a helmet.

It took him a minute to reach the bottom of the hill, and when he did, he felt his heart lodge itself in his throat. Breathing became uncomfortable as the sight of two women and a circling dog, entangled in a slow shuffle down the hill overwhelmed him. Gunning the bike, he reached them just as the flame began to tip itself down the side of the hill.

Dark, smoky, and with air containing little oxygen, he slid to a halt beside them. Justine quickly steered Aimee to sit behind Joey, then followed Joey's instructions to sit on the handlebars. It was awkward, and he nearly tipped them before he started off, but he would be damned if they were going to burn at the stake now.

Slowly, they pulled away, increasing the gap to the fire behind them. Aimee's sure grip around his waist like a comforting reminder that they needed to beat this. They needed to live.

He had to turn to avoid a rock, and everything unbalanced in an instant. Justine flipped off the bars to sail over the rock, and Joey extended his hand to brace the fall for Aimee and himself. The last thing he heard was his sister cry with pain, and then…then there was nothing but darkness as the rock rose up to greet the side of his head with a bang that could have deafened the dead.

Chapter Twenty-One

Blackness. Nothing but devastation and desolation across hundreds of thousands of hectares in the central west of New South Wales. Fires raged across many areas in the state as dry, fuel-rich ground fell to the fray as electrical storms savaged the countryside. The sobering news out of Condobolin reported that ten people had lost their lives to the fires the media was sensationalising as Black December fires. When Christmas came, Santa offered very little to those whose lives had been touched by flame and ash except hollowed remains and cinders where a home once stood.

It broke Sally's heart.

Stepping out of the stone homestead that offered the only piece of colour in a monotone landscape, she breathed in the heavy stench of charcoal and shivered despite the continued heat wave. A monotone landscape filled her view in every direction. Every direction but one. Around the pool at the Yarrabee Station homestead, sat everything she held dear in bright swimmers and gaudy towels.

The storm of fire had swept around the homestead her family fought so hard to protect. The stables suffered, as did the shearer's quarters, but remaining steadfast and untouched was the grand stone home her forefathers had built.

Some of their stock lost their lives on their property that day, but three thousand remained to feed off imported grain and hay. Their horses survived, as did Mitsy. Insurance, hopefully, would replace the rest. They got off lightly. The owners of the property next door had nothing but a shell to return to.

"Hey, need a hand with that?" Justine asked as she emerged from the long, cool hallway.

Sally gave her a smile. "Thanks. I got it." She shifted the platter of food in her hands. "How is she?"

"Still sleeping. I plan to leave her that way." Justine gave Sally a wink.

Chuckling, Sally led the way to the shaded porch by the pool where her children played under the watchful eye of their father. "She's always been a terrible patient. She'll be up and about again the instant she opens her eyes."

Justine nodded in agreement and watched her son tumble dive into the pool.

Sally's eyes scanned the thin crowd. Her brother's presence was sorely missed.

"Have you heard from Amber?" Justine asked quietly.

Sally put the platter on the table and sighed. "No change."

Joey had yet to recover. A week in an induced coma had let the swelling on his brain subside. Groggily he had re-joined the world, but as what, they had yet to discover. The doctors presiding over her brother promised big things, but seeing such a strong man reduced to grunting, drooling, and the occasional twitch of a finger was gut wrenching. Coming home for Christmas had felt like running away, but Sally needed to find some reprieve from the ghost who was her brother.

Sally felt Justine's hand touch her shoulder, squeezing in silent support. They had forged a bond close and tight since that awful Black Christmas day. Returning to the farm deep into the night when the road had cleared, Sally walked into a nightmare. Already panicked because none of her family had returned, she felt relief burn at her lungs when Danny emerged from the unscathed homestead to wrap her tightly in his arms and whisper words of love and forever. Moments later, fear gripped her. Limping, Justine had greeted her also. A large bruise marred her cheek and her wrist was being iced. She had waved the injuries off and showed her Joey and Aimee.

Covered with blood, Joey looked pale and lifeless. His head wrapped in bandages, Justine informed her the paramedics had been notified and they were waiting for the chopper. Beside her brother in the bed, was Aimee covered in soot, cuts, bruises and her leg oozing blood. A lump marked her forehead that had kept her unconscious since Danny had rescued them from the encroaching blaze.

Side-by-side, Danny, Justine, and Amber had kept vigil by the beds of those they loved. Quickly, Aimee recovered from her concussion, and slowly, her leg mended from the spike embedded deep into her flesh. Aimee had to be forcibly removed from her brother's bedside when she found out about his brain injury. Another reason coming to the farm for Christmas was a good idea. It kept Aimee from exhausting herself beside Joey and Amber.

"Shall we?" Justine said, indicating the Christmas lunch now fully laid out on the table.

Sally smiled and nodded. *Time to celebrate the fact that everyone was still alive.*

***

"Hey," came the whisper in her ear.

Aimee screwed her nose up at the sound.

"Time to wake up, sleepy head. Medication time."

This time, Aimee grimaced and groaned. "Go away," she said in a voice croaking with sleep.

She felt Justine's chuckling make the bed bounce, and then a hand ran through her hair. "You can go back to sleep right after you have something to eat and your tablets. Okay?"

Aimee sighed and peeled her eyes open with some trouble. Sleeping had apparently done nothing to restore her exhaustion. Since the fire, she'd been utterly drained of energy. The doctors blamed the concussion she sustained as well as the blood loss and trauma to her leg injury. Struggling, she accepted Justine's assistance to sit upright and lean against the headboard. "How long?"

"About three hours. You missed lunch."

"You should have woken me," Aimee said, not sorry that she had been left in peace. She sighed again. "Any word?"

Justine shook her head. "Here. I brought you Christmas lunch." Justine handed her a small plate of food. Knowing she needed to have something with her tablets, she forced down some of Sally's infamous Christmas ham. It tasted heavy and tiresome in her mouth. In years past, she would have fought her brother for the bulk of the delectable meat. Now, however, she was encumbered, the farm was in ruins, and her brother was fighting for quality of life in Sydney. Aimee pushed the plate away.

"Have some more in a bit, okay?" Justine said, handing over the antibiotics, painkillers, and a glass of water. Taking them dutifully, Aimee handed the glass back. Capturing the hand once disposing of the glass, Justine held it and ran her thumb over the back of Aimee's knuckles. At Aimee's heavy sigh, she said, "Everything's going to work out, you know?"

Aimee nodded slowly, but she didn't feel very positive about her answer.

Justine gave her a small smile and tucked a strand of hair behind Aimee's ear. "You want to know why?"

"Why?"

"Because we're all still here. The homestead is still here. Your family is alive. We're alive. We made it through hell, and nothing could get worse than that."

Aimee nodded and looked at their linked hands. Nothing but the fact that Joey was sick, and the woman she loved was only with her for a short time. Holidays would be soon over.

"What are you thinking?" Justine asked, smoothing out the frown on Aimee's forehead.

"Nothing," Aimee said with a smile and a shake of her head. "I'm just glad you're here."

"Good, because I plan to be for a long while."

Aimee sighed. "For a few weeks at least."

Justine smiled and shook her head. "No, honey, for a long while." Justine took a deep breath. "I have a filly to train, remember? Big commitment."

Aimee furrowed her brows. "Yeah. Yeah, you do," she said, tentatively following Justine's vague suggestion. "But—"

"She'll require constant attention. I don't plan to let her run wild."

"She could do with a firm, but kind hand."

Justine bit back a grin. "Yes, she could. She's strong-willed, stubborn, and full of mischief."

Aimee frowned, not certain whether Justine was referring to the horse she had named Pebbles anymore.

"And I love her very much," Justine said, reaching over and caressing Aimee's cheek.

Aimee collected the hand in her own. "Are you sure? Even after everything that happened?"

"I'm very sure," Justine said with a nod. "Even more so than before. We nearly lost each other, Aimee. I don't want to miss out on a thing. If you'll have us, then we'd very much like to stay."

"For real?"

"For good, actually."

Aimee's chin wobbled as she stared at those sweet, watery eyes in front of her. "For good, then," she said quietly.

"For good."

Bringing Justine's knuckles to her lips for a sweet kiss, Aimee smiled at the woman that meant everything and more and said, "I love you."

Justine smiled. "I know."

Six months later…

Aimee woke with a start and grimaced at the ache in her leg. According to the doctors, the trauma in her muscles was severe enough to expect a long recovery time. Every morning started this way, but if this was all she had to put up with, then she was happy enough. At least she could walk unassisted.

"Hey," came the whisper beside her.

"Morning," Aimee said softly back, kissing her girlfriend on the brow before leaving the bed. Stretching her leg and working out the stiffness, she moved to the newly renovated loft kitchen and prepared a cup of tea. Loud snores came from the added room off the main living area, and with a smile, she shuffled over and shut Aaron's door. The boy had shot up in the past few months. His voice broke and, like Robbie, he was becoming a man. A man Aimee was honoured to help shape. He was a great kid, a testament to Justine's ability as a mother, and he had adjusted to station life like he was born to it.

Making two cups when the kettle dinged, Aimee took one to her new, complete with doors and walls, bedroom, and handed it to Justine. Justine had lived up to her decision to move to the station and she had been an integral part of the rebuild. Summer rains had sparked growth across the property, and insurance claims replaced lost property and stock. They also paid for a new wing in the stable complete with two-bedroom loft. They had moved in together and hadn't looked back since.

"Ready for today?" Aimee asked.

"Yes. You? You have to wear a dress." Justine chuckled into her cup. Nothing like a wedding to make a woman frock up.

Aimee grimaced and sipped at her own tea. "Don't remind me."

Reclining against the headboard and relaxing into the feeling of Justine caressing her leg, Aimee soon took a deep breath. "I better go do the stables before all this la-di-da later."

"Don't forget, only one sugar cube for Pebbles. I swear that horse has a sweet tooth to rival Rolly's."

"Yes, ma'am."

***

Clomping downstairs a few minutes later, Aimee moved through her care routine of the horses and headed over to the house after swinging past the new chicken coop. Rebuilt to represent the homestead on the insistence of the children, the ten chickens kept them in enough eggs to feed an army. Rolly had mourned the loss of her birds thanks to the fire, but her new flock had filled the hole in her heart.

"Six eggs today," Aimee said, walking into the kitchen where Sally was bustling about. "That little bugger Henrietta nipped me again. You need to talk to your daughter about taming those chooks."

Sally chuckled. "Put them over there, for now, I'm out of egg cartons," she said, pointing to a cane basket. "Want a cuppa?"

"No thanks, had one already. Do you need a hand?" Aimee frowned at the clutter of containers on the bench. "What's all this for?"

Sally huffed. "The caterers gave us nothing but foil trays to hold everything. Useless. I'm going to spoon it all into those."

"I'll help."

Sally responded by getting an armful of foil trays with cardboard lids out of the fridge and placed them on the kitchen table. "Knock yourself out."

"I wouldn't recommend it," Joey's voice said from the doorway. He shuffled in on his walking sticks and sat beside Aimee. The hair had grown over the site where his head collected the granite rock all those months ago, and the colour had returned to his face.

"Nervous?" Aimee asked, spooning a glob of potato salad into a container.

"Nope," Joey said, his voice cracking.

Sally and Aimee shared a grin.

"Yeah, what's there to be nervous about," Aimee said with a shrug of her shoulder. "I mean, it's only forever. You know, until the end of time."

Joey narrowed his eyes at his sister. "You're next, you realise that?"

Aimee choked on an inhale of air. "Marriage? Me? Oh, hell no!" Joey and Sally chuckled. "Besides, it's not legal for me."

"And if it was?" Sally asked.

"Then no. You two hardly offered the best example of the benefits of marriage."

"Hey! My marriage is just fine, thank you very much," Sally said in protest.

"Yeah, now, maybe. But it took a disaster for you and Danny to snap out of your funk."

Sally pursed her lips and turned her back to her sister. Opening her mouth to deliver what was no doubt a scathing comeback, she was interrupted when Justine raced into the kitchen looking panicked. "Help!"

Aimee rolled her eyes. "Let me guess, the bride is having a wardrobe malfunction."

"More like her waters breaking all over the rug malfunction. She's in labour!"

"Yes! I knew it." Aimee fist-pumped the air before reining in her excitement. She cleared her throat.

Justine looked to Sally after giving her an unimpressed look. "Sal?"

"On it. Aimee, get clean towels and the baby blanket. Joey, call the doctor. He was invited, so maybe he's already on his way. Justine, get her on some towels and on the bed." Everyone stood there nodding at Sally thinking her orders sounded fair and reasonable. "Now, people!"

As Aimee ran down the hall, she could hear Sally shouting, "Danny! Find the bloody pastor! We have an emergency wedding to perform."

Aimee chuckled at his distant reply of, "What the hell are you on about?"

"Oh crap," Aimee said as she spotted the look on Amber's face when she delivered fresh towels to the bedroom where she was changing. Her off-white wedding dress was soaked in a curious liquid, and the tendons in her neck were taut and ready to snap. Her mother was sitting beside her brushing her sweat-drenched hair from her face.

"Put them here," Justine said, indicating the dresser across the room.

Aimee did so, but not without having to avoid a cameraman. "Seriously, mate, you gotta go," she said, shoving at the man covering the wedding for next years' success stories of *Romancing the Farmer*. "Justine, tell your minion to leave," she added when the man refused to budge.

"Dave, get the hell out. Australia doesn't need to witness this."

"But—"

Joey finally made it to the room after hobbling up the hall and grabbed the man by the scruff of the neck, shoving him towards the door. "Amber? Honey. Are you okay?"

Amber grimaced and groaned.

"I'm thinking no," Aimee muttered.

Sally bustled into the room with an assortment of equipment and took control. She had lifted Amber's dress to her waist and cut off her knickers before Aimee had a chance to escape. She'd witness thousands of lambs being birthed, but the sight of her soon-to-be sister-in-law's private areas looking like something out of a Freddy Kruger movie was revolting. "Oh, Christ," Aimee muttered before rushing from the room, leaving Sally, Justine, Joey and Amber's parents to deal with the carnage of childbirth.

"Where's the emergency?" Danny said, running down the hall with a flustered old man behind him.

"In there." Aimee thrust a thumb at the room and delighted in Danny's curse word of choice when he found what was going on.

"Pastor, marry these two, and hurry the hell up. This little bub is waiting for no one."

Aimee smiled as she leant against the wall listening to the harried clergyman rush through the wedding vows over the top of Amber's increasing groaning, screaming, and vitriolic insults at Joey. The moment Amber screamed 'I do', a baby's wail filled the airwaves.

"It's a girl," Justine said, as she joined Aimee in the hall. "A beautiful pink little girl."

Aimee grinned. "Does that mean I win the bet?"

"That depends on the weight," said a man's voice, joining them as he exited the bedroom after Justine. Amber's father, a portly greying man with a penchant for a wager, smiled at Aimee. "I won."

Aimee shook her head at Harold. "There's no way she's heavier than seven pounds. Amber is tiny."

"My family breed them big. You just wait, young lady, she'll be eight pounds or more, and then I'll soon be enjoying a nice nip of fine scotch."

"You wish."

"Just to remind you, anything less than eighteen years old is a waste of my time." Harold patted Aimee on the shoulder and walked back into the bedroom to meet his new granddaughter.

Justine rolled her eyes and returned to the room.

***

Introduced to online shopping by Justine and Aaron, Aimee was in the homestead office a few hours later looking for the perfect bottle of scotch for Harold when Joey shuffled in grinning.

"Well, here's the proud dad," Aimee said, returning his goofy smile. "How's Amber?"

"Enjoying a well-deserved rest," he said as he eased himself into another chair. "The little one is sleeping too."

"And her name is…?"

Joey hesitated for a moment. "Bridget."

Aimee's hand came to her chest. "Mum would have loved that."

Joey nodded. "I think so."

"Here you two are," Sally said, walking into the office. "Joey, the pastor wants a word before he leaves. Apparently you've yet to sign your marriage certificate."

"Sit down a sec," he said to his sister, patting the coffee table beside him.

"What?" Sally asked once she sat.

"I just wanted to let you know that Amber and I have decided to name our little girl after mum."

Sally's hand pressed against her chest like Aimee had done. "You named her Bridget?"

Joey nodded. "Bridget Aimee Turner, actually."

Aimee blinked. "You named your daughter after me? Why?"

"Because you're the strongest, most resilient, determined woman I know." Joe leant forward and touched Aimee's knee. "You're a hero and a woman who knows her heart. I'm sorry for everything that happened last year. I was an arsehole, and because of that, I nearly lost you all."

"I'm sorry for being an arsehole, too," Aimee said, covering her brother's hand.

Joey turned to Sally and gave her a smile.

She raised her hands. "I didn't act like an arsehole, so I'm not apologising. But it's good to see the knock on your head has made you see sense, though," Sally said, trying to be teasing, but the tears shining in her eyes betrayed her. Joey's rehabilitation wasn't over, but the hardest battle had been fought.

"I love you both, more than anything." He smiled at them. "Well, almost. I think my baby girl has succeeded you both."

"As it should be," Sally said, patting her brother on the arm. "And speaking of daughters, or sons for that matter, Danny and I…" She took a deep breath. "We're pregnant."

Aimee's jaw dropped and Joey frowned.

"You're happy about it?" Joey asked.

Sally nodded. "It wasn't planned, but…I think this is the start of a new beginning for us. I think we're all getting a second chance. Don't you?"

Aimee nodded. "Yes, I think we are."

The truth behind Danny's funk and Sally's erratic moods had come out after the fire levelled the property. Joey, while unconscious when it happened, made up for lost time when he did find out and punched Danny across the jaw. Weak from his incapacitation, the hit was more like a light tap on the face, but the sentiment behind it was significant. The couple had been driving into Roper Creek monthly for marriage counselling to get their relationship back on track. The one thing the fire had done in their favour was to remind them how much they didn't want to lose their family.

The fire had cleaned the slate for their entire family's future. Aimee had decided to continue into a Ph.D. by finally deciding to run her own breeding experiment on the farm. Justine had given up her city life, but had brought her love of horses with her, and thanks to Dreamer, was already on the way to breeding quality horses to train and sell. Aaron was training for the Australian Youth Equestrian team and had given Robbie a new outlet in the process. Both boys were now travelling the horse circuit, only Robbie's skills were better applied in the rodeo ring.

The family group smiled at one another, enjoying the renewed bond they had once shared. It was snapped a moment later when Aaron and Robbie came bursting into the room.

"Kite is having a baby!"

Mayhem ensued, and a little after midnight, new life was once again welcomed at Yarrabee Station. The new filly, Hope, had opened her eyes to see her future family gathered around her with smiles and tears in their eyes.

###

Acknowledgements

I would like to thank four extraordinary ladies who took time out of their lives to help make this story better for the world to enjoy.

To Sue, a new, but essential friend, thank you for offering to read through my story around your very hectic and emotional time. I owe you a significant debt of gratitude. To fellow author and friend, Tara Wentz (go check out her stuff), thank you so much for your last minute acceptance of my beta request. You are a pleasure to chat with, an honour to know, and I look forward to collaborating with you again in the future. To Fiona, an amazing and highly entertaining individual who has quickly become the best fan *ever*. Your generosity is unsurpassed…except by your impressive ability to talk fluent okka. You're a grouse sheila. And to the woman that has supported my writing since day dot, Lyn the-ever-amazing Gardner. She's a phenomenal writer, an outstanding editor, but more importantly, my beautiful friend. We've both come a long way since our fanfiction days, and we have many more roads to travel. Did someone say: Road trip!
Lastly, to my poor, neglected friends and family. Thank you. Writing can be a lonely endeavour, but you guys make it worth it.

Tricky Wisdom
Available in paperback or ebook

Darcy Wright is a closeted lesbian who has been infatuated with her best friend, Taylor, since junior high. Leaving her small northeast Minnesota town for Harvard in a quest to become a doctor, she moves in with med-student Olivia Boyd, a neurotic, anal, gigantic pain in the backside. The first year of juggling medical school is gruelling, but it's nothing compared to living with Olivia.

Coming out to her friends and family with an anti-climactic flop, Darcy uses her newly publicised sexuality to try and win Taylor's affections through an ill-hatched scheme that crosses uncomfortable lines. The result is as unexpected to Darcy as Darcy's affinity for medicine is to Olivia.

The first year of medical school is a nerve-wracking encounter in medicine, learning lessons the hard way, and finding what her heart desires.

The Woman Upstairs
Available in paperback or ebook

Ricci Velez is a fiercely independent woman that worked her way up from the poverty line to become a respected engineer and property developer. Mistaken as the little wifey by Tara Reeves, the new tenant at her Manhattan apartment building, Ricci wants to evict her before she even signs the lease. A slighted ex-tenant, a vandalized apartment, and an interfering best friend means that she's forced to offer Tara a room in her own apartment. Can she survive having the secretive hard-nosed executive judging her in her own home? Worse still, can she survive her match-making mother shamelessly besotted by the temporary housemate?

Made in the USA
Middletown, DE
24 September 2017